BLUE GOLD

ELIZABETH STEWART

annick press
toronto + new york + vancouver

Main cover photo: Shaker Paleja
Cover model: Paula Ayer
Cover photo (inset): Sean_Warren@istockphoto.com
Edited by Pam Robertson
Copyedited by Linda Pruessen
Proofread by Tanya Trafford
Cover design by Natalie Olsen/Kisscut Design

We acknowledge the support of the Canada Council for the Arts, the Ontario Arts
Council, and the Government of Canada through the Canada Book Fund (CBF) for our
publishing activities.

ONTARIO ARTS COUNCIL
CONSEIL DES ARTS DE L'ONTARIO
50 YEARS OF ONTARIO GOVERNMENT SUPPORT OF THE ARTS
50 ANS DE SOUTIEN DU GOUVERNEMENT DE L'ONTARIO AUX ARTS

Cataloging in Publication

Stewart, Elizabeth (Elizabeth Mary), author   Blue gold / Elizabeth Stewart.

ISBN 978-1-55451-635-3 (bound).--ISBN 978-1-55451-634-6 (pbk.)

    I. Title.

PS8637.T49445B58 2014   jC813'.6   C2013-907156-3

Distributed in Canada by:
Firefly Books Ltd.
50 Staples Avenue, Unit 1
Richmond Hill, ON L4B 0A7

Published in the U.S.A.
by Annick Press (U.S.) Ltd.
Distributed in the U.S.A. by:
Firefly Books (U.S.) Inc.
P.O. Box 1338
Ellicott Station
Buffalo, NY 14205

MIX
Paper from
responsible sources
FSC
www.fsc.org   FSC® C004071

ANCIENT FOREST ™
FRIENDLY

Printed in Canada
Visit us at: **www.annickpress.com**

Also available in e-book format. Please visit
www.annickpress.com/ebooks for more details. Or scan

For my girls,
Kim and Alexis,
and for John

BY THE TIME people finished texting the address of Jeff's party around to everybody they knew, eighty kids had shown up. The front door was wide open when Fiona and Ryan got there. Girls and guys were hanging out on the front porch, soaking up the late-evening sunshine. It was an older crowd, some from different schools. Fiona didn't know a lot of them, so she was doubly nervous about how she would fit in.

Inside, bodies crammed the living room. Fiona and Ryan wove their way through the crowd looking for Jeff, whose parents were away for the weekend. It was so loud that everybody had to shout, which just made it louder. In the kitchen, Fiona was relieved to find her friend, Rick Yee, chugging a beer while a bunch of other guys chanted, "Do it, do it, do it!"

Rick finished and wiped his mouth. "Fee!" he yelled when he saw her, slobbering a bit as he lifted the empty bottle in victory. "Pokémon!"

Fiona had known Rick since grade one, when Pokémon was their shared obsession.

"Pokémon!" she yelled back.

"You gotta catch up," Rick told her, wiggling the bottle in her direction.

But he was wrong. Fiona was already more buzzed than she wanted to be. Before the party, she and Ryan had stopped at the park to chug down half a water bottle of vodka Ryan had pinched from home. He said it would help her relax. Fiona wasn't into drinking, and the vodka was making her feel woozy and out of control—the opposite of relaxed—but she didn't want Ryan to know that.

Fiona had been dating Ryan for five weeks, since the beginning of May. Practically married, according to some people. But Fiona was still getting used to the idea of having a boyfriend. She liked Ryan—she just wasn't sure if she *liked him* liked him. He was pretty average looking, but then so was Fiona, with mouse-brown hair that was too bushy and a face that, in her opinion, was too broad and too freckled. Ryan was tall and ridiculously skinny. They were both B-list popular. Well, Fiona thought she might be more like B+.

Ryan found a couple of rum coolers in Jeff's fridge and handed her one. "You'll like it. It tastes like lemonade," he told her. He was right—in a few sips, half of it was gone. "C'mon," he said into her ear. "Let's check out downstairs."

He took her hand and led her toward the basement. *How are you supposed to know what you feel?* she wondered as he pulled her through the crowd of kids jamming the stairway, down to the family room, where the lights were low and the music throbbing. People were slow dancing, even though the music was fast. She could see couples kissing while they danced, and some were full-out groping. *What exactly is Ryan expecting from me?* Fiona's stomach fluttered in sudden panic. She could taste the rum cooler in her mouth, and the vodka behind it.

She spotted her friend Lacey along the wall, in the middle of a group of girls with their heads bent over their phones. Fiona leaned close and told her, "I don't feel so good."

Ryan threw her a questioning look, but with the music so loud, he couldn't hear what she was saying.

"Tell Ryan you want to leave," Lacey advised. She was sipping a beer, buzzed but not drunk. Trust Lacey—tall, model-thin, and confident—to look like she belonged here. "Do what feels right," she said.

But Fiona didn't want Ryan to think she was being a drama queen, so she let him lead her to a leather sectional in the corner, full of kids making out. He found a spot for them and pulled her down so that she was sitting on his lap. Then, without warning, he pushed his tongue into her mouth. His kiss was hard and wet. She tried to respond, but she felt like she couldn't breathe, and the music was giving her a headache.

Ryan broke off the kiss and whispered in her ear, "The bathroom's free."

At first Fiona wasn't sure what he meant. Then she glanced over and saw Jeff and his girlfriend emerging from a bathroom. Ryan and Jeff were a year older than Fiona and her friends, who were still in grade nine. Maybe grade tens were more into sex than her crowd was, but as far as Fiona knew, none of her friends had done the deed. Girls were expected to put out in other ways, though—blow jobs, hand jobs—neither of which she had ever done. She felt panic rising again, which made the nausea worse.

"I think I'm going to be sick," she said, and staggered for the staircase, her head spinning.

"Fee?" said Lacey as she passed her. But Fiona kept moving, craving fresh air.

Somehow she got outside. On her knees on the front walk, she gave in to her retching stomach and threw up under a bush. When she leaned back briefly, Lacey was by her side.

"Get it out," she told Fiona, holding her hair back. "All out."

Fiona puked again, and, when she was done, felt a bit better. When she sat up, she saw Ryan beside Lacey, watching her with concern.

"You okay?" he asked.

"Yeah. Sorry," Fiona told him, feeling gross and like an idiot. A gross idiot.

"Don't worry about it," Ryan replied.

"Want me to take her home?" Lacey asked Ryan.

"Nah, I'm good," he said. He put his arm around Fiona and helped her up. "Can you walk?"

"Yeah. Sorry," she apologized again.

"Happens to everybody," he said, but he seemed disappointed.

JEFF'S HOUSE was in the posh Point Grey neighborhood of Vancouver. Fiona lived with her mom further east, in Kitsilano. By the time they reached her place, she was a little less woozy. She glanced up to the fourth floor of the low-rise building and saw that the lights were on in their apartment. Her mom was probably waiting up for her.

"Can you smell it on my breath?" she asked Ryan, pausing at the security gate.

"The puke or the booze?"

He seemed a little disgusted, and he wouldn't look her in the eye. Fiona felt guilty for making him leave the party. She hoped he wasn't going to break up with her over this.

"I'm really sorry, Ryan."

"Hey, it happens."

"My mom is going to freak if she finds out," she said.

"Just go right to your room. Don't let her get a whiff."

"Is that experience talking?" she asked, trying to joke with him.

"Whatever," he shrugged. It seemed like he was in a hurry to get away from her.

"You should go back to the party," she told him, although she didn't want him to, not with all those other girls there. Maybe this was how you knew you were with the right guy—when the thought of him being with somebody else made you jealous.

"Maybe I will," he said, and started off down the sidewalk without even kissing her goodnight. Fiona supposed she could hardly blame him, considering she hadn't had a chance to rinse her mouth out. He tossed back, "I'll call you later," so casually that Fiona wondered if he would. Ever.

She took Ryan's advice when she went inside and kept the conversation with her mother, who was reading in the living room, to a minimum. *Yes, I had fun. No, I'm not hungry.*

She was pulling on pajamas in her bedroom when her cell phone pinged with a text. It was from Ryan.

"ok wth mom?" he asked.

"ok," she texted back. "sry about 2night"

"ddnt go xactly how i xpctd"

"wat did u xpct?"

"dunno. u r so sexy"

He thinks I'm sexy! So he wasn't mad at her after all.

"wat r u doing?" he asked.

"gting rdy 4 bed"

"wat r u wearing?"

The truth was she was wearing flannel pajamas with little skating penguins all over them. But in the safety of her bedroom, she *felt* sexy.

"nthing," she texted back.

"lets c"

Fiona hesitated. Really? Would she dare? Another text arrived.

"pls? u r so prty"

He thinks I'm pretty! Fiona felt warm all over. *This is what it means to have a boyfriend,* she realized. Sharing secrets—feeling hot for each other. Another text arrived.

"sho me u lke me"

I do like you! she thought. Maybe she even loved him. Before she could talk herself out of it, Fiona held her cell phone at arm's length, puckered her lips in a vampy kiss, yanked up her pajama top, and clicked a selfie. With another click, she sent the photo to Ryan.

"sb," he wrote. *Smiling back.*

Fiona smiled, too. It was only later, when she was lying in bed, her head spinning from the booze, that she started to worry about whether she'd turned herself into a sexting cliché, sending a shot of her bare boobs out into the cyberverse for anyone to see. Friends. Teachers. Her parents! *Get a grip,* she told herself. Ryan was her boyfriend. She trusted him not to send it to anybody else. Besides, it was just a joke. What harm could come from that?

SUNDAY MORNING, Fiona's alarm went off at eight. Her head was pounding and her mouth tasted like it was stuffed with compost. But there was no time to feel sorry for herself. Her dad was picking her up in half an hour for a softball game—he was the coach, she was the pitcher. She threw off her blanket and got to her feet, feeling the floor rock beneath her and her stomach rise. More than anything, she wanted to lie down again, but she knew her father was already on the bridge, driving over from West Vancouver. She couldn't let him down.

Fiona faked her way through the game, counting herself lucky to stay standing. In the end, she gave it up ten to three—not so bad, she figured, given that her brain was working at half speed.

"What happened out there?" her dad asked as they headed across the grass toward his car.

"I think I may have the flu," Fiona told him.

He put his hand to her forehead and then pulled her into a hug. "Poor pumpkin," he said. "Home to bed for you." Sometimes her dad was way too easy.

Inside the car, Fiona rummaged in her bag for her cell phone to see if Ryan had texted, but she couldn't find it. She was foggy about a lot of things that morning, but she was certain she'd put the phone in the bag. Had it fallen out, or had somebody taken it? There had been tons of people in the park, and the bag had been lying in the grass, where anybody could have gotten at it. Suddenly, Fiona really did feel feverish—with anxiety. Losing her phone was bad enough, but she was mostly freaking out about what was on it. What if somebody found the boob shot?

Wait, she told herself, *I erased it.* At least, she remembered *thinking* she should erase it. But had she? Yes, she was certain of it.

Fiona glanced over at her dad as he drove, so cheerful and clueless in his tidy white team shirt, tucked in, and wire-rimmed glasses. He'd flip if he found out Fiona had lost the phone—he was big on being responsible—but if he found out she'd sexted Ryan? He'd bust a vein.

When they pulled up in front of Fiona's mom's place, her dad gave her a funny look and asked, "Everything okay? I mean, apart from the flu?"

"Fine," she said.

It was only half a lie. Everything would be fine—*if* she got the phone back. As she watched her dad drive away, Fiona's head was suddenly crystal clear. She had to find that phone, before anybody else found it.

SYLVIE WALKED STEADILY AND CAREFULLY, balancing a heavy sack of ground maize upright on her head as she made the long trek back from the food distribution center. Her arms ached from the heavy bags of beans and rice she carried in each hand, and her flip-flops kicked up red dust from the bone-dry track, dust that parched her throat and coated her skirt and blouse.

Nyarugusu Refugee Camp was huge—over sixty thousand people in seven zones and more than fifty villages. Every two weeks, Sylvie had to make the half-hour walk to the food distribution center from Zone 3, where her family had lived since fleeing to Tanzania five years ago, to stand in a long line for their rations—maize, dried beans, cooking oil, and a little salt. Some said they were lucky to be here, away from the fighting back home in the Democratic Republic of Congo. But it was hard to feel lucky when every day was filled with work and worry.

As she got closer to the cluster of mud huts where she lived with her mother, brothers, and little sister, Sylvie could hear the shouts of young boys playing football. She listened for her brother Olivier's voice—easy to pick out

9

because he was the loudest of the boys in their village—but his was not among them. So he had not returned from wherever it was he'd disappeared to this time. Mama would somehow find a way to blame Sylvie for his absence.

When she came into the common space that served as a playing field, she saw that her younger brother, Pascal, had the ball. His bare feet controlled it effortlessly as he dodged the other boys, making steady progress toward the opposing goal, marked by two tin cans. Soon he'd be as good at the game as Olivier, although he was only nine. Olivier would be fourteen next month, old enough to come and go as he pleased, as he never tired of reminding Sylvie. But Sylvie was fifteen and still the eldest, even if she was only a girl. For now, at least, the boys minded her, their second mother.

Why do the boys get to play, when I must do all the work? Sylvie let the bag of maize slip to the ground. "Pascal!" she called. "Bring this inside."

With a swift kick, Pascal landed the ball between the rusted cans and scored. His teammates slapped his back and shouted his name. Sylvie's heart softened when she saw his broad smile. For a moment, she was back in their home village, watching their father playing ball with Olivier and Pascal in the yard of their house. It was a real house made of cement blocks, with two bedrooms, a sitting room with proper furniture, and a kitchen with a cook stove—nothing like the one-room mud and thatch hut they lived in here.

"You can't boss me, Sylvie," replied Pascal.

"I'll spit in your *fufu*," she threatened, referring to the sticky dough she'd make from the maize she was carrying.

"Then I'll eat yours instead of mine!" he said, laughing.

"Help me," she coaxed, "and I'll give you Olivier's share."

Pascal came over and struggled to lift the heavy sack, his thin arms barely reaching around it. "What if Olivier comes home?" he asked.

"I'll make sure you get more than him," she promised.

Sylvie carried the other rations into their hut, dipping down to clear the doorway. Inside it was dark, like always, the only light coming from the open door. They'd had to construct it quickly when they first arrived. There was no time to make windows, and since then, no will. Pascal followed her in with the sack of maize, dropped it onto the dirt floor, then ran back outside to join his friends.

Sylvie's mother, tiny and frail, propped herself on an elbow where she lay on a sleeping mat against the curved wall. "Did they have cassava?"

"You ask that every time, Mama," Sylvie replied, placing the beans and rice inside the metal bucket they used to discourage rats. "They never have cassava. Only maize."

"Ph!" she replied. "They expect us to eat that."

Today was a bad day for Sylvie's mother. Her mind was only half with them in the present, and she had barely stirred from the mat. Lucie, who was six, looked up from where she was playing on the dirt floor with the doll Olivier had carved for her out of a piece of wood.

"I'm hungry, Sylvie," she said.

"You think I'm not hungry?" she chided. "I just walked for an hour, and had to line up for another!" She picked up the yellow plastic can that they used to carry water from the communal tap and swished the contents around. "You and Pascal must go and get more water later." Kneeling down she took their battered pot and began mixing maize and water. She could hear the boys' shouts from outside. They were playing again. "Pascal!" she called through the open door.

"What?" he said a moment later, popping his head through the doorway.

"Start the fire."

"That's Olivier's job!"

"Do you see Olivier here?" replied Sylvie sharply, and immediately regretted giving her mother the opening.

"It's because of your bad temper, Sylvie," she pronounced from the woven mat. "That's why he stays away." Sylvie wanted to bite back that it was misery, not her, that kept Olivier away. "When Patrice arrives," Mama continued, "he will beat sweetness into you."

Sylvie and Pascal shared a look. So it was one of *those* days—a day when Mama refused to believe that Papa was dead, insisting instead that he was only delayed in joining them.

"Please make the fire so we can eat," Sylvie told Pascal evenly.

Mama gave a short nod of approval. With a shrug, Pascal gave in. He took the matches from the bucket where the beans and rice were kept and headed back outside.

Sylvie poured water into a second pot they had rescued from another family's castoffs and added some beans to let them soak. As she worked, she made a silent vow that she would never become like her mother—depressed, defeated, even crazy some days. Sylvie was determined that she would have a different life, a better life.

"Men like women who are sweet-tempered," her mother lectured. "Just ask your father. But maybe it doesn't matter," she added. "Maybe you'll never have a husband anyway."

"Why will Sylvie never have a husband?" asked Lucie.

"Because of this," replied Mama, dragging her finger in a diagonal across her face.

At the mention of it, Sylvie could feel the long scar on her face—from above her right eyebrow, across the bridge of her nose to her left cheek. Was she actually feeling it, or only imagining she did, the way other people imagined limbs that were no longer there? The way Mama imagined Papa. Either way, Sylvie told herself she didn't care about how she looked. She was glad she'd never have a husband. Instead, she'd stay in school. Her father had been educated at a university, and she would be, too. Maybe she'd even become a doctor, just like Doctor Marie in the camp hospital. She would make Papa's spirit proud of her—as proud as her mother was ashamed.

"Olivier's here!" called Pascal from outside.

A figure filled the doorway, blocking the light so that for a moment the hut was in darkness. Then Olivier stepped inside, lit from behind like a god descending from heaven—and just as pleased with himself.

"Olivier!" squealed Lucie, jumping for joy.

"You think I'd been gone a week!" he said.

"A whole night and a whole day is enough!" complained Mama, sitting up from the mat. "Where have you been this time?" Her words were angry, but her pleasure was undisguised.

"That's my business," declared Olivier. He was already taller than his father had been, with a broad face and handsome features.

"He's been hunting!" announced Pascal, who had followed him inside.

Olivier made a face at Pascal for giving away his surprise. "Here," he said triumphantly, tossing a sticky lump wrapped in a large leaf to Sylvie. "There's more where that came from."

The package gave off the sweet, tangy odor of fresh red meat. She unwrapped the leaf to find enough to feed them for two days. It made her mouth water, but she frowned.

"Where did you get this?"

"It's bushpig," Olivier told her proudly. "I caught it."

Lucie blurted in awe, "How?"

"I dug a hole and laid a trap. Then I chased it into the pit."

"How could you be so stupid?" admonished Sylvie, getting to her feet. The Tanzanian police shot people for poaching animals from the bush around Nyarugusu. The Congolese weren't even allowed to go outside of the camp.

Olivier threw her an angry look. "All the men do it. We'll have meat every night for a week, and I'll sell the rest for lots of money."

"You think the police won't find out?"

"I was careful. No one saw me."

"The camp guards will find out when you sell it. And people will smell it cooking."

"They won't find out," Olivier insisted, wounded that his gift was unappreciated. "You can watch us eat it, Two Face."

At the nickname, Sylvie turned away to hide her scar—a stupid habit she'd developed, because she knew there was no way to hide it.

Mama struggled up from the mat and took Olivier's prize from Sylvie, weighing it in her hands. She held it up to her nose and sniffed it as though she was shopping at the market, just like in the old days.

"Cut the meat into small pieces and cook it with the beans," she instructed Sylvie. "No one will smell it, and for once we'll eat well." Olivier looked triumphant. "But be careful who you sell the rest to," she told him, wagging her finger. "We can trust no one here but ourselves."

Anger clouded Olivier's face. "You should trust *me!*" he said, and strode out of the hut—gone again for who knew how long, this time.

"Your temper has done it again, Sylvie!"

Something else to blame on me! thought Sylvie. Without answering, she knelt back down and began sharpening the one knife they owned against a stone. *Where does Olivier disappear to?* she fretted. *Who is he with?* There were many bad people in the camp, people who would rob and even murder. With Mama the way she was, it had been up to Sylvie to keep Olivier safe from people like that, but she couldn't do it anymore, not when he wouldn't listen to her.

How much longer could she keep Pascal safe, or Lucie? *Worry and work, work and worry*, she chanted to herself in rhythm with the knife strokes.

Then another chant bubbled up, catching her off guard. *Someday we will be free.* Every refugee knew how dangerous it was to hope, but there hope was, anyway, keeping time with the knife, demanding equal attention with worry. *Someday we will be gone from here. Someday we will be free.* She chanted it over and over, until the knife was sharp enough to cut the meat. Until she almost believed it.

LAIPING

ASIA

FROM THE CROWDED RAILWAY CAR, Laiping craned her neck to get a first glimpse of the city of Shenzhen through the window. Older Cousin Min said that fourteen million people lived here. Back in her village, Laiping had tried to imagine what a city of that size would look like. Min, who went out from their village two years ago, told her when she came home at the New Year that Shenzhen was like Hong Kong or Shanghai—shiny and new, lit up by skyscrapers and the neon glow of the shops. That was in February, just four months ago. Laiping could barely believe that she was already on her way to the city.

It was night when the train reached the outskirts of Shenzhen, but Laiping saw no bright lights. Rain was falling, obscuring the view. All she could make out were squat buildings—endless rows of them receding into the drizzle and haze. Laiping wondered if the skyscrapers were hidden by the clouds—or whether they existed at all. Maybe Min had invented them, wanting to impress everyone in their village. Maybe she'd made up her stories of swimming pools and restaurants and shopping malls built especially for the workers. Suddenly, Laiping felt a pang of homesickness. She thought of her mother wiping her eyes on her sleeve as the train pulled away from the station, of Baba at her side, frail, but waving to her bravely. What if Min wasn't waiting for her as she promised? Where would Laiping turn in a city of fourteen million strangers? But she caught herself. If Min *was* waiting for her and she saw tears in her eyes, she would call her a baby.

As they'd waited for the train that morning, Laiping's father told her that when he was young, Shenzhen was just a fishing village. "Now it is the third largest city in all of China," Baba said. "A place of opportunity, where even a country girl can find a good job."

"I'm glad you are going, Laiping," her mother added through her tears. "There is no future for you if you stay here."

Laiping knew what her mother *wasn't* saying—that with Baba's health failing, it was up to her to send money home. Min had promised that if Laiping came to Shenzhen, she would help her find a well-paying job making computers or mobile phones—even though, at fifteen, Laiping was still a year too young to work legally. Min said she would take care of that, too.

Over the loudspeaker, the conductor shouted out the name of Laiping's station. The train slowed down, rocking the passengers as it rolled to a stop. Laiping could see crowds of people outside, flowing along the brightly lit platform like crosscurrents in a stream. Most of them seemed fashionably dressed, making Laiping self-conscious about the old T-shirt and baggy jeans she was wearing. She scanned desperately for Min as the conductor's voice shouted out over the loudspeaker, ordering passengers to disembark.

She grabbed the handle of the plastic zip bag containing her belongings and maneuvered her way toward the car door, bashing her knee against the hard corner of a large cardboard box sticking out into the aisle. It belonged to a man who was staying on the train. The man made no motion to move the box, or even to look her way. Fortunately, Laiping was tall for a girl and was able to step over it to join the press of people making their way out onto the platform.

Soon Laiping was in the flow of the stream. From platform level, it was impossible for her to search the crowd for Min, so she allowed herself to be swept along with other people leaving the train in the hope that they knew where they were going. They inched their way through a wide doorway, bumping each other with bags and backpacks. The inside of the station was a vast hall. The swarm thinned a little as people went their separate ways, allowing Laiping to take in her surroundings. Everything was new and beautiful—sleek glass and steel. She noticed *gweilo*—Westerners—among those scurrying for trains. Foreigners were seldom seen in Laiping's village, but Min said they were not uncommon here, less than an hour's train ride from Hong Kong.

Laiping saw signs giving directions. In addition to Chinese characters, there was writing that she took to be English. Even in Chinese, Laiping didn't know the street names and had no idea which exit to take. A woman knocked her shoulder as she passed, reminding Laiping that she couldn't stand there gawking forever. She felt panic rising. Where could Min be?

"There you are!"

Laiping heard Min's shrill voice above the crowd and turned to see her pushing her way across the flow of people. Min was the opposite of Laiping in appearance—short and sturdy. She bulldozed her way to Laiping, a blunt force.

"What are you standing there for?" she barked. "Here's your first lesson about life in the big city—you have to keep moving!"

"I'm sorry. I was looking for you."

Min thrust her hand through the crook of Laiping's arm and pulled her along.

"Come on," she said. "We need to catch another train."

Min held fast to Laiping's arm as she guided her down a stairway to a different platform, this one with many tracks and many more people.

"This is the subway," Min explained over the squeal of trains stopping briefly to offload passengers and take on new ones. "This will take us to where I live."

A car glided to a halt in front of them. Doors opened. Min pushed Laiping inside while other passengers fought their way out. With no place to sit, the cousins found a corner where they could set Laiping's bag down and within seconds the train was moving again, into a dark tunnel.

"Where are the skyscrapers?" Laiping asked.

Min pushed air through her teeth in a short burst. "*Ai ya!* Why do you think they call it a subway, you goose? We're traveling underground!"

I'm not a goose, thought Laiping, a little cross with Min's bossing. *I know we're underground!*

"I mean," she explained, "when will I get to see them?"

"Not tonight. We are traveling away from downtown, to the campus."

"What do you mean, 'campus'?" asked Laiping, disappointed.

"I told you back home—the factory is like its own city. You'll see."

With that Min fell silent. Laiping became aware that no one in the car spoke or even made eye contact. She noticed that her cousin was wearing eyeliner and lipstick, which she would never have done back home. She had on a short denim skirt and on her T-shirt there was a picture of a kitten wearing sparkly sunglasses. Laiping wasn't sure she liked this look on Min. For one thing, her legs were short and a little plump. When their grandmother was alive, she used to say that Min would grow up to be a great brain, and Laiping would be a great beauty.

Laiping glanced around to see that most of the girls her age were wearing makeup, plus pretty tops and sundresses that showed off their necks and arms. The guys wore tight jeans and T-shirts. It was how Laiping imagined people in Los Angeles or London might dress. She had been in Shenzhen for only fifteen minutes and already she had learned three lessons. The first was to keep moving.

The second was to pretend you were alone, even in a crowd. The third was to dress the way people in magazines do.

SOON, AS THEY CLIMBED THE STAIRS up from the subway station, Laiping saw for herself what a campus looked like. The rain had tapered off, but the air was still heavy and humid as she followed Min along a broad walkway, passing shops and restaurants full of chattering people. It was late—nearly midnight—but the tables were full, and guys and girls were waiting outside in long lines for their turn to go in. Everyone was young, in their teens or twenties.

"When do they sleep?" asked Laiping. In their village, there was nothing to do in the evenings, so everyone went to bed early.

"If you're on the night shift, you sleep in the day," explained Min. "The factories never stop. There is always someone working, and someone sleeping."

Further along, the walkway ended at a wide boulevard. They got caught in a crowd of people shuffling forward on the sidewalk to get onto a bus that had stopped, while just as many people were trying to get off. Laiping fought her way through, afraid of losing Min. Once they were past the crowd, Laiping could see that the boulevard was lined with huge white-tiled box-shaped buildings, much like the ones she had seen from the train on her way into Shenzhen. Each building was four or five storeys tall and as wide as several rice paddies.

"Which one is the factory?" she asked.

"They're *all* factories," Min replied. "The company has lots."

Laiping followed Min as she veered onto another walkway, and her face opened in delight.

"Skyscrapers!" she proclaimed as a row of tall buildings came into view.

"Those aren't skyscrapers!" corrected Min. "They're just the dormitories."

Min led Laiping into the lobby of the third dormitory and onto an elevator, explaining that this dorm was for women only. Laiping had never been on an elevator before. She experienced a thrill of fear each time it lurched to a stop at a floor to let people on and off, like a train car that went up and down instead of sideways. On the fifth floor, Min and Laiping got off and headed down a dark, narrow corridor. Every few steps there was a door. Every door was exactly the same, except for its sequential number. Min stopped at a door midway down the corridor and inserted a key card into a lock.

"We have to be quiet when we go inside," said Min, making her voice soft. "If someone complains that you stayed overnight, I'll get fined."

Inside, a weak ceiling light revealed a narrow path flanked by walls. Once Laiping's eyes adjusted, she saw that they weren't walls at all, but bunk beds stacked from floor to ceiling, three to a section. Curtains were hung across each bunk for privacy. It wasn't so different from home, where Laiping's house was one large room, divided by curtains. The only difference was that, here, the curtained areas were stacked vertically. A couple of bunks toward the end of the row were lit up from within, creating enough spill that Laiping could discern a large window. Silently, Min took Laiping's bag from her and placed it under the window, where several other bags and boxes were stored.

Min cupped her hand over Laiping's ear and told her, "The toilet is in there," nodding toward a tiny cubicle to the left of the window. Laiping was impressed—back home, the toilet was an outhouse. Min climbed a ladder up to the third tier and crawled in behind a curtain. Laiping saw a light go on from inside Min's bunk. Placing her foot on the bottom rung of the ladder, Laiping followed her cousin up. She pulled the curtain back slightly to find Min seated cross-legged on the narrow mattress, stooping so as not to hit her head on the ceiling.

"Welcome home!" she whispered.

AFRICA

ON MONDAY MORNING, as she did every weekday, Sylvie put on the white blouse and blue skirt of her school uniform and, leaving Lucie with Mama, walked with Olivier and Pascal to make sure they went to class. There were four high schools in Nyarugusu Refugee Camp. The one that Sylvie and Olivier attended was in a one-storey cinder block building consisting of two large rooms, one for the high school and the other for the primary grades, where Pascal went. The building was located in between the food distribution center and one of the camp's medical clinics, where Sylvie had an after-school job.

"It's boring," Olivier complained, as he so often did, as they walked the red dust track. "And the teachers know less than you do!"

Secretly, Sylvie agreed with him. She had always been a good student, eager to make something of herself, but the teachers at Nyarugusu offered little inspiration. They were Congolese refugees who taught because the Tanzanians wouldn't let them leave the camp to find better jobs. Sylvie herself taught math to the younger children, although she wasn't paid for it at all, because the regular math teacher so often got the lessons wrong, and she wanted Pascal and the other children to have a decent start.

Congolese refugees had been living in Nyarugusu for almost twenty years, but the Tanzanians didn't want them in their country. Every day there were rumors that the Tanzanian officials were going to close Nyarugusu—just this year, they shut down the Nyarugusu market, where people used to make a little money selling vegetables they'd grown, or soap and candles they'd made. The Tanzanians wanted the Congolese to go back to their own country, across Lake Tanganyika, but there was still fighting there. Besides, Mai-Mai soldiers burned down the village where Sylvie's family had lived, so, for them, there was no home to go back to. There was only Nyarugusu—until the Tanzanians shut it down. Then where would they go?

"Papa would want us to get an education," Sylvie told Olivier. She was certain that was what Papa would say if he were here. She tried not to dwell on the fact that being educated hadn't saved him. In fact, it may have cost him his life.

Sylvie's father was the teacher in their village school in North Kivu province. It was never a safe place, their village. Armed militias belonging to one group or another had come through many times, some of them raiding from the hilly forests along the border with the neighboring country of Rwanda. Others, like the Mai-Mai, were Congolese, sometimes working for the government, always working for themselves. Wherever they came from, they were all alike—taking what they wanted, burning homes, brutally raping girls and women—boys and men, too. And murdering those, like her father, who stood in their way. Coltan was what they were after—the blue-black nuggets of columbite-tantalite ore that was plentiful in the highlands surrounding their valley. Some people called it blue gold. Her father was helping the miners who eked out a living gathering coltan from the hillsides and panning for it in streams to file claims for their plots. Then the Mai-Mai came.

Sylvie wasn't at school that day. She had stayed home to help Mama with Pascal and with Lucie, who had just been born. But Olivier was there. He never talked about what he saw, just as Sylvie and Mama never talked about what happened to them when the Mai-Mai came into their house. At any rate, what more was there to say, except that the Mai-Mai found Sylvie's father at the school, and they shot him? Then they set fire to the whole village, as a warning to other villages. Sylvie knew better than to ask Olivier, but she wondered sometimes what Papa's last moments were like. He would have been brave, she was sure of that. He would have stood up for what was right and fair, because those were the things he believed in.

But she tried not to think about her father's death too often, because she would start imagining herself in his place, facing the soldiers' rifles, feeling the bullets enter her body—making her heart pound so painfully and her breathing so tight that she feared she might actually die. Post-traumatic stress disorder is what the doctors at the clinic called it. Just about everyone in Nyarugusu suffered from PTSD, reliving in their minds and hearts and bodies the horrors that they'd been through back home.

Sylvie wished she could be brave like Papa, but instead she locked all the bad memories away deep down inside and tried to ignore them. That was what Olivier did, too, and Mama—she was sure of it. But the weight of those memories tugged at them anyway, pulling each of them down. Keeping them prisoners of the past.

"I like school," said Pascal, pulling Sylvie back to the present. He was scuffing through the red dust in bare feet. Pascal was only four when the Mai-Mai attacked and didn't seem to remember. For this, at least, Sylvie was grateful.

"Good. What do you like best?" Sylvie asked.

"Playing football!"

Sylvie clucked her tongue. "There's more to school than playing!"

But Pascal lived for the game. And all that he remembered about Papa was kicking the ball around the yard. *No wonder*, thought Sylvie, *that he loves the game so much.* Glancing to Olivier as they neared the school, Sylvie wondered what good memories *he* had about Papa. But there was no point in asking him. If Pascal was an open book, then Olivier was a closed one.

Sylvie saw that Olivier was turning something shiny over and over in his hand. "What's that?"

"Nothing." He slipped the object into his pocket.

"Show me," she said.

"It's none of your business!"

She grabbed at his pocket, but he dodged away.

"Leave me alone!"

Throwing up his arms in anger, he turned and headed away toward the empty dustbowl that used to be the Nyarugusu market.

"Olivier!" Sylvie called after him, angry that he was wasting the precious shillings it cost to go to school.

He disappeared behind a collection of makeshift food stalls that refugees had put up in defiance of the Tanzanians.

"I'll bet he's going to see Mr. Kayembe," remarked Pascal.

Sylvie's eyes narrowed with concern. Hervé Kayembe came from North Kivu, too. In the fighting over coltan, the Mai-Mai accused him of working with the Rwandan rebels. They killed his wife and sons, but he escaped by fleeing the country. In Nyarugusu, he set up a business selling radios and mobile phones and calling cards, which was shut down with the rest of the shops. But everybody knew his business was much bigger than that. He ran the black market, supplying drugs and guns—and doing anything that would line his pockets with money.

"How do you know that?" Sylvie asked Pascal.

"Because Jean-Yves and I followed him." Sylvie disapproved of Pascal's friend Jean-Yves, an orphan who came to Nyarugusu with his older brothers, who let him run wild. "Olivier sold the rest of the bushmeat to Kayembe," reported Pascal.

Hearing this, Sylvie knew she had reason to worry. Kayembe was well known for the small army of thugs and criminals he employed. Was Olivier becoming one of them?

"I told you to stay away from Jean-Yves," Sylvie scolded Pascal.

"He's my friend!" he protested.

Before she could argue with him further, he ran over to join some boys kicking a ball around outside the school. *If we stay in Nyarugusu*, thought Sylvie, *how long before Pascal is swallowed up by Kayembe, along with Olivier?* A familiar wave of panic rippled through her, making her heart race and her stomach twist with nausea. Sylvie felt certain that, if Papa was with them, he would have found a way to get their family out of this camp, where there was no life and no future—only day after day of waiting. The Tanzanian officials liked to tell the Congolese that it was safe to go home, but every day more refugees arrived with horror stories of death and maiming and rape. They couldn't go back, and with vultures like Kayembe about, they couldn't stay in Nyarugusu, either.

If Papa was here, they would have been in Europe or America by now. But Papa wasn't here, and many days Mama was only half with them. If they were going to leave this place, Sylvie knew it was up to her to find the way.

AFTER SCHOOL, Sylvie went to the Zone 3 medical clinic, where she earned a little money three days a week helping the nurses and doctors with basic chores like cleaning and stocking shelves. Sometimes she held the tray of gauze and instruments while the medical staff attended to patients with cuts or broken bones. She liked this job the best, because she could imagine herself in their place one day, as a doctor or a nurse.

"*Bonjour*, Sylvie!" chimed Doctor Marie as Sylvie entered the clinic.

"*Bonjour!*" replied Sylvie.

Marie was in an examining area, where she was giving an injection to a small child being held firmly by his mother. The baby wailed as the needle penetrated his arm, but Marie was quick, cooing to him, "I know, it's not nice, is it? There! All done!"

The nurses at the clinic were mostly African, but many of the doctors came from Europe or North or South America, working with one aid organization or another. They took turns rotating between the Nyarugusu hospital and the outpatient clinics. The head doctor was Bernard Van de Velde, a scowling white man from Belgium. Doctor Marie came from Canada. Her skin was as dark as Sylvie's and she spoke French, Sylvie's second language next to Swahili.

"Is it polio vaccine?" Sylvie asked Marie, about the injection.

"Something new, to prevent malaria."

The word triggered a distant memory of Sylvie's cousin, Josue, who died of malaria when he was five. *If only we had this medicine*, she thought. *Maybe he would still be alive.*

"Are you okay?" asked Marie. She had a look on her face that Sylvie had come to recognize—still smiling, but also assessing, probing, wondering what horror she had stirred from Sylvie's past.

"Fine," she replied.

The baby had stopped crying now. His mother thanked Marie in Swahili.

"His arm will be sore for a couple of days," Marie said in French, turning to Sylvie, who translated her words into Swahili.

"She says she understands," Sylvie translated back into French from the mother to Marie.

"Doctor Marie," Sylvie asked as she disposed of the syringe in the sharps bin, after the mother and child had gone, "does everyone in Canada speak French?"

"Not everyone," she replied. "In Quebec, where I come from, French is the official language. That's why my parents decided to immigrate there from Haiti, which is also French-speaking." She got a quizzical smile. "Why do you ask?"

"Just wondering," said Sylvie with a shrug.

"Have you thought more about what we talked about?"

"No," she replied, lying. The truth was she had thought of little else.

"The best thing you can do for your family is go to Canada and get an education. Once you're settled, you'll be in a better position to help them join you there."

When, months ago, Sylvie first confided in Marie her dream of becoming a doctor, Marie immediately began pushing the idea that Sylvie must go to Canada to finish her education. Sylvie had always insisted that leaving her family behind would be impossible. Mama would never forgive her. But today, when she was feeling so desperate to escape, she said nothing—which Doctor Marie seemed to take as agreement.

"Stay right here," she said with a grin.

She headed into the doctors' private office, returning a moment later with her mobile phone.

"Come out into the light," she told Sylvie, leading her outside through the open doorway of the clinic. "Now smile!"

Before Sylvie had time to stop her, Marie took her photo with the phone. Sylvie burned with embarrassment —she hated having her picture taken, just as she hated looking in mirrors.

"It's nice," said Marie, examining the photo on the mobile's screen. "Look."

"I don't want to look!" protested Sylvie, temper flashing.

But Marie was too busy fidgeting with her mobile to notice Sylvie's shift in mood. "With your permission," she said, "I want to send this to a friend of mine back home."

"No!"

Marie looked up with surprise. "Sylvie, you're so beautiful," she told her, pitying and patronizing, which Sylvie hated most of all.

She held the mobile up. All Sylvie could see was the hideous scar across her face, and, without warning, a memory burst from its hiding place. Her heart was racing. Anxiety twisted her stomach. She was ten years old again, trapped under the soldier's sweating body. Suffocating. Weak, helpless.

Marie touched her arm. "Sylvie?"

Sylvie recoiled at her touch. Panic turned to anger.

"I didn't say you could take my picture!"

"Please, just listen. My friend's name is Alain. We've

been talking. He thinks he might be able to raise sponsorship money. He has a plan."

"No! Don't send it," Sylvie told her. Why wouldn't she listen?

"Sylvie, the Canadian government won't accept you as a refugee as long as you're living in a safe country like Tanzania—unless somebody in Canada is willing to sponsor you."

"No!" she repeated, and started walking away.

"Sylvie, just think about it!" Doctor Marie called after her.

Sylvie didn't look back. A black rage had seized her. She was helpless against a flood of living memories—the soldier groping, hurting, pushing his thing inside her. Then his machete raised over her face. And through it all, one thought: *Why is this happening to me?*

She stared without seeing as she walked, lost in the horrors of the past. But all at once the sight of Olivier brought her crashing into the present. He was standing by one of the food stalls in the former marketplace, sipping a Fanta—purchased, no doubt, with the money Kayembe gave him for the bushmeat—and he was turning the shiny object he had hidden from her that morning over and over in his hand. It was a mobile phone, Sylvie now realized, like the one that Papa used to have. That phone had been a prized possession—nobody but her father was allowed to touch it. "But it's a blessing and a curse," Papa told her. "People in America and Europe and China are willing to pay a lot of money for the coltan mined here, so they can use it to make phones and computers. That is the reason rebels and soldiers attack our village and so many others—so they can get hold of the coltan and get rich."

Where did Olivier find the money for a mobile phone? Sylvie wondered. Suddenly it rang. He opened it and held it to his ear. Whoever was calling him must have been important, because he quickly lost his lazy slouch. He closed the phone and headed briskly away into what used to be the market street, as though following orders. *Kayembe's orders*, thought Sylvie. So what Pascal said was true: Olivier was becoming one of Kayembe's brutes. They were all the same—the Rwandans, the Mai-Mai, Kayembe. She would never forget the swagger of those soldiers entering their house, like they owned everything, even people. It sickened Sylvie to see it now, in her own brother.

Papa, she prayed silently to the spirit world, *tell me how to save him from becoming one of them!*

LAIPING LAY AWAKE most of her first night in Shenzhen, squished on the narrow mattress between Min and the wall, listening to her cousin's gentle snores. Her mind buzzed between the dual frequencies of excitement and anxiety. All night, she was aware of restless sleepers tossing, of girls padding along the narrow pathway between the rows of bunks, of the toilet flushing in the tiny cubicle. It seemed to her that she had just nodded off when Min sat up, jostling the mattress as she crawled to the ladder.

"Wake up, lazy!" Min whispered when Laiping lifted her head.

"Is it morning?" she asked.

"It's seven o'clock."

"I hardly slept."

"I know! You kept me awake all night," retorted Min. Laiping thought this was rich, considering Min's snoring. "My shift starts at eight," Min told her, keeping her voice low. "I won't be able to take you to the employment office. Just ask somebody where the main building is—everyone knows it. Here, take this with you." She reached into a plastic bag hanging from a hook on the wall and handed Laiping a sheet of paper. "It's a new birth certificate for you."

Laiping stared with surprise at her name on the certificate. "But the date is wrong."

"Of course it's wrong, dummy! It's a fake—because you're underage. When you get paid, you owe me ten yuan for that."

As Min disappeared down the ladder, Laiping stretched out her cramped limbs. She must have fallen asleep again, because the next thing she knew she was startled awake by the sound of a shrill whistle coming from some distance—loud enough to wake the ancestors. She was disoriented for a moment, unsure where she was or what she was doing here. Then she found the fake birth certificate beside her and everything came back to her. She'd come to Shenzhen to find a good job in a factory, like Min's. Unless Laiping wanted to spend her life like her parents, knee deep in muck in the rice paddies back home, it was time for her to get up and apply for that job.

At the elevator, she asked a girl how to find the factory's employment office. When the girl heard Laiping's country accent, she was a little snooty, but she gave Laiping the directions she needed. Laiping waited for the girl to press the button on the elevator, not yet trusting herself to push the right one. Inside the elevator car, girls chattered about which cafeteria they would go to for breakfast, which reminded Laiping that she was hungry. She was tempted to follow them and try to get something to eat, but she was afraid of being caught and somehow spoiling her chances of being hired.

The morning sun was baking hot as Laiping retraced her steps, making her way back to the broad boulevard where the busses stopped. There were even more people on the sidewalk now, lining up for busses. There were more girls than boys, many of them with neatly styled hair, makeup, and frilly tops. Min had mentioned that the really good jobs weren't in the factory, but in the office. She wondered if that's where these girls worked. There were a few couples holding hands as they strolled down the sidewalk—a public display that wasn't done back in the village. But here, stylish girls seemed to show off their boyfriends the same way they did their pretty blouses and new shoes.

Laiping followed the wide boulevard past one of the giant white factory buildings, the sun gleaming off its large square tiles. She saw a sign for the employment office, just as the girl in the dorm said she would, and followed it down a street flanked by more blockish white-tile buildings, all of which looked the same. But she could tell she had reached the employment office by the long line of job-seekers outside. Laiping followed the line around the corner of the building. Most of the people looking for jobs appeared to be a little older than Laiping, but a few looked younger. She took her place at the end and waited for her turn to be called inside the building.

"How long have you been waiting?" she asked a tiny girl in front of her who looked like she belonged in middle school.

"Not that long," she replied. "But they're only taking a

few people at a time. I hope we're not here all day."

The girl looked anxiously up the line, craning her neck. From her plain and worn clothing, Laiping guessed that she, too, had come out from a village to find work in the city. Laiping could tell from her accent that she was from Guangdong Province, just like her.

"My name is Laiping," she said.

"Yiyin," replied the girl.

"Are you here alone?" Yiyin gave a quick nod. "I'm staying with my cousin," Laiping told her. "If they won't give me a job, I'll have to go home to my parents near Heyuan."

"My mother told me not to come home unless I send money ahead of me," confided Yiyin. "All she cares about is paying for my brother to go to school. I was better in school than he is, but she made me leave after grade seven."

Laiping remembered how her own mother cried at the train station, and thought, *Yiyin's mother must be mean.* But then, Laiping's parents didn't have a son to favor. She was their only child.

"Where are you from?" she asked.

"Dongzhou, a village near Shanwei," Yiyin replied. Laiping had heard Min talk about girls she'd met from Shanwei—it was one of a dozen manufacturing cities, like Shenzhen, in the broad Pearl River Delta. According to Min, though, the factories there were lower quality and didn't pay as well as Shenzhen. "My father was a fisherman," said Yiyin. "Then they started filling in the bay to build more factories, and the fish disappeared."

In front of them, a girl of about twenty was fanning herself in the growing heat of the sun. She gave Yiyin a sharp look. "I'd keep quiet about being from Dongzhou, if I were you. They don't hire protesters and troublemakers."

Yiyin was suddenly fierce. "Mind your own business," she fired back. "I'm not a troublemaker."

The older girl made a face and turned away, still fanning herself. Laiping didn't understand why she was calling Yiyin and her father troublemakers just because they were from Dongzhou, but she admired the way Yiyin stood up for herself and her family.

"What does your father do, if he can no longer fish?" she asked.

For a moment, Yiyin turned the same fierce look on Laiping, but when she saw that Laiping meant no offense, she dropped her eyes. "He went away," she said, then she fell silent. Laiping wondered what she'd said wrong.

"What's taking so long?" grumbled Yiyin after another half hour went by, the hot sun beating down on them. "I have to pee."

"Go. I'll save your place," replied Laiping.

Yiyin gave Laiping a distrusting look, but her bladder seemed to decide for her.

"Don't go in without me," she said, then darted away.

The line suddenly lurched forward and rounded the corner of the building. Now Laiping could see the entrance to the employment office, where several people were being ushered inside. She was starting to feel anxious. What if her turn came and Yiyin had not come back? She didn't want to risk her chances by letting others go ahead of her, but she had promised to save Yiyin's spot. Laiping shifted from foot to foot, glancing over her shoulder every few seconds for Yiyin.

Down the line toward the corner of the building, Laiping noticed a guy in a blue hoodie approaching people. She thought it was strange that he was wearing a hoodie in this heat. She noticed how people turned away from him.

"Keep moving!" shouted a security guard up near the entrance.

The line moved forward again. Laiping closed the gap with the girls in front of her. When she turned back to look for Yiyin, the guy in the blue hoodie thrust a pink flyer into her hands.

"If they hire you, there are things you need to know," he said.

His eyes were intense and his face lean and handsome. Laiping glanced at the sheet and saw written in large characters: *Know Your Rights!* She looked around and noticed that nobody else had taken the flyer. Then she heard someone shout,

"You!"

The security guard at the entrance had spotted the guy in the hoodie and was blowing a whistle. Several other guards emerged from the building and started chasing the guy, who took off running. Just before the guards reached the spot where Laiping was standing, the girl with the fan snatched the pink paper from her hand and threw it to the ground. The guards ran right past Laiping. The guy in the hoodie was yards ahead of them now, sprinting like a deer—losing himself between the buildings before the security team could catch him.

"Stupid hick," said the older girl in disgust.

It took Laiping a moment to realize she meant her.

"Did I miss anything?" asked Yiyin when she returned to the line several moments later.

Laiping saw the flyer on the ground near her feet and was about to tell Yiyin about the guy and the security guards, but the words "stupid hick" rang in her ears.

"No," she said. "Hopefully it won't be much longer."

AT LAST LAIPING and Yiyin's turn came to enter the employ-ment office. They were told to line up again, this time in a large room with several wickets. The woman behind the wicket in their line asked them if they were together when they reached the front. Before Laiping could speak, Yiyin answered for both of them that they were.

"Have you worked in a factory before?" asked the woman. Her manner was severe and suspicious. She was seated on a stool behind a desk, while Laiping and Yiyin stood.

"No," answered Laiping, "but I am a very hard worker and I learn quickly."

"I have!" declared Yiyin. "I worked in a factory in Shanwei making purses."

Laiping wished she had factory experience to boast about.

"Why did you leave there?"

Yiyin didn't miss a beat. "Everybody knows that Shenzhen is the place to be. In Shanwei there are posters everywhere saying so! Besides, I want to make high tech."

"There are posters in my village, too," Laiping piped up, hoping to appear every bit as eager as Yiyin. The image of a girl on an assembly line rose in her mind, smiling with pride above a caption that read, "*Come out to the city to work!*" Laiping had always admired the girl's smart white smock and cap.

The woman made notes on their application forms. Without looking up she said, "Identification papers."

Laiping pushed the fake birth certificate Min gave her under the glass. The woman gave the girls' documents a quick glance. "Which one of you is Fen?" she asked.

Laiping was confused. Who was Fen? But Yiyin answered promptly, "I am."

The woman looked her up and down, seeming to note for the first time how tiny she was. She read Yiyin's identity card to confirm, "You are sixteen?"

"Yes."

The woman seemed satisfied with her reply. She didn't even bother to question Laiping about her age.

"Education?"

"I finished middle school," replied Laiping, which was true—she had graduated from the ninth grade last month. But to support the lie about her age, she added another lie: "A year ago."

"So did I," concurred Yiyin.

Laiping and Yiyin spent several anxious minutes while the woman made notes on each of their forms. "Since you are both from Guangdong Province," she said, "we will place you in the same division. Report to Building 3 for training at one o'clock today."

Laiping and Yiyin were over the moon. The woman placed them in the same dormitory, too, and although Laiping was disappointed that she wouldn't be in the same building as Min, she was happy she'd be with her new friend.

"Because you are inexperienced, you will be paid the basic wage," the woman continued. "You must sign a contract stating that you will stay here and work for two years."

Laiping's smile faded slightly. She had been so caught up in the excitement of working in Shenzhen that she had never considered she might be required to stay for a certain period. Two years seemed like a very long time to be away from home.

"I'll stay here forever!" declared Yiyin. "I love the big city."

"You will stay here until the company gives you permission to leave," stated the humorless woman, "and you will stay in the dormitory we assign to you. There's a list of rules posted on every floor of each dormitory. Make sure you obey them. Do you understand?"

"Yes," replied Yiyin, chastened.

"Yes," replied Laiping, forcing a smile.

The woman pointed toward another room to her right.

"Go in there and have your pictures taken for your company ID tags, then you may eat in the cafeteria before reporting to the Training Center."

BY THE TIME LAIPING AND YIYIN LEFT the employment office, they had just enough time for lunch, so they headed immediately to the nearest cafeteria, proudly wearing company ID tags on plastic strings around their necks that would allow them access to the company's facilities. They entered to find a vast room lit by high windows, with row upon row of tables at which thousands of people were seated, eating quietly. A worker checked their ID tags before they were allowed to get in line. On Yiyin's tag, she was identified as Fen.

"Why are you called Fen when your name is Yiyin?" asked Laiping as they chose the shortest lineup they could find to wait for their food.

Yiyin shrugged. "That's the name on my ID card."

"Is that you?"

"It is now." Yiyin grinned.

Now Laiping understood—the card was a fake, just like her birth certificate.

"How old are you really?" she asked.

"Fourteen. You?"

"Fifteen. Where did you get that ID card?"

Yiyin took a fraction of a second before answering, "I found it." Her hesitation made Laiping think she was lying.

"Did you really work in a purse factory in Shanwei?" she asked, wondering what else Yiyin had lied about.

"No, but my mother does," she replied. "That's how I know it's better to work here in Shenzhen, making high tech. By the way," she added, "from now on, my name is Fen."

Laiping and Fen slowly shifted forward in the line, worrying that they would be late for their training. At last they reached a steam table where a worker behind the counter filled their plates with rice and vegetables and a portion of meat that looked like chicken, but might have been pork. To Laiping, it was a feast, but Fen complained that the portion of meat was small. They found a spot at a table of girls. Both were so hungry that not a word passed between them while they clacked chopsticks.

At a nearby table, a girl raised her voice in protest at something another girl had said. A security guard, a middle-aged woman wearing a severe expression, stepped toward the offending girl, pointing to a sign on the wall that read, *Eat Quietly and Quickly*. The girl bowed her head.

"Sorry," she said softly. "Sorry."

The matron retreated to her post by the wall, but she kept her eye on the girl. Laiping and Fen, mouths full, exchanged wary looks. Laiping counted a fourth lesson she had learned since arriving in the city: obey the rules, and avoid the attention of the security guards.

AFTER LUNCH, Laiping and Fen scurried to find Building 3. They had to show their ID tags to a security guard before they were allowed to enter, then they followed hundreds of other new employees into a space that was even bigger than the cafeteria, with tables running in rows along the entire length of the massive room. Everything was white—the walls, the linoleum floor, the tables—giving Laiping the sense she was entering a huge, open hospital.

A foreman shouted for the newcomers to find a work station. Fen pulled Laiping with her to two free spots along one of the tables, where they stood awaiting further instructions. On one wall, Laiping saw a huge portrait of an important-looking man with a confident smile. He was Chinese, but he seemed Western—maybe because of the expensive-looking suit and tie he was wearing, and because of the smile. Posters on the wall beside the portrait proclaimed, *Take pride in your work!* and *Duty leads to prosperity!*

Once all of the new workers were settled, a woman in a business suit entered, accompanied by fifty or more men and women in white smocks and caps—just like the ones the girl in the poster back home was wearing.

"I'll bet they're going to give us more rules," said Fen.

The woman in the suit took a microphone from a stand. "Hello, and welcome!" she said, smiling so that all her teeth showed—her voice echoing around the hall. "We are happy you are here, and we hope that you are happy, too."

The woman cupped her hand around her ear, waiting for a reply. Laiping was startled when hundreds of new employees—including Fen—obliged her in unison with a resounding, "Yes, we are happy!"

"You have had the good fortune to be hired by the most successful company in China. Almost half a million people work at this location alone, and this is just one of many factory complexes around the world. You owe your jobs to this man," she said, sweeping her arm toward the giant portrait on the wall. "Mr. Steve Chen is the founder and chief executive officer of this company. He is like a father, and you are like his children—many, many children he looks after and cares about. Let's hear it for Mr. Chen, who is giving you prosperity and a future you could never have dreamed of!"

A loud cheer welled up. Laiping joined in, even though she had never heard of Mr. Chen. "Mr. Chen has provided for your every need, from good food to comfortable beds. He has even built a movie theater and swimming pool for you to enjoy!"

The workers cheered, Laiping included. The woman with the microphone let them applaud for a bit, then motioned for them to be quiet. Her tone turned serious.

"Mr. Chen is very kind to his employees, but in return for his kindness he expects something from us."

Fen leaned into Laiping. "Here come the rules! I told you so!"

Laiping wished Fen would keep quiet and pay attention to what was being said.

"First, he expects hard work." The woman's voice echoed off the walls.

"More like slave labour," Fen chimed in.

Laiping edged away from her slightly, wanting to listen to the woman instead of Fen's smart remarks.

"Second, he expects quality work and quality products."

"Then give us quality food!" countered Fen.

Laiping noticed several people around them glancing at Fen. A foreman standing nearby shot her a warning look, holding his finger to his mouth—but Fen didn't see him.

The speaker's expression darkened; her tone became dire. "Thirdly," she said, "Mr. Chen expects loyalty. The products we make are secret, the very latest technology. Should they fall into the wrong hands before they reach market, those responsible will be punished for humiliating Mr. Chen, and for putting everyone's prosperity at risk."

A hush had fallen over the training hall, but Fen couldn't resist whispering into Laiping's ear, "Who would be that stupid?"

Suddenly, a hand locked around Fen's arm. The foreman swiftly and quietly marched her out of the hall. Laiping watched them, alarmed. But then she noticed that no one else had even turned her head, and decided it would be smart to pretend, like the rest of them, that nothing had happened. The woman in the business suit was jolly and smiling again.

"Let us care for each other to build a wonderful future!" she proclaimed.

Everyone applauded, including Laiping, but she barely listened to the rest of what the lady had to say. *What if Fen never comes back?* she worried. Fen might have been loud and a liar, but other than Min she was the only person Laiping knew in all of Shenzhen.

IT TURNED OUT that the men and women in white smocks were instructors who were there to teach the new workers how to do their jobs. Laiping's instructor was Mr. Huang, who told the half-dozen workers lined along their section of table, "You will be trained to work in the mobile phone factory. Specifically, you will learn to solder capacitors onto printed circuit boards."

Laiping experienced a moment of panic. She had no idea what a capacitor or a circuit board was, or what "to solder" meant. But her anxiety lessened a little when Fen returned to the hall and took her place beside her. Laiping tried to welcome her back with a small smile, but Fen—pale and serious now—kept her eyes on the instructor.

Mr. Huang had the group gather around him while he demonstrated how to use tweezers to pick up a tiny flat square with a geometric pattern on it from one bin, which turned out to be a circuit board, and a far tinier component from a second bin, which was the capacitor.

"The tantalum capacitor is an essential part of the cell phone," explained Mr. Huang. "Tantalum powder is made from columbite-tantalite, or coltan, a special mineral that stores energy and releases it quickly, with very little energy loss. Tantalum powder is what allows high-quality electronics to become smaller and smaller in size. But if the capacitor is not secured perfectly to the circuit board, the mobile phone won't work properly and the company's customers will be unhappy. Mr. Chen's reputation will suffer!"

Using tweezers, he carefully placed the capacitor onto a designated spot on the circuit board, stepping back so that each of them in turn could examine where he had positioned it. Next, he picked up a small pointed tool with an electrical cord in one hand and a thin strand of metal in the other.

"This is the soldering iron and solder," he said. "You will touch the hot tip of the soldering iron to the place where the capacitor meets the circuit board to heat them, then you will use the iron to melt the solder, like this." Mr. Huang touched the iron to the strand of metal until it liquefied and coated the tip of the iron. "Be careful not to get too much or too little solder," he said, applying the molten tip of the iron to the circuit board with a quick, deft motion, "Or the joint will not function properly." Mr. Huang lifted the iron away from the board. "There!" he pronounced. "Now you try!"

For the next four hours, Laiping and Fen tried their hardest to solder capacitors onto circuit boards. Laiping went hot with embarrassment whenever Mr. Huang checked her work. The first time, the instructor was able to break the capacitor off the board with the slightest tweak of the tweezers—"The joint is weak," declared Mr. Huang. "The board and capacitor weren't hot enough when you applied the solder"—only to complain during his next inspection that Laiping had applied too much.

Laiping's fingertips were burned from the soldering iron. Her neck and shoulders ached from being hunched over the work table, and her legs were stiff from standing. But she was pleased when at the end of the day Mr. Huang held up one of her circuit boards to the group as an example of good workmanship.

"That's enough for today," he announced. "Be back here at eight o'clock tomorrow morning. By the end of the week, we expect you to be ready to move onto the factory floor."

Fen was unusually quiet as she and Laiping found their way from the Training Center to Dormitory 2, where they had been assigned.

"What happened when that foreman took you away?" asked Laiping. Fen threw her a hostile look, just as she had done that morning in line at the employment office when Laiping asked about her father. "Sorry," said Laiping, realizing she was causing Fen to lose more face than she already had.

With that, Fen softened a little. "He just yelled at me," she said sullenly. "In my mother's factory, the bosses yell at the workers all the time. Sometimes she works every day of the week, for twelve hours. I don't want her life. I want to make something of myself, to be more than just an ordinary worker."

Again Laiping wondered what happened to Fen's father, but she knew better than to ask. She tried to change the subject.

"What are those nets?" she asked as they approached their dormitory. There was broad webbing surrounding the building, raised two storeys off the ground.

Fen threw Laiping a wary look. "You don't know?"

"Know what?" replied Laiping, Fen's tone making her feel stupid.

"Never mind."

"Tell me," replied Laiping. She had to know these things, so people would stop calling her a country hick.

Fen dropped her voice so the girls around them going in and out of the dorm couldn't hear. "They're to catch people who jump."

Laiping was confused. "Why would people jump? From where?"

Fen rolled her eyes and kept her voice low. "Didn't your cousin tell you anything?"

"Tell me what?"

"That workers have killed themselves, or tried to."

Laiping went cold. "Why?"

"I guess you'll find out, won't you?" answered Fen.

While Fen went inside, Laiping lagged behind. *With good jobs and movie theaters and swimming pools,* she thought, *why would anyone want to kill herself?* Then she remembered what the guy in the blue hoodie had said to her. *There are things you need to know.*

Laiping followed Fen into the building with a nagging sense that there was another lesson to be learned here. She just wasn't certain what it was.

NIGHTTIME WAS THE WORST IN NYARUGUSU, when there was nothing but mud walls and the old sacks they used to cover the doorway to separate the family from rats and thieves. But the terrors Sylvie feared most were in her jumbled dreams—the soldier on top of her, Mama screaming from the bedroom, Papa's face when the bullets hit. This night, like so many others, she woke in a cold sweat, her heart racing. She could see nothing, but she heard Mama muttering and fretting in her sleep and could only guess at what nightmares she was reliving. Sylvie dozed fitfully for the rest of the night, until at last dawn framed the sacks in the doorway with soft light.

But the mat where Olivier usually slept was empty. He hadn't been home in two days—the last time Sylvie had seen him was in the marketplace, when she'd watched him take a call on his mobile phone.

Mama stirred and sat up. "Has he come back?" she asked.

"No," said Sylvie.

"You must have said something to keep him away, you and that temper of yours."

Without replying, Sylvie got up and took the lid off the cooking pot, encouraged to see that bugs and rats hadn't gotten into the cold porridge she'd saved for their breakfast. Pascal and Lucie were soon awake and scooping the porridge from the pot with their fingers, while Mama continued to blame Sylvie for Olivier's absence—"What did you say to him? You must have said something!" Sylvie gave Pascal a warning glance to stay silent about Kayembe.

"Olivier doesn't listen to me, no matter what I say," Sylvie told her, yawning.

She was tired from lack of sleep—too tired to care that her mother seemed to take pleasure in accusing her. But to Sylvie's surprise, Mama's eyes suddenly filled with tears. Through everything they had endured, Sylvie had rarely seen her cry.

"We're just women and children!" she wailed. "With Patrice gone, Olivier is the man of the family. What will become of us without him?"

Sylvie wasn't sure which were worse, the days when Mama forgot that Papa was dead, or the days when she remembered. She looked at her mother sitting up on the sleeping mat, head in her hands, her thin shoulders heaving with each sob. Married Congolese women took pride in wrapping their hair in a colorful cloth, but Mama hadn't bothered in months. Her hair sprung in clumps all over her head, as chaotic as the brain inside. Sylvie knew she should try to comfort her. But the truth was that Mama's weakness made her angry. She wanted to shout, *Haven't I provided for the family by working at the clinic? Me—not Olivier!* Instead she promised, "I'll try to find him."

PASCAL WAS GLOOMY as he and Sylvie walked to school.

"Olivier is never coming back," he said. "Why should he, when he can make money working for Mr. Kayembe?"

"Because family comes first," Sylvie replied.

Pascal brooded over this as they walked. Then he asked, almost in a whisper, "Sylvie, how did your face get cut?"

If anyone else had asked the question, she would have snapped that it was none of their business. But this was Pascal. He was there. He saw.

"You don't remember?" she asked.

He shook his head. He was watching her with frightened eyes, as though the memory was lurking somewhere in his mind, waiting to jump out.

"A bad man did it," she told him.

"The same man who killed Papa?"

"No." Then she revised, "Maybe. I don't know."

It was possible it was the same soldier, she supposed. He could have gone to the school after riding away from the house with the other soldiers—after they'd finished with her and Mama. She wasn't sure she would recognize the man, except by his greasy smell of sweat and diesel fuel. And by the weight of his body. Pascal pulled her back to him by slipping his hand into hers, something he hadn't done in forever.

"Sylvie, why did he cut you?"

Why? She had tried to accept that there would never be an answer to that question. But she thought she understood what he really wanted to hear.

"I don't know if Olivier is coming back, Pascal," she

told him, squeezing his hand. "I promise you this, though. I will never leave you."

They continued walking in silence, hand in hand. When they got to the school, she told Pascal to go in by himself, and she'd be back soon.

"Where are you going?"

"To find him."

With that Sylvie veered off toward the old market-place. She glanced back to see Pascal standing in the dust, watching her.

"Go to school!" she called to him sternly, and he obeyed her. But would he for much longer?

MOST OF THE TIME, Sylvie tried not to think about what had happened in their village, but as she walked past the abandoned stalls of the market, the ghosts of the past seemed to walk with her. When the Mai-Mai came five years ago looking for her father, they went first to the house. Mama was in her bedroom, resting with the new baby, while Sylvie played with Pascal in the sitting room. She remembered the rumble of the truck pulling up outside. When she looked out the window and saw the soldiers climbing out of it, she rushed to the door and locked it, but the soldiers burst through it. It was good that Pascal couldn't remember, but she would never forget—how Pascal screamed in fear, and how she held him tight, trying to comfort him, until one of the soldiers tore her away and pushed her down on the floor, pulling her skirt up, her underwear down.

She could hear the baby crying and her mother's shouts from the bedroom, "We have done nothing wrong!

Take what you want! Let us be!" And then her silence—
more frightening than her screams.

The whole time the soldier was on top of her, Sylvie
listened for her mother—even through the searing pain of
being split open, the smell of diesel, his crushing weight.
When it was over, Sylvie saw the blood on her dress. Pascal
was sitting against the wall, knees pulled up to make himself small, eyes wide and unseeing. Then she heard Mama
sobbing in the other room, and felt a wave of relief that she
was still alive. Soldiers came out from the bedroom, swaggering, laughing. One of them saw the crucifix on a silver
chain around Sylvie's neck—a gift from Papa for standing
first in her grade.

"Take it from her," he told the man who had raped her.

"No!" Sylvie had cried, still on the floor, her legs sticky
with blood. Hadn't they taken enough?

The man knelt down to her. "Give me the necklace
and I won't hurt you."

Sylvie slapped her hand over the crucifix to protect
it. In nightmares, she still saw the sudden anger in the
soldier's face, and how swiftly he drew the machete from
his belt. After that, she remembered nothing. She woke up
later, being jostled by a moving vehicle, a thick smell in the
air from their burning village—blinded by the rag someone
had tied over her face. She pulled the rag up enough to
see that it was nighttime. She was in the back of an open
truck with many other people, including Mama and the
baby. Pascal was sound asleep against Mama's side. Olivier
sat apart, sullen and staring at nothing. She felt for the
necklace. It was gone.

"That's what you get for being so stubborn," Mama said, and those were her last words about what had happened to them that day inside their house.

"Where's Papa?" she asked.

Olivier, only nine years old, told her, blank-faced, his eyes cold, "Papa is dead."

His words cut deep, as though he meant them to wound. Sylvie remembered willing herself back to sleep in the hope that when she woke up, she would be in her own bed, with Papa close by in the other room, but that wasn't what happened.

She shook these thoughts away as she crossed a dusty open area into a road, heading toward the shack that was Kayembe's shop before the Tanzanians shut it down. Nyarugusu wasn't safe for girls walking alone—she had to stay alert for trouble. Men lingered in small groups by the food stalls sipping tea, or leaned against scrubby trees, smoking. Some were on crutches, others were missing an arm or a leg. Sylvie kept her eyes forward as she passed them, but she could feel their leering stares. She ignored lewd comments from those who were shamefully drunk. One of them offered her a few shillings to have sex with him.

Sylvie saw Kayembe standing outside his old shop, deep in conversation with two of his men, one short and scrawny and the other tall and round. Everybody knew that Hervé Kayembe was the most powerful man in Nyarugusu, and the armed men he employed were the reason why. They were dressed like makeshift soldiers, in camouflage pants and mismatched shirts. The skinny one had a handgun tucked under his belt, and the fat one a long machete.

When Kayembe saw Sylvie approaching, he dismissed the men with a nod of his head and they ambled off.

"*Mademoiselle* Sylvie!" he greeted her with a sweeping bow. Sylvie thought he was making fun of her. He was a big man of fifty, maybe even sixty years. His full cheeks were rutted with deep lines. "To what do I owe the pleasure?"

"How do you know my name?" she asked.

"We are clansmen, from the same village. I knew your father, and I knew your mother. She was so beautiful when she was young. Just like her daughter."

Now Sylvie was certain he was making fun of her, calling her beautiful. Her face grew hot and prickly. She felt the scar tighten. "I'm looking for my brother, Olivier," she told him.

He pretended to become serious. "Businesslike and to the point. I like that. Unfortunately, *Mademoiselle* Sylvie, I am not at liberty to disclose Olivier's whereabouts."

"Then you know where he is."

"Suffice to say he is doing a little work for me."

Sylvie shouldn't have been surprised to have this confirmed, but it shocked her nevertheless. "What kind of work?" she asked, forcing herself to be bold.

"If I told you that, I would have to kill you," he replied, and then he laughed so hard she could see his belly fat jiggling through his shirt. Kayembe must have seen how Sylvie feared him, because he hastened to add, "It's a joke! Have you never seen American movies, girl?"

"Please tell me where Olivier is," she repeated, wishing nothing more than to be gone from his presence.

"You are a stubborn one, you are. Like your father. Tell your mother not to fear for her son. He will be back with her by tomorrow."

Sylvie saw she would learn nothing more from Kayembe. She drew herself up, remembering her manners, and her dignity. "Thank you," she said.

He nodded his head in a slight bow. "One moment, fair *mademoiselle*." He went inside the shack that used to be his shop and came out with a small paper sack. "Please accept this with my compliments," he said, handing it to her.

"What is it?"

"Cassava flour, from back home."

Sylvie thought how happy the flour would make Mama. Now she could make real *fufu*! Then she wondered how it was that Kayembe received goods from the Congo, here in the refugee camp. Or any of the goods he traded in, really. She knew better than to ask.

"Sweets for the sweet, as it were," added Kayembe.

As Sylvie walked away, she wondered why an important man like Kayembe found it necessary to mock her. But quickly her mind was filled with the question she had come to ask him, still unanswered: *Where has Olivier gone?* Now she had a new question: *Is it too late to save him?* She knew where she had to go next, if she had any hope of doing so.

"SYLVIE!" exclaimed Doctor Marie. She took Sylvie's hand and squeezed it in the overly friendly way of North

Americans, then checked herself and let her hand drop. "I'm so glad you're here," she said, smiling.

In the waiting area, one of the nurses was taking a man's temperature. Otherwise it was quiet inside the clinic. Not even the hum of the generator out back disturbed the calm. They were saving petrol—one of the cutbacks that had taken place recently, along with food rations.

"The picture you took," Sylvie began. "Do you still have it?"

Marie took her mobile phone out of her pocket and with a flick of her finger found the photo. "Here it is," she said, showing the picture to Sylvie.

Sylvie studied herself. If people saw past the scar, she wasn't so bad looking. She might even look intelligent. Tears sprang to Sylvie's eyes.

"*Cherie*, what's wrong?"

Marie moved toward Sylvie to give her a hug. By reflex, Sylvie pulled back.

"Sorry," said Marie.

Sylvie had never told Marie the reason why she didn't like to be touched, but with the militias raping women, children, and even men in the villages they terrorized, she supposed Marie must have guessed.

"Please, can you send the photo to your friend?" asked Sylvie, her voice choking.

"I'll send it to Alain right away," Marie told her. "He and some friends of his have a website they set up to tell people what's happening in the Congo, because of coltan."

The idea that people somewhere knew about the suffering of the Congolese made her feel a little better.

"I'm sorry for losing my temper the other day," Sylvie apologized, and she meant it.

"No, Sylvie, it was my fault," replied Marie. Now she was crying, too. "I had no right to make presumptions like that, to pressure you. Everything's going to be okay," she said, forcing a cheerful smile. "Alain will find a way to get you to Canada, where you'll be safe."

Safe? Sylvie tried to imagine what that would feel like, to be in a place where there were no militias, no Kayembe. A worm of hope was taking hold inside her, that most deceiving of emotions that could lift the spirit but dash it just as quickly when promises fell through. *Someday we will be gone from here. Someday we will be free.* Could it be true? Could she trust this feeling?

"What are you thinking, Sylvie?" asked Marie.

"It's cold in Canada, isn't it?" she replied.

Marie laughed. "It's summer there now. It's not as hot as here, but it's warm. If all goes well, you'll see for yourself before long."

She tried to imagine what it must be like there. She knew so little about Canada, except for what Marie had told her. But Marie was a happy person, and her family had immigrated to Canada, so perhaps Sylvie's family could be happy there, too. For just this moment, she allowed hope to lift her heart a little higher.

ON THE WAY TO SCHOOL on Monday morning, Fiona asked Lacey if she thought she should go looking for Ryan at his locker—he hadn't been in touch since Saturday night. But Lacey talked her out of it.

"You don't want to look like you're chasing him," she said. "Especially after sexting him."

As they walked along the sidewalk of the leafy Vancouver neighborhood, Fiona had confided all to Lacey—about the boob shot, and about Ryan not calling.

"You think it was dumb to send him that picture, don't you?"

Lacey shrugged. "It depends how much you trust him not to send it around to his friends."

"I *do* trust him," replied Fiona. But did she? She'd thought she did when she sent him the selfie, but since then she'd been having second thoughts. He *had* kind of pressured her into sexting. That wasn't very nice.

"Maybe he tried to call your cell," Lacey suggested, "but the phone thief answered."

Fiona had to admit it was a possibility. She had gone back to the ball diamond on Sunday to search for her missing cell phone, but it was nowhere to be found. Maybe it had fallen out of her bag and somebody picked it up. Or maybe somebody took it out of her bag while nobody was watching. Anybody could have it. Fiona felt sick about it. But a missing phone didn't let Ryan off the hook.

"I still have a laptop," Fiona said. "He could have Friendjammed. Or emailed."

"Who emails?"

"We have a land line, too."

Lacey's eyes went wide with a sudden vision of disaster. "This boob shot, did you send it from your cell or from your laptop?"

"My cell, but I erased it!" Fiona added quickly. She'd been over it a hundred times in her head since discovering the phone was missing. She was positive she'd deleted the shot immediately—just as she was positive she was never mixing vodka and rum coolers again.

"So don't worry about it then," Lacey concluded.

But by now all Fiona could do was worry. How well did she know Ryan, and how much could she trust him?

Fiona spent the rest of the day looking for Ryan in the hallways between classes, and at lunch in the cafeteria. Since she didn't have her cell, she had to borrow Lacey's smartphone to check her Friendjam account, but by mid-afternoon study hall there were still no messages from him. The longer he went without contacting her, the more worried she became that maybe she had misjudged how much she could trust him. Then, at the end of the day, when Fiona was at her locker getting ready to go home, he at last appeared, sauntering up to her with gangsta cool. "Whassup?" he asked.

"Where have *you* been?" she replied, trying to match his apparent indifference.

"I been busy," he said with a shrug.

"Doing what?"

"Stuff. So, what's going on?"

"Well, I lost my phone."

"Yeah? That sucks."

Ha! Fiona had him. "Obviously you didn't try to call me, or you would have known," she said.

"Are you mad or something?" Ryan asked, at last clueing in to her mood.

"I just think you should have called me."

"About what?"

"You know," she said, prompting him. When he still didn't get it, she dropped her voice so that kids around them wouldn't hear. "After I sent you that picture and everything."

"Oh."

"Oh?" Was that all he had to say? Ryan was being so annoying. "You think I do that all the time?" she said.

"You didn't have to do it." Fiona noted that he was avoiding her eyes.

"You asked me to!"

"That didn't mean you had to."

Fiona couldn't believe what she was hearing. She waited until the last of the kids around them had closed their lockers and headed away, and kept her voice low. "So now you think I'm a slut?"

He shrugged again. "No…"

Ryan was blushing, struggling for words. But his "no" definitely sounded more like a "yes." Fiona felt her blood boil.

"That is *so* judgmental," she said.

"I still like you," Ryan offered, feebly.

"Don't do me any favors!"

"What are you getting so upset about?" he asked, annoyed now, like she was being some kind of drama queen.

"I don't know. Because you're a two-faced hypocrite?"

Ryan's face got pinched and angry, but Fiona didn't care. Suddenly she was wondering what she ever saw in him.

"So…what? Are we, like, breaking up?" he said.

Fiona wasn't sure if he was asking or threatening. Either way, she found herself jumping at the suggestion.

"Maybe we should," she replied, and before he could respond, she slammed her locker shut and started away. She took two steps, then spun back to where he stood glued to the floor, gape-faced.

"Give me your phone," she demanded.

"Why?"

"Just do it!"

He dug in his pocket and fished out his cell. Fiona grabbed it out of his hand and in three seconds flat had found the selfie—which, naturally, he had saved. With the tap of her finger, she deleted it.

"There," she said, handing it back to him. "Just in case you get any ideas about spreading it around."

As she headed down the front steps of the school, breathing in the fresh spring air, Fiona felt a surge of freedom. She also felt relief—she'd totally dodged a bullet with the boob shot. It had seemed like such a nothing thing on Saturday night, but the anxiety she had felt since then wasn't worth it. She'd learned her lesson—from now on, she was going to be more careful.

FIONA HAD TOLD HER MOM about the lost phone on Sunday, but on Monday night after softball practice, she had to face telling her dad. The phone had been a Christmas present from him. Her dad was a super-conservative business guy, the vice president of communications for a mining company. Balding, glasses, polo shirt tucked neatly into chinos—there was no way she was going to avoid a lecture.

"Fiona, you were supposed to look after that cell phone," he said.

They were sitting in his car outside her mom's place, the engine running because he had to get home to his other family in West Vancouver, across the bridge. Fiona's parents had been divorced since Fiona was three, time enough for her dad to produce another whole family with Wife #2, also known as Joanne. Brandon was eleven and Katie was seven. At first Fiona had been jealous of the competition from kids who were only half-related to her, especially when Katie, his second daughter, arrived, but the upside of her dad being super straight was that he was also super conscientious. He made the trip across the bridge twice a week to coach softball and he always included Fiona in family vacations to Whistler and Hawaii, which her mom could never have afforded.

"I'm sorry," she said, duly regretful.

"I hope you don't think I'm just going to go out and replace it."

She didn't expect that. On the other hand, her cell phone was her life.

"I was thinking I'd get a job this summer," she replied, "and pay for it myself."

"Good idea," he nodded. She could tell that he was proud of her. "If you get a job," he said, "I would be willing to get you a new phone, for your birthday."

My birthday's in September, and it's only June! calculated Fiona. That was a long time to go without a phone.

"By that time," he said with a wink, "the next generation of these babies is supposed to be out." He slipped his smartphone out of his pocket—top of the line, the phone that people camped out overnight in front of electronics stores to buy. "I know a guy who can jump the queue."

"That would be awesome!" *Beyond awesome!* Fiona hugged him. "Thanks, Dad."

"Better not mention it to your mom," he added.

He didn't need to say more. Fiona's mom had a tendency to flip out when she came home with expensive presents from her dad. Her mom was a writer for a consumer magazine. Fiona knew her rant by heart—*"For every electronic gadget we buy, somebody, somewhere is being exploited!"* But Fiona thought that her mom's mini-meltdowns were really about the fact she didn't make much money, and she felt bad that she couldn't compete with Fiona's dad.

"Don't worry," Fiona agreed.

She climbed out of the car and waved while he drove away in the late-evening light, feeling that all was right with the world once more. She could hear kids playing at a nearby park, their voices ringing out last shouts of freedom before their parents packed them off home. Soon the summer holidays would be here, two whole months of freedom. As she turned her key in the gate, Fiona wondered what kind of job she would be able to find, considering she wasn't quite fifteen.

"Ryan called," her mom told her when she walked into the apartment. She was at the kitchen table, working at her laptop. Fiona's expression must have betrayed her, because her mom peered over her glasses at her. "Everything okay?" she asked.

"We broke up," Fiona told her.

"Oh, Fee, I'm sorry," she replied.

"*I'm* not," said Fiona.

Fiona could see her mom willing herself not to ask what happened, knowing that Fiona hated to be interrogated. She leaned back in her chair and ran her hand through the mass of brown-gray curls that covered her head. "Are you going to call him back?" she asked.

"I'm pretty tired. I'll see him tomorrow at school. Goodnight."

"Goodnight, hon."

As she headed to her room, Fiona was curious about why Ryan had called. But whatever the reason, he was the last person she wanted to talk to. She was amazed by how quickly she was over him. *I guess that's how you know what you feel*, she realized. Now that she understood she'd never really had feelings for him, something else was dawning on her. She'd sent a nude photo of herself to a guy it turned out she didn't even like that much. Thinking about it made her burn with embarrassment. No, she really didn't want to talk to Ryan—ever. If she was lucky, she'd get through the last couple of weeks of school avoiding him. After that, she would put the whole business behind her, like it never happened at all.

ASIA

LAIPING AND FEN inhaled a breakfast of rice and vegetables in the cafeteria, then hurried along the sidewalk to the Training Center. As they walked, they chatted about how they would spend their first paychecks, even though they wouldn't be paid until they'd finished their training and been on the job for two weeks.

"I want to buy my own phone," said Laiping as they rounded the walkway to the broad boulevard where the busses ran. The air was stinky with exhaust, and a gray, humid haze hung over the campus.

"I'm saving my money to take a computer course," countered Fen.

"Why bother?"

"A computer course will allow me to move up to an office job," she replied. "Do you think I want to be stuck on the assembly line forever, going numb, like my mother?"

To Laiping, Fen was getting ahead of herself. "I just want to become good at this job," she said.

"Laiping," lectured Fen, "in order to be successful, you have to have a plan to improve yourself."

Laiping was discovering that Fen had a talent for making her feel ignorant, even though Fen was a year younger. "I do have a plan," she said. "I plan to make lots of money."

"That's what everybody says when they come out from their villages. But do you know how many wind up going back after a couple of years, worn out and just as poor as when they arrived?"

"How many?" Laiping asked, challenging her a little.

"Lots," replied Fen vaguely. "That isn't going to happen to me."

It sounded to Laiping as though Fen was making things up again. But as they walked through the shadow of a white-tiled factory building, she did start to think. *What plan do I have, other than to work and send money home?* Even her plan to buy a mobile phone would have to wait, she realized, until she had wired money to her parents—and until she had paid back Older Cousin Min. Someone in Min's dorm had told on Min about Laiping sleeping there. Min was fined one hundred yuan—almost a day's pay! When they saw each other at breakfast, Min shouted at Laiping that she would have to pay her back, plus the ten yuan for the fake birth certificate—only to then be fined another twenty-five yuan by the cafeteria guard for causing a disturbance!

"That's another twenty-five yuan you owe me!" Min had snapped at Laiping, keeping her voice low.

Fen, who was sitting with them, had butted in with, "It isn't Laiping's fault you have a temper like a sow in heat!"—which made Min even more cross.

Now Min wasn't speaking to Laiping. Laiping felt sick when she thought about it, first because her cousin was angry with her, but mostly because she had planned to put her first one hundred yuan toward buying a mobile phone so that she could call her parents whenever she wanted. Her money was disappearing before she even earned it!

FOR THREE MORE DAYS, Laiping and Fen reported to the Training Center to practice soldering capacitors to circuit boards. *Circuit board-capacitor-solder; circuit board-capacitor-solder*—once Laiping had mastered this rhythm, the work became as monotonous as planting rice. But at least, she reflected, her feet were dry, not being sucked into the mud of a farm field.

By the end of the fourth day, Mr. Huang pronounced Laiping and Fen ready to move onto the factory floor. The next morning, they found their way to Building 4, which turned out to be even bigger than the white-tiled factories they passed every day on their way to the Training Center, a squat but massive concrete structure of six storeys that took up two campus blocks. They showed their ID tags to a security guard at the entrance. Inside, they were given smocks to wear over their street clothes, caps to put over their hair, and booties to cover their shoes, the last of which they were required to put on before entering the factory floor in order to prevent dust and dirt from outside from getting into the electronics. Laiping felt a thrill as she pulled on her smock and cap—just like the girl in the poster! Except that Laiping's smock and cap were blue, not white.

Laiping and Fen climbed a wide staircase alongside hundreds of other workers up to the fourth floor, where they had been assigned. They went through a broad doorway and found a vast factory, bigger than two cafeterias put together, divided by long rows of work stations, and lit by glaring fluorescent tubing that hung down from the high ceiling. The floors were spotless concrete, and there was a slight chemical smell—perhaps from whatever was used to clean the floors. Laiping looked up and saw sealed windows placed up high along the walls. They provided a little daylight, but no fresh air.

In the open aisles between the rows of work stations, workers in blue smocks and caps identical to Laiping's and Fen's were lined up in formation, eyes forward—like soldiers at attention. There must have been over a hundred people in each line, and four lines in each aisle—more than a thousand workers altogether on this floor alone.

"What should we do? Should we join them?" Laiping whispered to Fen.

Fen shrugged her shoulders, *yes*. The girls hurried to the end of the nearest line of workers, almost to the back wall. Someone they couldn't see blew a whistle. Over a loudspeaker, a cheerful but firm female voice told them, "Good morning!"

"Good morning!" the thousands of workers repeated, as one.

"How is everyone this morning?"

"Fine! Fine! Fine!" replied the workers in unison.

"On the count of three, we will march on the spot, right foot first. One…two…three!"

The workers began marching on the spot in near-perfect unison. Laiping and Fen joined them.

"Lift those knees!" warned the pleasant voice from the loudspeaker. "Remember what our leader Mr. Chen says, 'Fit body, fit mind—fit for work!'" Laiping looked up to a giant portrait of Steve Chen, the company's founder, on the wall, smiling down on the factory floor, like a father smiling down on his children. Laiping's glance strayed to a giant poster near the portrait of Mr. Chen: *Work hard today, or work hard to find another job tomorrow.* She lifted her knees higher, anxious to show her willingness to work hard. The lady told them to run on the spot, then to march again. After ten minutes or so, she told them to stop marching and to punch their time cards in a machine. New workers, like Laiping and Fen, were to find a supervisor to be assigned work stations.

The supervisors were not hard to find—they were the ones walking up and down the aisles, telling the workers to hurry up and get to work. Fen nudged Laiping toward one of them, a pudgy man in his forties. His eyes were set too close together for his broad face and he had a big mole near his nose that Laiping tried not to stare at.

"Excuse me," she said politely, "but we don't know where we're supposed to go."

"Country mice, eh?" replied the man. "Let me see your hands."

The girls held out their hands.

"Yours are nice and small," the supervisor told Fen. Then he shifted his attention to Laiping's hands. "Your fingers are like sausages! Big and clumsy!" he pronounced.

"What are they thinking sending you here? This is very delicate work."

Blushing, Laiping pulled her hands back. But Fen spoke up.

"My sister does the finest embroidery," she told the foreman. Once again, Laiping marveled at Fen's quickness with a lie. "Back home, everyone admires how delicate her work is."

The supervisor looked from tiny Fen to Laiping, who was taller than he was, and got a crooked smile. "If you're sisters, I'm a millionaire," he said with a laugh, but not un-kindly. "I get it. You want to stay together. Come with me."

The supervisor, whose name was Mr. Wu, led them down the production line where worker after worker was seated in an identical pose, head bent over tiny squares on a mat in front of them, to a spot where there were two open stations. Laiping was happy to see that there were stools at each work station, so they wouldn't have to stand while they worked. Mr. Wu told her and Fen to pull on plastic gloves and face masks to cover their mouths and noses, like the other workers were wearing.

"Show me how you work," he said, waiting expectantly.

Laiping took her seat, her hands shaking with nerves. Gingerly, she used tweezers to lift a circuit board from a bin onto the mat. The tiny capacitor was hard to pinch. She hoped that Mr. Wu didn't notice her hands trembling. From the way he was focusing most of his attention on her, she assumed that Fen was faring better than she was.

"Now the soldering iron," he prompted, noting Laiping's hesitation.

Laiping picked up a soldering iron, its fine tip giving off a wisp of heat. She took a deep breath, willing her hand to be steady. Bending close to the circuit board, she managed to touch the soldering iron to just the right point. Next she took a string of solder and melted the tiniest amount on the tip of the iron, applying it to the exact spot where the capacitor joined the circuit board, just as she had done a hundred times in training. She looked over at Mr. Wu for his reaction. He nodded his head slightly, eyeing Laiping as though he suspected she was cheating somehow. Otherwise, how could her fat fingers have managed such a delicate task?

"For today," he pronounced, "take your time and make sure to do your job perfectly. But by tomorrow we expect you to work as quickly as everyone else."

Laiping glanced down the line and saw how the other workers performed the procedure in seconds, without ever looking up. *Circuit board-capacitor-solder; circuit board-capacitor-solder.*

"Your shift is ten hours," said Mr. Wu, "with a half-hour break for lunch. Any questions?"

"No, sir," said Laiping.

"No, sir," said Fen. "Thank you, sir."

"Then get busy." He gave Laiping an appraising look and added, "Sloppiness will be punished."

"Yes, sir," she said, and bowed her head.

After Mr. Wu walked on, Laiping reached her tweezers into the first bin and laid a circuit board on the mat. She took a tiny capacitor and dropped it onto the proper spot on the board. She picked up the soldering iron and touched it to the capacitor and the circuit board to heat them. She melted the solder with the iron just as she had practiced and applied just the right amount to create the joint. Perfection! Pleased with herself, Laiping glanced down the line of blue-capped heads bowed to their task in quiet efficiency—in the shared certainty of three meals a day and a warm bed at night—and pondered what on earth could make workers so unhappy with their lot that they would throw themselves off the roof of a dormitory rather than face another day.

SYLVIE

AFRICA

OLIVIER DIDN'T COME BACK the next day as Kayembe promised, or the day after that. When finally he returned late in the afternoon of the third day, he was angry that Sylvie had been to see his boss.

"How does it make me look, to have my sister checking up on me?"

His offended pride filled the small hut up to bursting. He seemed to have grown suddenly taller, and broader through the shoulders. From his body odor, he obviously hadn't washed in the few days he'd been away.

"It makes you look like you have a family where you belong," snapped Sylvie, refusing to be bullied.

"Stop arguing with him, Sylvie, and give him some food," commanded Mama.

But Sylvie noticed that, as relieved as Mama was that Olivier had returned, she had not gotten up from the sleeping mat to greet him. She was keeping her distance, almost as though she was afraid of him. Sylvie knew what she was thinking, because she was thinking it, too. *He's beginning to look like a soldier.*

Pascal and Lucie came in, lugging the plastic jerry can full of water between them.

"Olivier!" shouted Pascal with excitement. "Where have you been? Is it true you learned how to drive a truck?"

Sylvie turned a sharp look on Olivier. "You're driving for Kayembe? Where to?"

"None of your business!" He took a tin of meat from the sack he was carrying over his shoulder and tossed it to her. "Mr. Kayembe sent this for you," he said, and headed outside.

"Where are you going now?" Sylvie called, but he didn't bother to reply. In a way, Sylvie was relieved that he was gone. Pascal started after him. "Pascal!"

He stopped, turned—frowning with annoyance. "What?"

"You stay here."

"No! I want to go with Olivier!"

"Stay here, and I'll make *fufu*. Real *fufu*," she cajoled.

"How," asked Mama, suddenly interested, "without cassava?"

Sylvie took out the small bag of flour that Kayembe had given her from where she'd hidden it, under the dried beans.

"I bought some," she lied. "I got paid at the hospital."

Mama struggled to her feet and came over to help Sylvie mix the flour with the water that Pascal and Lucie had brought.

"But we don't have a fire to cook it on!" Lucie pointed out.

"From now on," said Sylvie. "Making the fire is Pascal's job."

Sylvie met Pascal's eyes. For a moment, he looked as though he was going to complain. But then his expression became thoughtful, and he seemed to understand that he'd been promoted within the family. Without arguing, he fished the matches out from the battered cooking pot and went outside to start the fire. Sylvie was grateful that he, at least, had listened to her.

ON SATURDAY MORNING, Mama felt well enough to go with Sylvie the short distance to the communal laundry tubs, located in an open area at the center of their block of huts. Sylvie filled a bucket with water from a pump and poured it into a tub, while Mama sat under the sparse shade of a eucalyptus tree and supervised. Sylvie lathered a bar of soap she'd bought with her clinic money, then swished the few pieces of clothing the family owned through the sudsy water. She was careful to keep the school uniforms clean, especially after one girl in her class had left school because she couldn't afford soap to wash her uniform, and the teacher told her she was dirty. Sylvie heard she was selling herself now, as so many girls in the camp were forced to do to bring in a little money for extras that the food center didn't supply.

"You're not scrubbing hard enough," complained Mama.

Sylvie managed to hold her tongue. Getting no reaction from Sylvie, Mama began chatting with the other women who had brought their family's laundry to the tubs, comparing notes about what part of the Kivus they had come from. But nobody talked about what tragedies they had endured there. It was taken for granted that every-one in the camp had lost someone they loved—a child, a spouse, sometimes a whole family. Talking about it was too painful. It seemed to Sylvie that everyone here was waiting for pain to end and for life to begin again.

As she wrung out Lucie's spare dress against the concrete tub, Sylvie listened to her mother boasting to the other women about how clever Sylvie was, how she regularly stood first at the high school. Sylvie was at once thrilled and mortified—thrilled because her mother so rarely praised her; mortified because she hated to have attention drawn to her.

"What are you staring at?" Mama said sharply to a little girl who had become fixated with Sylvie's scar. The little girl hid behind her mother's ample skirt.

"There's no need to scare her," replied the woman indignantly. "She's just curious."

"Where I come from, we teach children to have man-ners," Mama stated bluntly.

For a moment, Sylvie was reminded that her mother hadn't always been this thin shadow of herself. Once she'd been a proper lady who took pride in her house and her family, the wife of an educated man who, while never wealthy, knew how to behave in the world.

"You should have seen how pretty my girl was, before," Mama told the frightened child in a warmer tone. "Pretty like you, *and* smart," she added, trying to make amends but at the same time managing to imply that while the girl might be pretty, she was probably a dimwit compared to Sylvie.

Without commenting, the other mother packed her damp laundry into a woven basket and, lifting it onto her head, herded her little daughter away. The remaining women scrubbed their families' clothing in silence. Mama went silent, too, seeming to understand that she was the source of an unpleasant shift in the mood around the tubs. Sylvie was sad for her—feeble and lost, and barely thirty-five.

"I'm finished," Sylvie announced, packing the last of their sodden garments into their basket.

Mama got to her feet and gave an uncertain half-nod to the other women, who kept their gazes averted, pretending not to see her farewell glance. They walked side by side back to their shanty in silence, Sylvie balancing the laundry on her head. All the while, Sylvie was thinking of how to tell Mama about her plans. However she put it, she knew Mama would call her selfish for thinking of leaving the family behind.

"Mama," Sylvie said as they drew near to the hut, "something's happened."

"What is it?"

"I may have a chance to leave Nyarugusu. To go to Canada."

Mama stopped walking and turned on Sylvie, speechless at first—then furious. "What about going home?" she said.

It was exactly the reaction that Sylvie had feared.

"We don't know if we'll ever be able to go home," she

replied. "And even if the fighting stops, there's nothing to go back to."

"Of course there will be nothing if everyone leaves! You think you are so much better than us that you would leave us here, and save yourself? Move to a rich country so you can live in a big house and buy fancy cars, while we starve?"

"I'm trying to save all of us!" she protested, setting the laundry basket down on the ground. "Once I'm there and I get an education, then I can bring all of you to join me."

"And how many years will that be? Who's going to help me with the children, unh? How am I supposed to manage, with you and Olivier both gone?" Tears of rage and helplessness rolled down her cheeks. Then, abruptly, she struck Sylvie hard against her cheek.

It took every ounce of Sylvie's self-control not to slap her back. "Listen to me!" she said fiercely. "What is there for us if I stay here, stuck like this? Nyarugusu is bad enough, but what happens when the Tanzanians send us back?" Mama covered her face with her hands and wept openly, but Sylvie wouldn't stop. "Mama, how long before Kayembe turns Pascal into one of his soldiers, the way he's doing with Olivier?"

At this, Mama dropped her hands. Her eyes were wide with terror, her gaze blank and far away. Sylvie knew where she was. She was back in their village, in their house, the day the soldiers came—the day they never talked about. But today, Mama surprised her.

"He looks just like them," she said.

"I know," whispered Sylvie. She watched as Mama

inhaled a deep breath and let it out, her thin frame rattling. "Mama, it may be too late for Olivier, but it's the only way to save Pascal."

Mama's eyes met Sylvie's without spirit, used up. She gave Sylvie a short nod, then resumed walking, as though putting one foot in front of the other took all the energy she had. Sylvie lifted the basket of laundry onto her head and followed, asking herself for the hundredth time, *How can I leave her?* And, for the hundredth time, *How can I stay?*

ASIA

THERE WERE EIGHTEEN BUNKS in Laiping and Fen's dorm room. Laiping's was the middle bunk in the fifth row on the left, and Fen's was at the bottom of the third row on the right. All of the other girls in their room came from Guangdong Province, like them. Choilai was the eldest at twenty-two, and had been working for the company since she was seventeen. Choilai was a big sister. Her job was to make sure the girls obeyed the dormitory rules, such as not spitting and not having food in the room and being quiet after midnight. She also taught Laiping and Fen about the *unwritten* dorm rules. For instance, when the Guangdong girls outnumbered the Sichuan or Fujian girls in the common room, the Guangdong girls got to decide which program to watch on the television.

"If you have a problem, you must come to me," Choilai told Laiping and Fen kindly.

"Don't tell her anything!" advised Older Cousin Min when the girls met her on Sunday, their day off. "Big sisters work for the company. Anything you tell them, they'll pass on to the bosses."

Min was speaking to Laiping again after forgiving her for getting her into trouble, and had taken her to one of the campus Internet cafés to show her how to use a computer to call home. Fen had tagged along, to Min's annoyance. The three of them were seated at a table with cups of coffee, which Laiping found bitter and too strong.

"But Choilai is nice," replied Laiping, swallowing a small sip.

"They're all the same. Don't trust them," insisted Min. "Who do you think fined me a hundred yuan for letting you sleep in my bunk? A big sister. By the way," she added, "don't forget you owe me that money."

"How could she forget when you keep reminding her all the time?" Fen remarked.

"Who asked you? And why do you follow my cousin around like her shadow?" snipped Min, naturally suspicious of anyone outside her and Laiping's family. "Maybe you're a company spy, too," she said, her hand trembling slightly as she lifted her coffee mug to her lips.

"Please don't fight," pleaded Laiping. She wanted Min and Fen to get along.

"*I'm* not fighting," protested Fen. "Anyway, I think Min is right about Choilai. I don't trust her, any more than I trust those supervisors in the factory."

"Mr. Wu is nice," Laiping pointed out.

Despite Mr. Wu's initial doubts about Laiping's suitability to work on his line, by the end of the week he was praising her for her accuracy and speed. In fact, Mr. Wu praised Laiping's whole line for their work, and scheduled

Laiping, Fen, and the rest of them for a day of overtime on Saturday at extra pay.

Fen wrinkled her face in disgust. "Mr. Mole Face?! Maybe you want him for your boyfriend."

Min burst out laughing just as she set her mug down, and coffee slopped all over the table. "*Ai!*" she exclaimed. "You made my hand slip!"

"You're lucky you have me to blame for everything," said Fen.

"Yes, lucky me," replied Min sarcastically, but her mouth twisted in a smile. "And Laiping is lucky that she has both of us to stop her from trusting everyone she meets."

"Yes, she is," agreed Fen.

They were making fun of her—Laiping was annoyed. "I have to go to the washroom," she announced, and got up from the table.

She walked to the back of the café, where she joined a line of girls waiting for a toilet. A couple of girls had their heads bent over their mobile phones. Laiping started to calculate when she'd be able to afford a mobile of her own, after she paid Min the 110 yuan she owed her—she refused to pay her twenty-five yuan fine she received for yelling in the cafeteria!—and after she sent money home.

"Those are crappy phones."

Laiping snapped back to reality to find a boy of about twenty standing beside her—the same guy, she realized, who'd handed her the flyer in the employment line.

"Now this is a phone," he said, showing off the shiny

new touch-screen phone in his hand. It looked similar to the smartphones they made in the factory. Laiping had heard they cost more than two months' salary to buy.

"My name is Kai," he told her.

"I'm Laiping," she replied, a little tongue-tied. She wasn't used to talking with boys, especially good-looking ones like this Kai. Curiosity helped Laiping find her voice. "Did they catch you?" she asked.

"Who?"

"Those security guards at the employment office, a couple of weeks ago."

Kai let out a laugh. "If those goons knew who I was, do you think I'd still be working here?"

He's so full of himself! thought Laiping, but she was aware that Fen and Min were watching with interest from their table. She hoped they were jealous.

"How's it going?" he asked. "Are the bosses treating you okay?"

"Yes, fine," she replied.

His face took on a knowing look. "Just wait," he said. "Word is there's a new product launch coming. When that happens, the bosses turn into slave drivers."

Suddenly, Fen appeared at Laiping's elbow.

"Can I see that?" she asked, reaching for Kai's smartphone.

"Who are you?" Kai frowned, and folded his hand over the phone.

"I'm her friend," explained Fen with a nod toward Laiping. "How much did you pay for that?"

Kai turned to Laiping. "Tell your friend she's nosy."

Laiping gave Fen a wide-eyed look intended to tell her to go back to the table, but Fen ignored her.

"That's a cheap knockoff," Fen told Laiping dismissively. Then, to Kai she remarked, "Are you trying to impress people? Make them think you're a rich American?"

"I don't want to be a rich American," retorted Kai. "I just want to live like one." He turned to Laiping. "If you want to get a good deal on a phone, let me know," he said. "You can find me here most Sundays."

Before he walked away, he gave Laiping a charming smile that made her heart flutter, just the way girls wrote about in magazines. Laiping had never felt that way before.

"Wait until I tell your mother you have a boyfriend!" laughed Min, joining them.

"Yes, Mr. Wu will be jealous," added Fen.

"He's not my boyfriend!" exclaimed Laiping, fed up with their teasing. "He recognized me from the employment line, that's all. He was handing out flyers. The security guards chased him away."

"What did the flyer say?" asked Min, losing her smile.

"Something about workers knowing their rights."

Min and Fen exchanged a wary look.

"Don't talk to him anymore," warned Fen. "He's a troublemaker."

That was exactly what the girl in line in front of them had called Fen's father, back when Fen was Yiyin, Laiping remembered, but she kept this thought to herself. Despite their warnings, Laiping decided that maybe she *would* like

Kai for her boyfriend, just to show them that she was more grown up than they seemed to think she was.

MONDAY MORNING BEFORE EIGHT, another week on the factory floor began with marching and running on the spot, following the instructions of the loudspeaker lady.

"How is everyone today?" she asked.

"Fine! Fine! Fine!" replied the workers in unison.

Then the workers punched time cards in the machines and took their stations. *Circuit board-capacitor-solder; circuit board-capacitor-solder.* Laiping liked the work well enough, but at night she was beginning to dream about capacitors and solder. After ten hours bent over the bench each day, her shoulders and neck ached.

"There's a hot tub at the campus swimming pool that's good for sore muscles," Min told her when they met at the cafeteria Monday evening.

"Can I borrow your swimsuit?" asked Laiping.

"No!" replied Min. "You'll stretch it all out of shape!"

One more thing to save for, thought Laiping.

When she got back to the dorm, she stood under the hot shower until Big Sister Choilai came in and told her to turn it off—even though no one else was waiting for a turn. Laiping was beginning to think that Fen was right about Choilai. She pretended to be caring, but all she ever talked about were the rules.

On Tuesday, Laiping worked hard, willing herself to focus when her mind began to wander. *Circuit board-capacitor-solder; circuit board-capacitor-solder.* At noon she went to the cafeteria with Fen and lined up for lunch. The food was the same at each meal—rice, vegetables, and a little meat or fish. Fen grumbled about the portions and the blandness, but Laiping barely had time to taste it anyway, so quickly did they have to eat to get back to the factory floor within half an hour.

On Wednesday, Mr. Wu complained that Laiping and Fen's line hadn't made its daily quota and forced the whole line to stay for an extra half-hour, without pay, until they had soldered enough capacitors to enough circuit boards.

On Thursday, Mr. Wu pulled a girl from their line and yelled at her for making a sloppy solder.

"A pig can only give birth to the brainless!" he shouted, loudly enough for everyone to hear. The girl hung her head and promised to do better.

On Friday, Mr. Wu announced that the line next to Laiping and Fen's would be given the honor of earning overtime pay on Saturday. Laiping and Fen's entire line lost face, considering that just last week they had been the praiseworthy ones. Burning with shame, Laiping made a silent vow, *Next week I will work harder!* She wanted Mr. Wu to be proud of her. She wanted Steve Chen to be proud of her, too. She remembered what Fen had said about the importance of having a plan, and made one up on the spot. *My plan is to be a good worker for the company, and then the company will be good to me.*

AFRICA

· ·

SATURDAY WAS RATION DAY. Leaving Mama at home with
Pascal and Lucie, Sylvie made the long trek to the food
distribution center, an open structure with a tin roof
supported by posts. She had to stand under the hot sun
for almost an hour in a line that snaked out into the dusty
open space where the marketplace had once been. When
at last it was almost Sylvie's turn, the woman in front of
her started arguing with the aid worker behind the table, a
young American with a scruffy blond beard.

"I want my share!" demanded the woman, swishing
the contents of her half-filled jug of cooking oil—and
drawing the attention of one of the United Nations peace-
keepers standing guard, his rifle poised for trouble.

"I'm sorry," explained the aid worker in broken
French. "The shipment was short. Everyone is getting less
this time."

"Animals are treated better," retorted the woman.

She gathered her oil, maize, and beans and headed
away. Sylvie stepped up to the young American, whom she
had come to recognize. Usually he was friendly, but his

94

patience was wearing thin today. Sylvie could imagine that he had been taking the brunt of the refugees' anger over the shortage of rations.

"*Bonjour*," he said, mangling the greeting as he poured three cups of oil into the can she had brought instead of the usual five.

"*Hello*," replied Sylvie, practicing one of the few English words she knew. Then, in French, "What's the problem?"

"I don't know. They don't tell me. Every week there are more people, but the same amount of food. And this week there's less."

As he poured dried beans into the sack that she'd brought, Sylvie felt a familiar knot in her stomach. How would they eat if they were cut back any more? As it was, the rations barely lasted two weeks. She remembered the cassava that Kayembe had given her, and the can of meat that he'd sent with Olivier, seeing the trap that lay in his generosity. Is that how Kayembe came to own people?

The American put a sack of maize on the table for Sylvie. Lifting it onto her head, she thanked him and took the oil and beans in either hand. Thus balanced, she started away to take the red dust track back home to the hut. But she was only halfway across the old marketplace when she heard someone shout her name.

"Sylvie!"

She glanced around to see Kayembe calling to her from one of the makeshift food stalls. He was seated at a small table under the shade of a tree. Two of his guards were at another table, their AK-47s slung over their shoulders. Sylvie kept walking, pretending she didn't hear. But carrying the rations slowed her down. In another moment, one of the guards—the round man she had seen Kayembe talking with before at his former shop—stepped in her path.

"Mr. Kayembe wants to speak with you," he said.

This one wasn't like Kayembe's other men. He was polite, taking the oil and beans from her to lighten her load. On the other hand, Sylvie realized, holding onto the rations was a good way to force her to come with him.

"Did you get the meat I sent?" asked Kayembe as Sylvie approached him with the soldier as her escort. He rose slightly from a rickety folding chair, indicating with a sweep of his hand that she should take the one across from him.

"Yes. Thank you," she said, making no move to sit.

"Please, have a seat," he insisted.

Reluctantly, she sat down, easing the sack of maize from her head to the ground while calculating how to get the rest of the rations back. The soldier solved that problem by putting the beans and oil down beside the maize.

"Has Olivier talked to you?" Kayembe smiled and bent closer, his old man's breath sour in her nostrils. "Let me buy you a Fanta, my dear," he said, waving to the large woman in a traditional *pagne* and matching turban who ran the food stall to bring a second bottle to the table. "I promise I won't touch you."

Sylvie was worried by his need to make such a

promise. Why should he touch her? "What was Olivier supposed to talk to me about?" she asked.

He spread his hands wide, as though offering her a blessing. "About becoming my wife, my dear," he said.

He waited with an expectant smile for Sylvie to absorb the enormity of the honor he was doing her. But Sylvie was in shock. How could Olivier even consider such a revolting proposition? Neither of them spoke while the woman in the colorful *pagne* placed a bottle of Fanta in front of Sylvie.

"I take it that Olivier has not yet had the discussion with you," Kayembe said, reading her expression.

"I don't want to marry you," she told him flatly.

Seeming not to have heard her, he took a long drink from his Fanta. Sylvie refused to touch hers. Kayembe belched up a little gas before explaining, "Here's how it is. I need someone I can trust to help me with my business affairs."

"I don't know anything about business," Sylvie countered.

"I will teach you. Olivier tells me you are very smart, and good at maths." He waited for her to reply, but Sylvie sat mutely. "Once we are married, I will look after you and your family," he continued. "I will help them and protect them, just as I am helping Olivier."

"How are you helping Olivier?" she asked.

He smiled. "Let's just say Olivier and I are helping each other."

Sylvie repeated, bluntly, "I don't want to marry you."

He reached out and gently ran his fat fingers along her chin. Sylvie pulled back, and he withdrew his hand.

"Don't be so hasty," he said. "You will be the wife of Hervé Kayembe. People will look up to you. Besides," he added, lifting his index finger to her face and tracing her scar with it, "beggars can't be choosers."

Repulsed, Sylvie jerked away from him and jumped to her feet, toppling the table and sending the Fanta bottles into the dust. Outrage stormed across Kayembe's wide face. He looked ridiculous, a big man perched on such a rickety chair, but all the same Sylvie found she was terrified.

"Who do you think you are?" he bellowed. His guards quickly righted the table in front of him. He brought his fist down on it with enough force to almost shatter it. "I could buy a hundred girls like you in the street!" he ranted. "I am offering to make you my wife!" He took a moment to catch his breath—and his temper. Abruptly, he was charming again, although violence pulsed just beneath his smile. "Forgive me, my dear. This offer comes as a surprise to you. I understand you need a little time to get used to the idea." He leaned toward her. "Listen to me, Sylvie," he said, looking up at her, a hand on one knee. "There are business opportunities happening back home. For a while, the Americans stopped the coltan trade in the Congo, but now the Chinese want to buy it—and I know how to get it out of the country and sell it to them. One day soon I will be returning to North Kivu as a rich man, and I will build a big house for you there."

"But the Mai-Mai will kill you if you go back," she said.

"The Mai-Mai are busy holding off the Rwandan fighters coming across the border," he replied with a shrug. "They can use my help, in exchange for an appropriate share of the profits."

Sylvie's stomach lurched. "The Mai-Mai killed my father, and they killed your family, too!" *And* they'd raped her and her mother, but this part she kept to herself.

Kayembe opened his hands wide before him. "Things change. Enemies become friends. Business is business. There is coltan in our country waiting for a market. Why shouldn't we get rich, instead of those Rwandan devils?" Getting to his feet, he reached out and stroked her cheek, seeming not to care when she pulled back in disgust. "We will be rich together," he said.

Sylvie felt a suffocating weight on her chest. "You can have any girl," she said. "Ask someone else."

His smile vanished. He drew himself up so that Sylvie could see how powerful he was, how dangerous.

"Your brother is the man of your family," he declared, "and he has given me his word. Men rule women, not the other way around."

"You are a devil!" Sylvie blurted.

She grabbed the oil and beans and ran, leaving the heavy bag of maize behind in her haste to get away. Kayembe didn't come after her, but she knew—and he knew—that he didn't have to. He owned this place—owned Olivier, and, if he wanted her, he owned her, too. *If only Papa was alive!* she thought. Her father would never have forced her into marriage. But as long as she remained in Nyarugusu, Sylvie was Kayembe's for the taking.

The maize! What would the family eat for the next two weeks? Her pride wouldn't allow her to go back for it. But she couldn't go home without it either. Instead, she headed for the clinic, desperately hoping that Doctor Marie was working today. She needed her help, and she needed it now.

ASIA

FRIDAY WAS THE END of Laiping's second week in the factory, and Saturday was payday! Laiping joined a lineup at an automatic teller just before noon, one of a dozen in a row outdoors near a busy restaurant that sold American-style food, like hamburgers. Laiping's stomach growled as she caught the scent of grilled meat. It was tempting to follow the lead of many in line who, once they received their yuan from the machine, went immediately into the restaurant to spend some of it. But Laiping decided she would eat for free in the cafeteria instead, and save her money.

The line was long and slow-moving, but everyone chattered excitedly. Not even the scowling presence of security guards with billy clubs holstered in their belts could dampen the mood. Recently, the company had given all of its workers in Shenzhen a pay raise. Laiping earned 450 yuan per week—so she counted nine hundred yuan she should have in her account from the last two weeks, plus the overtime she'd worked last Saturday. She should have enough to pay Min the 110 yuan that she owed her, plus send money home—maybe even money left over for a mobile phone if Kai could get the good deal he promised!

At last it was Laiping's turn. She'd been watching carefully how other people pushed their bank cards into a slot in the machine. She did the same, punching in her security code when the screen told her to. Her heart beat a little faster as the machine processed—and then her face fell. Instead of over nine hundred yuan, the machine told her she had none!

"Hurry up!" called a man in line behind her.

Flustered, Laiping took her card back from the machine and moved on.

"Fen!" she called, spotting her just as she finished at another machine. "There must be a mistake. There's no money in my account."

"Mine either!" replied Fen, upset. "My mother will say I'm cheating her!"

"There's Choilai," said Laiping, spotting their Big Sister in one of the lineups.

"Wait!" warned Fen, but Laiping didn't listen.

"Choilai, we have a problem," she said, running over to her. "There's been a mistake in our pay. Can you help us?"

"Read your contract, stupid!" retorted Choilai, with no trace of her previous kindness. "The company deducts 110 yuan per month for the dormitory and three yuan per meal. Did you think they would feed and house you for free?"

Fen tallied quickly in her head and blurted shrilly, "They charge sixty-three yuan a week for that slop they feed us?"

"You don't understand," said Laiping, "There's no money in our accounts at all!"

One of the security guards stepped toward them.

"What's going on here?"

"Nothing," said Fen, bowing her head and moving behind Laiping.

"If you don't like the pay here, find another job!" he said, gripping the handle of his billy club threateningly. "Now move along."

Fen pulled Laiping away from the guard and the machines.

"But our money—"

"Stop making a fuss!" hissed Fen. "He'll hear you!" She pointed to a surveillance camera fixed to a light pole. The camera was aimed directly at them. "It's easy for them to find out who you are, you know."

Fen pulled Laiping past the restaurant where workers were filling their stomachs with hamburgers. A few moments ago, Laiping had thought about joining them. Now she realized that, with the money she'd brought from home almost gone, she could barely afford to buy tea, let alone a meal—or a mobile phone. Laiping wanted to shout out loud that the company was cheating them, but she let Fen lead her away, tears of frustration burning her eyes.

THEY'RE NOT SUPPOSED TO, but the company holds onto your first month's pay, in case you get any ideas about quitting," Older Cousin Min explained when Laiping visited her in her dorm that afternoon.

"That doesn't make any sense!" protested Laiping. "Why would I want to quit? I just got here."

"Lots of people quit. Why do you think they keep hiring so many new workers?"

Min was rinsing her nightdress out in the sink in the toilet compartment, with Laiping stationed at the door in case anyone came in. It was against the rules to wash clothes in the dorm room, and Min didn't want to have to pay another fine. But Min's roommates were in the factory working overtime. *Or they're out spending their paychecks,* thought Laiping, bitterly. For the time being, they had the room to themselves.

"It's your problem, too," Laiping pointed out. "I can't pay you the yuan I owe you." Min just shrugged. All at once, Laiping realized what was going on. "You knew this would happen. Why didn't you talk about this back home, at New Year?"

"I didn't want to frighten you off," Min admitted. "I thought it would nice if we were here together. It gets so lonely."

Laiping should have been angry, but when she looked at Min, lifeless and bone-weary, all she could feel was sorry for her. Where had her bold Older Cousin gone?

"I thought you liked it here," she said. "You made it sound like so much fun."

"It was fun at first," she replied, pressing the night-dress into the sink to force out the water. "But it seems like as soon as you make a friend, they quit and you never see them again. They withheld my pay when I went home at the New Year, just in case I had any ideas about not coming back. They still haven't paid me that money."

Laiping noticed Min grimace in pain when she squeezed her hands around the nightdress to wring it out. Her grasp was too weak to have much effect—the nightdress was still a sodden lump. She remembered that Min's hands had trembled in the café last week, too.

"Are you all right?" asked Laiping.

Min looked away, trying to hide her face from Laiping.

"Min? What's wrong?"

Laiping watched in alarm as her normally tough cousin burst into tears.

"I feel awful! I'm so tired all the time. My hands shake, and my eyes get blurry."

"It's the flu," said Laiping, holding her hand to Min's forehead. But her forehead was cool.

"I guess so," replied Min, drying her eyes with the back of her hands. "Everybody on my line has been getting sick."

"You should stay in bed."

"I can't. I'm working overtime tomorrow. The bosses keep telling us that if we don't show up for work, they'll replace us with robots."

Laiping shook her head. "And Grandma always said you were the smart one!"

Min let out a laugh, chasing the last of her tears away. "Do you remember how she used to nag us? 'Study! You must study hard in order to become rich!'" she said, in a perfect imitation of their grandmother.

"She never told *me* to study," protested Laiping. "I wasn't university material!"

"You were always the pretty one! This will have to do," declared Min, giving her nightdress a final twist in the sink.

While Min carried the damp bundle to her bunk to hang it to dry, Laiping went to the window. She was facing south, toward downtown Shenzhen, but it was a muggy day and the horizon was obscured by a brown haze. Laiping had to go on faith that Shenzhen's skyscrapers were out there. She remembered how as a little girl she had dreamed of the big city, imagining herself as a famous actress, or a fashion model. She'd made it as far as the big city, but those dreams seem further away today than they had when she was little.

"Maybe we'll find rich Shenzhen boys with their own apartments to marry," she said, only half joking. "Then we could stay in the city and let them look after us."

Suddenly she was thinking of Kai. Was he from Shenzhen, or was he a migrant worker like her and Min? She knew nothing about him.

"You think every girl here hasn't had the same thought?" Min remarked, climbing the ladder and hanging the nightdress on a hook so that, when she closed the curtain, no one would see it. "Just our luck that this is the one place in all of China where girls outnumber boys."

"Just our luck," agreed Laiping, turning back from the window in time to see Min climbing down from her bunk. Every step seemed to cause her pain. "Min, you can't keep working if you're sick," she told her.

"What choice do I have?" she sighed. "I can't go back to the village. I'm different now. It's too boring there— there's nothing to do. Nobody there can understand how I've changed."

Min and Laiping listened to the nightdress dripping onto the mattress.

"Looks like I'll be sleeping in a soggy bed," remarked Min, making a face.

"You know what Grandma would tell you," said Laiping.

Min forced a smile. "She would say I must learn to eat the bitter first, then the sweet."

"Actually," replied Laiping, "I was thinking, 'You can't conceal fire by wrapping it in paper.' If you're sick, the company should give you time off, or you'll just get sicker. And while they're at it, they should give Fen and me our money."

Thinking about her empty bank account made Laiping angry all over again. She had made a plan to work hard for the company, in the belief that the company would in turn be good to her. But now she felt cheated.

"There's something else that Grandma used to say," Min pointed out, growing serious. "'The bird that sticks its head out is the first to get shot.' I'm not going to stick my head out, and you shouldn't either."

Laiping thought again of Kai, who wasn't afraid to stick his head out. *There are things you need to know*—she was beginning to understand what he had meant by that. If the company wasn't going to treat her fairly, then Laiping needed a new plan. From now on, she decided, she would try to be smart, like Kai.

"You deserve better than this," she told Min. "We all do."

AFRICA

HOLDING TIGHT to her family's rations of oil and beans, Sylvie entered the medical clinic to find Neema, one of the nurses, seated at the admitting table reading a novel. There were no patients waiting, and Neema was one to take full advantage of a lull.

"Is Doctor Marie here?" asked Sylvie.

"She finishes at three on Saturdays," Neema replied, barely acknowledging her. Sylvie knew that Neema didn't like her, probably because Neema was Tanzanian and thought that a young Congolese like Sylvie had no business being so friendly with one of the doctors. "Come back on Monday."

"I can't wait until Monday!"

Neema tilted up her ample chin so that she was looking down her nose at Sylvie. "Well, you're going to have to wait."

But Sylvie knew where to find Marie. She left the clinic and set out for the compound reserved for foreign workers. Sylvie was reluctant to disturb her there, but she had to see her. Marie was her only hope for escaping the marriage trap that Kayembe had set for her, apparently with Olivier's help. She followed a track that led from behind the clinic into Zone 1 of the camp, keeping her head down to avoid the stares of the men she passed. Women preparing food over cook fires threw hostile looks her way, knowing she didn't belong in this part of Nyarugusu. The smell of cooking reminded Sylvie of the sack of maize she'd had to leave behind.

The foreign workers' compound was surrounded by a high fence of thorn branches. Ordinarily, refugees weren't allowed to go inside, unless they were delivering food or other supplies. A UN soldier was posted at the gate, an Asian man with the flag of some country Sylvie didn't recognize stitched on his uniform. Sylvie swallowed her fear, trying to be brave as she approached him.

"I need to speak to someone inside," Sylvie told him.

"No refugees," he replied in halting French

"But I work at the clinic," she explained. "I need to see one of the doctors."

The soldier didn't seem to understand. "Go!" he commanded, shaking his rifle at her.

"Is there a problem?"

Sylvie turned to see the American aid worker, returning to the compound. He must have finished his shift at the distribution center.

"I need to see Doctor Marie," Sylvie told him. The American looked wary. Perhaps he'd had enough of complaining Congolese for today. "Please," Sylvie pleaded. "My name is Sylvie. She knows me. I work for her at the clinic."

He thought it over for a moment, then said to the guard, "She's okay."

Beyond the gate, Sylvie saw green canvas tents instead of mud huts. It looked…temporary, as though the foreign workers might pack up their tents and leave Nyarugusu at any moment. Several white people, men and women, sat in camp chairs, sipping beers in the late afternoon sun. Among them was Doctor Van de Velde, the head doctor. When he saw Sylvie enter with the aid worker, he got up from his chair and came over.

"She's not supposed to be in here," he scolded the American. "What do you think you're doing, Martin?"

"She says she works at the clinic," Martin replied with a shrug.

Doctor Van de Velde looked at Sylvie, recognition dawning. "Only regular staff is allowed inside the compound," he said.

"She only wants to talk to Marie," said Martin—suddenly her ally—earning a glare from the much older doctor.

"Please," said Sylvie. "I just need to speak with her for a moment, then I will be gone."

Doctor Van de Velde frowned while he thought it over. Then, reluctantly, he turned and shouted, "Marie!"

Marie emerged from one of the tents. She looked younger than she did in the hospital. Sylvie was surprised to see her wearing shorts and a skimpy top—a Congolese woman would never have dressed like that.

"Sylvie! What's wrong?" she asked, crossing to her.

"I need to talk to you," whispered Sylvie urgently.

Marie picked up on Sylvie's plea for privacy. "Come inside the tent."

"Don't make a habit of this!" warned Doctor Van de Velde as the two of them headed away.

"I'm sorry I got you in trouble," Sylvie whispered to her.

"Don't mind him," replied Marie. "What's he going to do? Fire me?"

Inside the tent, there were two cots and a plastic storage bin with drawers. On top of the bin there was a framed photograph of a nicely dressed African-looking family— an older man and woman and two girls who looked like Marie.

"My parents and sisters," explained Marie.

Sylvie stared at the photo. Marie's family looked nice—happy, like Marie.

"What's wrong, Sylvie?" asked Marie. "What did you want to talk to me about?"

"When can I go to Canada?" she blurted. "I need to go soon!"

"Why?" Marie asked in confusion. "What's going on?"

"Please, how long will it take?"

"I don't know exactly, but these things take time."

"I don't have time!"

Marie held up her hands to slow Sylvie down. "Not long ago you were mad at me for pressuring you to go," she said. "What's happened?"

Sylvie began to tremble. "Olivier told Kayembe I'll

marry him. My brother has given me away."

Surprise played across Marie's face, then anger. "I'll speak with your brother—"

"No! It's too dangerous. Olivier has become one of Kayembe's men."

"How? What's he doing for him?"

"He won't say," said Sylvie, the words tumbling out now. "But Olivier knows how to drive a truck now, and Kayembe told me he's bringing coltan out of North Kivu. Maybe Olivier is working for him as a driver."

"Kayembe is breaking the law by bringing coltan over the border," said Marie when Sylvie stopped to catch her breath. "I'll report him to the Tanzanian authorities and they'll expel him. If he's not here, he can't force you to marry him."

"No! If you stand in his way, he will make you suffer." As Sylvie spoke, she realized her warning to Marie applied to herself as well. *If I say no, he will make me suffer. Not only me, but the whole family, too.*

Marie shook her head in disgust. "He thinks he runs the place!"

"He *does* run it," replied Sylvie.

Marie stared at Sylvie, the complications sinking in. "C'mon," she said at last, heading out of the tent. "There's someone we need to talk to."

Sylvie kept up with Marie's brisk pace as they crossed an open area to a rounded metal hut. Inside, Marie sat down at laptop computer, like the one Sylvie's father used to have back in their village, only newer.

"Have you ever Skyped before?" she asked.

"What?" replied Sylvie.

"You'll see."

Marie's fingers were dancing over the keyboard. There was a ringing sound, and after a few moments a young white man appeared on the computer screen. He was thin-faced, with reddish hair. On a shelf behind him there were many books.

Marie smiled. "Alain! Thank heavens you're there!"

"Is everything okay, *cherie*?" the young man asked. "You're calling early."

From his eager concern, Sylvie wondered if the man was Marie's boyfriend.

"Don't worry. I'm fine," she reassured him. "I have someone here who would like to talk with you." Marie got up and indicated that Sylvie should sit in her place. "This is my friend Alain, in Montreal," she told her. "He already knows a lot about you." Suddenly timid, Sylvie hesitated. "Go on!" said Marie with an encouraging smile.

Sylvie sat and looked into the screen. She could see her own image in a small square in the corner. Alain's face lit up when he recognized her.

"Sylvie!" he said, his voice slightly delayed and the video of his face jumpy. "I was just talking about you with some friends of mine."

Sylvie didn't know what to say in reply. Marie leaned down so that they were both visible in the little square box.

"Alain, tell Sylvie what's happening."

"Sure, okay. Sylvie, we've started a web campaign on the Internet to raise money for you to come to Canada."

"A what?" asked Sylvie. She knew about the Internet,

but she had no idea what a "web campaign" was.

Marie saw Sylvie's confusion. She explained, "Alain runs a website keeping tabs on mining operations in the Congo, to raise awareness about the suffering that results from the fighting over coltan and other minerals."

"We're starting a campaign on the website about you, Sylvie." Alain picked up from Marie. "About your situation as a refugee."

"Basically," continued Marie, "in order for you to go to Canada you have to be sponsored by people who are willing to look after you. My parents want to do that, but they're retired and not wealthy. So Alain is using the website to raise the money you'll need for travel, and to finish high school in Montreal."

Sylvie's heart leapt. "Thank you!" she sputtered to both Marie and Alain. "Thank you so much!"

"We can't get ahead of ourselves," cautioned Marie. "We figure we'll need fifty thousand dollars to cover your expenses until you finish high school, more when you continue to university."

To Sylvie, it was an unimaginable amount of money.

"When people see your photo on the website, Sylvie," said Alain, "they start to understand what is going on there."

Suddenly, Sylvie's face fell. She knew that the Internet went all around the world. Now people everywhere could see the ugliness of her scar. Her heart was pounding, her stomach lurching. Seeing her panic, Marie rested her hand lightly on Sylvie's shoulder.

Alain looked worried. "What's wrong?"

"It's the photo," explained Marie. "Sylvie's sensitive about…"

She didn't need to finish the sentence. Alain seemed to understand.

"Sylvie, I'm sorry," he said. "I thought we had your permission to use it. We'll take it down."

"No, don't," replied Marie flatly. Sylvie turned to her in surprise. Whose side was she on? "Look, it's your decision," Marie told her, "but when people see you and find out about your life, they start to understand what's going on in the DRC, how lives are being destroyed because of blood minerals like coltan. People need to understand the human cost of the things we take for granted. When they see your picture, they *get* it. Sylvie, you could help lots of other Congolese." Sylvie turned her head away. "If only you could see yourself the way others do," Marie coaxed gently. "A beautiful girl. A smart girl. A *strong* girl."

"I don't care about others," Sylvie said, her voice thick with emotion. "I care about my family."

"Remember, eventually you'll be able to help them, too."

Hope and fear tugged at Sylvie, pulling her in opposite directions. Seeing her torment, Marie squeezed her shoulder.

"It's okay. I'm pressuring you too much," she said. She turned to Alain. "Let's give Sylvie some time to think."

But Sylvie was already thinking. She had to do whatever it took, she realized, to save the family from Kayembe, and from Nyarugusu—it was what Papa would have wanted her to do, even if it meant exposing her ugliness to the world. She looked into the computer screen and told Alain, "You can use the photo."

"Good!" replied Alain.

"But my family needs to come, too," she said. "All of us. My mother, my sister, and my two brothers. "

Sylvie and Alain both hesitated.

"Sylvie, that's a lot more complicated," replied Alain.

"I'm not leaving without them," she told them. "All of us must come."

Marie took in a deep breath. "Okay," she nodded, after a moment.

"But Marie—" Alain began to argue with her.

"I know it won't be easy, Alain," Marie told him, "but we have to find a way."

Alain didn't look convinced, but Sylvie saw the determination in Marie's face and took heart. In the tug-of-war going on inside her, she allowed hope to pull her away from fear.

IT WAS ALMOST DARK by the time Sylvie reached home with the beans and oil, jumping at every shadow as she hurried along the track that led to Zone 3. If it wasn't safe for a girl to walk alone through the camp in the daytime, a girl alone at night was assumed by many to be a prostitute, and free for the taking. All the way, she worried about how to explain to her mother that she had no maize. But when she entered the hut, she was surprised to find Mama seated on the dirt floor with Lucie, the two of them measuring handfuls of cornmeal from a full sack by the light of a kerosene lamp. There was some tinned meat and fish stacked beside the sack of meal, even fresh tomatoes and an eggplant.

"Where did all this come from?" asked Sylvie, half suspecting.

"Soldiers brought it!" reported Lucie, the sticky dough webbing her small fingers.

Sylvie realized, *This is how Kayembe thinks he can buy me!* She wanted to take the food and toss it outside, but then what would they eat?

"Were you too lazy to carry the maize yourself?" remarked Mama as Sylvie set down the oil and beans. When Sylvie didn't reply, she made a clucking sound with her tongue. "Gifts always come with a price."

She thinks I slept with him! Sylvie's face went hot with humiliation.

"I don't want his gifts, and I did nothing to get them!" Sylvie snapped back. She saw Pascal seated on the sleeping mat, tossing a small stone back and forth between his hands, sulking. "What's wrong, Pascal?" He didn't reply.

"Mama says you're going away. Is it true, Sylvie?" asked Lucie.

Now Sylvie understood why Pascal was pouting—she had promised him she would never leave him. She turned an angry look on Mama, who continued shaping dough balls for frying, avoiding Sylvie's eyes. What had she hoped to gain by telling the children? Did she want to turn them against her?

Pascal looked up at her, glaring defiantly. "Go where?"

"To Canada."

"What's that?" asked Lucie.

"It's a country, in North America. Across the ocean.

We're all going," she told them. "Pascal, do you hear me? All of us will go."

"We should be going home," stated Mama, keeping her gaze fixed on the dough. "Think about your father. What if there's no one here when he comes? I'll die waiting for Patrice, if I have to. If you go, you'll go without me."

Sylvie looked from Mama to Pascal, tossing the stone between his hands harder and faster, his hurt and anger building. She couldn't break her promise and leave him, any more than she could leave Mama. Either they all went to Canada, or they all must stay here. And if they stayed here, the only way to protect the family would be for her to give herself to Kayembe. She cursed hope for tricking her into believing there could be another way. But it was her own fault. She had let hope lift her heart, and now it had so much further to fall.

ASIA

ON SUNDAY, Laiping got to the Internet café early to call her parents on one of the computers, the way Min had showed her. She'd come alone because Fen was studying English from a tattered book she had found in the dorm common room—*Speak English to be Successful!*, another part of her self-improvement plan—and Min still wasn't feeling well.

"Auntie hasn't heard from Min," her mother told her over Auntie's cell phone. Her parents had no phone of their own, so they had to borrow the phone that Min had bought for her parents. "Is everything all right with her?"

"She's fine," Laiping replied with a white lie. "Just busy." She intentionally waited until her father came on the line to explain about the company holding back her pay. It was her mother who worried the most about money. "I won't be able to send anything until next month, Baba," she told him.

"Send it when you can," he said, easing her mind. "You're a good daughter."

Without warning, Laiping's eyes welled up. Until this

moment, she hadn't realized how much she missed her father's kindness.

"Soon I'll have a mobile of my own and I can call you any time," she promised.

"Just make sure you work hard," he advised her. "Make the bosses feel important. That's the path to success."

Laiping wished she could speak with her parents longer, but they were unused to talking on the phone and quickly ran out of things to say. Besides, the people in line waiting for their turn at the computer were giving her impatient looks. After she said goodbye, she looked around the café full of chatterboxes. All the things she had found so exciting when she first arrived on the company campus —the crowds, the noise, the activity—were annoying to her this morning. Maybe it was that after working two full weeks in the factory, she felt so tired. Or maybe it was that all these strangers made her feel lonely. Then her heart took a small leap. In the press of people placing their orders at the counter, she spotted Kai. Gathering her courage, she went up to him.

"Hello," she said, suddenly shy and awkward. What if he didn't remember her?

"Laiping!" he said with a grin. "I was hoping to see you here." Even when he was smiling, there was an intensity about him that missed nothing—including her sadness. "What's the matter?" he asked.

Laiping shrugged. "Just tired."

"You need a coffee," he replied.

"I don't have enough money," she told him. "I was

supposed to get paid, but there's nothing in my bank account."

"I get it," he said knowingly. "The company is holding your money hostage. Go find us a table. I'll buy you a coffee."

"Thank you." Laiping didn't tell him she preferred tea.

Laiping waited for a table to become vacant, and found one just as Kai carried over two mugs of coffee. She added enough sugar and milk to make it drinkable.

"How was your week?" asked Kai, sitting across from her. "Other than not getting paid."

"It's so unfair," she complained.

Kai glanced around to make sure he wasn't being overheard. "The company doesn't care about being fair. They care about making money."

"But what can I do to get what they owe me?"

Kai shrugged. "They say that if we have issues about working conditions, we should take them to the union. But the union is a joke. It's supposed to fight for the rights of workers, but it's run by the government, and the government is Steve Chen's biggest fan."

"I don't even really know who Steve Chen is," said Laiping.

"*Ai ya!*" exclaimed Kai at her ignorance.

"I know he owns the company," she replied, "but who is he?"

"He's one of the richest guys in China. He owns factories all over Asia that make electronics for big brand names. Rich people in America and Europe spend big money for the stuff we make, while we get treated like slaves—and Steve Chen pockets billions. Even the Americans think it's wrong. There've been all kinds of protests over there."

Kai took out his knockoff smartphone and with a few touches of his fingertip brought up what looked like an American news site on the screen, written in English. Laiping was shocked. The government was very strict about blocking sites people weren't permitted to see.

"Are you allowed to look at that?" she asked, guessing from the way that Kai held the screen so that no one else could see it that this was a prohibited site.

"Watch this," he said, ignoring her concern.

He tweaked the screen to enlarge a video box. Laiping watched a small group of *gweilo* walking in a circle outside a store, carrying picket signs and shouting something in English. The video zoomed in on one of the picket signs, on which there was a photo of a girl who looked African. Laiping saw a long diagonal scar across the girl's face. The video zoomed out again to show the shop and the protestors. There was a logo on the storefront, just like the logo on some of the products the company made.

"They're demanding fair wages for us, and better working conditions," Kai explained.

"Who's that girl?" Laiping asked. "What happened to her face? And why is she on that poster?"

"It isn't just us in China who are getting a bad deal. Her name is Sylvie. She's a refugee from the war in the Congo, where the factory gets tantalum."

Laiping remembered learning about the tantalum powder used in capacitors during her training. "They're protesting about her, as well as us?"

Yes. There's a website about her, here," said Kai.

He tapped the screen and a page of text appeared, with the same photo of the girl that was on the picket sign.

"You can read that?" she asked.

"Some," he replied. "This is in French as well as English."

"Are you breaking the law looking at that?" *Am I breaking the law, too?*

"They treat us all like ignorant peasants," Kai continued, without answering her question. "I've been to university, the first one in my family to go. When I took this job, I thought I'd be doing something interesting, something creative. But instead I'm like some robot." Kai dropped his voice and leaned closer, so that his face was inches away from hers. Laiping had never been this close to a boy before. It was unsettling, but exciting, too. "I like you, Laiping. Anybody can see how bright you are," he said. "You deserve better. We all deserve better."

"That's exactly what I said to my cousin!" she told him. "My cousin is sick, but the company won't give her time off."

Kai's eyes darted about, as though he was looking for company spies, then he focused his intense gaze on Laiping. "If you're serious about changing things," he whispered, "you and your cousin should come to our next meeting."

"What meeting?" she asked.

"A group of us is getting organized. If the union won't help us, then we'll have to help ourselves."

Laiping thought about the first time she saw Kai, at the employment office, and how the security guards chased him. *Birds sticking their heads out.* Yesterday, she had wanted to be brave like him, but today…today she saw that talking about this group was making him nervous, and that made her nervous, too. "How many are going to be at this meeting?" she wanted to know. "Who are they?"

It was the wrong thing to say. She could see Kai assessing her—something shifting in his eyes. He leaned back in his chair, away from her, suddenly cold and distant. "You ask a lot of questions," he observed, "like your nosy friend."

He looked around—anywhere but at her. Laiping wanted him to look at her again.

"Do you live on campus?" she asked, then kicked herself—another question! She'd do anything to make him like her again. "I'll be here again next Sunday," she told him. "Will you?"

He glanced at her and said, "Don't tell anybody."

"About the meeting?"

He got to his feet, with half of his coffee left in the cup. "What meeting?" he asked, and walked away.

He thinks I'm a spy! Laiping realized. Or, worse, stupid. People were waiting for her table, giving her impatient stares. She got up and left the café, feeling lonelier still.

MONDAY MORNING in the factory following exercises, the loudspeaker lady made a special announcement.

"Our leader, Mr. Chen, has very exciting news for us!" she trilled. "As of today, we will be making a new mobile phone—so new and cutting edge that its construction must be kept very secret. Customers all over the world are waiting to purchase this phone, so we will have to work extra hard to meet our shipping deadline so that there are enough for everyone to buy."

A low murmur started among the workers.

"Be silent and listen, pig-brains!" shouted Mr. Wu.

Laiping could hear supervisors in other aisles giving similar commands. She kept her eyes forward, resisting the urge to exchange glances with Fen, who was standing at attention beside her.

The loudspeaker lady continued in her pleasant tone. "Starting today, everyone will be working overtime with extra pay!" Laiping thought, *What good is extra pay if the company won't give it to me?* But she kept her face blank as the loudspeaker lady went on to explain, "Mr. Chen has generously authorized this factory to work in shifts around the clock, and on Saturdays and Sundays. Your shift today will be eleven and a half hours."

"Eleven and a half hours!" Fen whispered to Laiping as they took their seats at their work stations. "I can barely see straight after eight!"

Mr. Wu explained to the workers that they would find a new kind of circuit board and a new kind of capacitor in their bins. These components were even tinier than the old ones, and two capacitors instead of one had to be fixed onto each board to make the new product operate faster. Laiping had trouble picking up the tiny new capacitor with her tweezers. She managed to solder one in place—but there was too much solder on the iron for these smaller components. It balled up in an unsightly blob—just when Mr. Wu, strutting up and down the aisle, happened to glance over her shoulder.

"Sloppy idiot!" he yelled so that everyone could hear. "If you can't learn to keep up with the latest product, somebody else is waiting to take your job!"

"Sorry, Mr. Wu," breathed Laiping, head bowed. "It won't happen again."

"Sorry doesn't lead to success," he said, and moved on down the line.

Fen, to Laiping's left, stole a glance her way. "Still think he's nice?"

Hot tears formed in Laiping's eyes, but she willed them away. She took a circuit board and a capacitor and tried again, this time melting half the amount of solder she would normally have used onto her iron, and managed to make a perfect joint. She grew accustomed to a new rhythm: *Circuit board-capacitor-solder-capacitor-solder; circuit board-capacitor-solder-capacitor-solder.* Working slowly and carefully, by the end of an hour she had mastered the new components.

At lunch, all the girls on Laiping and Fen's line complained that focusing on the smaller capacitors was making their eyes hurt and their shoulders stiff from hunching over the mat. "You're working too slowly!" complained Mr. Wu as he paraded the aisle after the lunch break. "Pick up the pace!"

At five thirty they had another half-hour meal break, then they hurried back from the cafeteria and worked until eight to finish their eleven-and-a-half-hour shift. Laiping's shoulders and hands were numb by the time the end of shift buzzer sounded. But before they were allowed to leave the factory, the loudspeaker lady spoke.

"Well done!" she said. "You have made a good start. But in order to deliver on time, we must double our production. As of now, half of you will begin working the night shift and the other half will work the day shift. It will be up to the night shift to help train new workers who will join you shortly."

Laiping and Fen exchanged ominous looks.

"The night shift starts *now*?" whispered Laiping. "But we've been working all day!"

"I'm not working the night shift!" replied Fen. "I'm going home to bed."

"You will start counting from the head of each line," instructed the loudspeaker lady. "One, two. One, two. Ones will be night shift. Twos will be day shift."

At the head of each line, the workers began counting. One, two. One, two. Laiping's heart raced as the count came closer to her and Fen. The fifth girl ahead of her said "two"—and then Laiping knew. One, two. One, two. One…

"Two," said Fen when her turn came.

"One," said Laiping, her heart sinking.

Fen gave Laiping a pitying look as she headed away from her work station, mouthing, *Sorry*.

AFTER FEN and the other day-shift workers left the factory floor, a crew of new workers came in to take their places. Some had been transferred from other parts of the factory and others were fresh out of training—just like Laiping had been only a few weeks ago. Before they started the shift, a voice over the loudspeaker—a man's voice this time— made them line up in the aisles and do marching exercises. *Fit body, fit mind—fit for work!* For once, it was a relief to Laiping to march on the spot. She cranked her neck as she lifted her knees, trying to loosen her stiff shoulders.

A guy of about twenty took Fen's place. He said his name was Bohai, and he told Laiping that her line had it easy, compared to where he used to work in the metal processing department.

"Look," he said, pushing up a sleeve of his smock. Laiping saw scratches all over his arm. "That's from the machines we use to polish laptop cases."

"No talking! Get to work!" called Mr. Wu from up the line.

"She's showing me what to do," replied the guy.

With Mr. Wu watching, Laiping demonstrated for her new workmate where to solder the dual capacitors onto the circuit board. He leaned close to watch her work, making her gag at the smell of his greasy hair. She was already queasy enough with fatigue.

Despite the pain in her shoulders, Laiping fell into the now-familiar rhythm—*circuit board-capacitor-solder-capacitor-solder*. Long stretches of time went by before she snapped awake and realized she'd been working half-asleep. She prayed that her hands knew what they were doing, even if her brain did not. Otherwise, the inspectors would complain about her work.

At ten p.m. they got a washroom break. At midnight

they took their first meal break. Laiping was astounded that the cafeteria line was as long in the middle of the night as it was at noon. She found a spot at a table and ate ravenously, envying Fen, sound asleep in her bunk.

By four a.m. Laiping's head was pounding. The midnight meal sat like a dead weight in her stomach. At five a.m. the workers were given another half-hour meal break, but Laiping felt too ill to eat. Her headache was worse and her shoulders were so stiff that she could no longer feel them.

At seven a.m., the sun started to seep through the high narrow windows that rimmed the factory, lifting Laiping's spirits a little. Just one more hour and she could go back to the dorm and sleep. *Circuit board-capacitor-solder -capacitor-solder; circuit board-capacitor-solder-capacitor-solder.* It seemed to Laiping that this had always been her body's rhythm, more natural than her own heartbeat.

At eight a.m. the factory whistle blew. Laiping sat back, waking from a sleepless dream. The guy beside her pulled off his mask.

"I take it back about the metal processing plant," he said. "This is worse. My head hurts from concentrating so hard."

Laiping stood up, staggering on stiff legs. She rotated her head to stretch her throbbing neck muscles, and saw Fen coming in with the day-shift workers.

Over the loudspeaker, the pleasant lady was back. "Good morning, everyone!"

"Good morning," mumbled the workers around Laiping. She moved her lips, but no sound came out.

"Night-shift workers, please leave the factory floor promptly," said the loudspeaker lady. "Your next shift begins today at eight p.m."

"How was it?" asked Fen as Laiping passed her.

"Very hard," replied Laiping. "I feel sick."

"No talking!" shouted a supervisor. "Move along!"

Fen and Laiping exchanged fleeting looks from their respective streams of workers, one flowing in and the other out.

MANY OF THE WORKERS from Laiping's shift headed immediately to the cafeteria to eat breakfast, but Laiping wanted only her bed. The day was already hot and the air was humid, adding to her drowsiness. She stepped off the elevator at the seventh floor and was hit by a wall of stale, hot air. The sun glared through the common room window and glanced off the stark white surfaces of tables and chairs, raising the pungent odor of a thousand girls who had sat and chatted with their friends and roommates, mingled with the chemical smell of cleansers used to scrub away all trace of those girls, thousands of times.

Laiping swiped her pass card through the magnetic lock on the door to her room. Inside, it wasn't so bad. Someone had left the window open and the hint of a breeze brought in a sweet smell from outside. The curtains on the bunks were all pulled closed, so Laiping couldn't tell whether they were occupied—but she sensed that she was alone in the room. How heavenly. She went to the toilet, peed, washed her face—and later would have no memory of climbing up the ladder to her middle bunk.

When Laiping woke up nine hours later and opened her curtain, dusk was falling. She had a moment of panic that she'd be late for her shift and checked the clock on the wall: 6:33. She had just enough time to shower and eat and get back to the factory for eight.

THE WEEK WENT BY with dual rhythms: *work–sleep–eat, work–sleep–eat; circuit board–capacitor– solder–capacitor–solder, circuit board–capacitor–solder–capacitor–solder.* The shifts were long, but after working twenty-four hours straight, they didn't seem so bad. She went for whole days without saying more than a few words to anyone, seeing Fen only when they crossed paths at shift changes. She missed her parents and wished she had time to go to the café and call them.

On Sunday, Laiping thought of Kai and wondered if he was at the café. She wanted to tell him that she was working like a slave on the new product, just as he had warned her would happen. But the way they left things, who knew if he would ever speak to her again?

On Wednesday, Laiping got up early so she had time to meet Min for dinner before her shift. Min's health was no better—her hands still trembled and her cough was getting worse.

"Some people think it isn't the flu," Min said, keeping her voice low. "They think it's the new cleaner they're making us use on the laptops. It dries faster on the screens, so we're more productive—but it stinks."

"Do *you* think it's the cleaner?" Laiping asked.

Min nodded. "I think it might be. One of the guys even went to the union, but they take months to do anything."

"You should ask for a transfer."

"Everybody's asking for transfers! That takes months, too." She leaned closer and asked Laiping in a whisper, "Some of the workers on my line were talking about doing something about it, maybe protesting somehow. Do you know how to get in touch with that guy, the one who was handing out the flyers?"

"Not really," Laiping had to admit. She couldn't resist adding, "I thought you said I should stay away from Kai."

Min's chin dimpled. She wiped budding tears away from her eyes. "I don't know what else to do. Somebody has to make the bosses listen!"

Alarmed, Laiping glanced around and saw a security guard watching them intently from a few paces away. She remembered one of the first rules she learned when she started at the company—*Avoid the attention of the security guards.*

"Don't cry, Min," she told her cousin. "They're watching."

Min took in a deep breath and got up from the table, being careful to keep her back to the guard. "I'd better go," she said.

Laiping hadn't finished her meal, but she followed Min outside, happy to leave the swampy heat of the cafeteria behind. It was past seven thirty, almost time for her to go to work. The last rays of the sun sifted through brown haze, creating a rosy hue that almost made the white-tiled factory buildings look pretty.

"Kai belongs to a group. There's going to be a meeting," Laiping told Min when they had reached an open stretch of walkway where no one could hear them. "We should go."

Min gave her a fearful glance. "I don't know."

"Do you want things to change, or not?" said Laiping, echoing Kai.

"When is the meeting?"

"I'll find out," she promised, giving Min a hug before they parted ways at the main boulevard.

Laiping watched Min walk out onto the road to avoid the crowds on the sidewalk, as though she was too fragile to mix with them—no trace left of the bulldozer who met her at the station just a few weeks ago. She had no idea how to find Kai, or, if she did, how she would convince him to trust her. But she had to, for Min's sake—and for her own. *Anybody can see how bright you are*, Kai had told her. Laiping vowed to prove to him she was smart, and the first way to do that was by finding him, like a needle among a hundred thousand strands of straw.

SYLVIE LAY ON THE MAT with her eyes closed, thinking how nice it would be to go on sleeping. The nightmares had been bad, startling her awake with jumbled visions of soldiers and machetes, and raging fire. Now, when she could see the light of day through her eyelids, it felt safe to sleep. But it was a school day and she had to get herself and Pascal fed and washed. Olivier she didn't have to fuss over—he had stopped going to school entirely, and was never at home.

When she sat up, she saw Mama and Lucie curled beside her, but the other mat, where Pascal normally slept beside Olivier, was empty.

"I saw him leave," reported Lucie, stretching. "It was still dark out."

"You have to find him, Sylvie," Mama fretted.

"I will," she said, pulling on her white school blouse and blue skirt. Pascal had been sulking ever since Mama let slip Sylvie's plan to go to Canada, but it was unlike him to run off. Olivier was the quick-tempered and impulsive one—Pascal was usually easygoing and eager to please. She wondered what the nine-year-old could be thinking.

"Lucie," she said in a rush, "slice some of that fruit for breakfast."

"The knife is gone!" said Lucie, rummaging through their small collection of pots and implements.

So wherever Pascal was, he had taken the knife with him. Quickly fastening the buttons of her blouse, Sylvie wondered if he pictured himself a soldier, like Olivier, and the thought of it made her hurry all the more.

She ran most of the way to the school, hoping to find him playing football in the patch of red dust that served as a pitch. When he wasn't there, she decided check with his friend, Jean-Yves, who didn't attend school. She knew where he lived in Zone 5 with his brothers, and made her way there—suffering the usual lewd stares and comments from bored men loafing under trees and in doorways.

She found the eldest brother, Luc, chopping wood outside their hut. A little older than Sylvie, he was the head of the family since the parents were killed in the fighting back home. Sylvie knew from Pascal that they had been small-time miners, gathering loose coltan from the hill-sides. The government had allowed people to make a living that way for a while, until things changed and the Mai-Mai arrived to chase them away. They were the sort of people that Sylvie's father had been trying to protect—the reason he was killed.

"Jean-Yves is gone, too," Luc informed her indifferently.

His right hand was missing—taken by a soldier, Sylvie guessed. He was using his left hand to chop firewood, his right foot to keep the log in place on the ground. Sylvie shuddered as Luc brought the ax down on the log, a toe's width from his foot.

"You should be more careful," she said. He looked at her with lifeless eyes that seemed to say he didn't care what happened to him anymore. "Did Jean-Yves say anything about where he was going?" she asked, refocusing on Pascal.

"He does errands for Kayembe's men sometimes. If you find him, tell him to bring back our machete."

A missing knife and a missing machete. Sylvie feared her instinct had been right. *They've gone to become soldiers!* She knew where she had to look next.

There was a zone in Nyarugusu, a half-hour's walk north of the old market, where decent women didn't go, day or night. It was where Kayembe's men lived—where Sylvie assumed that Olivier had been staying, and where Pascal might have gone to join him. As Sylvie walked into Zone 7, she was stared at by groups of men gathered outside crude lean-tos. They didn't speak to her or offer to buy sex, which somehow made them more frightening than the drunks and loafers in other parts of the camp. There was a desperation about them that made Sylvie's skin crawl. Her head was light with dread that one of these men might attack her. She pulled her blouse down at the back to ensure modesty at the front. Keeping her eyes downcast, she forced herself to keep walking.

She came into a circle of abandoned, falling-down huts. The charred bones of animals were scattered out from an old fire pit, long gone cold. She recognized two of Kayembe's men—the scrawny one and the round one who had carried her beans and oil for her—leaning against a jeep, smoking cigarettes. Gathering every ounce of her courage, Sylvie went up to them.

"Do you know Olivier?" she asked.

The skinny one looked her up and down. Sylvie saw a handgun in his belt.

"Why do you want to know?"

"I'm his sister. I need to find him."

"Lucky girl," he said with a lecherous grin. "You found me instead."

"Mind your manners," said the big man, cuffing the smaller one. "Don't you know her? She belongs to Kayembe."

Sylvie bristled, but didn't argue.

"Don't mind Arsène," the larger man told her. "But you shouldn't be here. It isn't safe." He opened the passenger door of the jeep, as though he fancied himself a gentleman. "Allow me to take you back to your home."

"I must see my brother," she insisted. "Please. It's important. Our little brother is missing. I think he may have gone to find him."

The big man hesitated. "The boss won't like it."

"He said it's all right," she told him. "He said to ask you to take me to him."

The fighter's eyes narrowed. Sylvie could see he knew she was lying, but he also saw her desperation, and there was a kindness about him.

"Get in," he said at last, ushering her into the jeep. He jabbed his finger toward the man he called Arsène, warning him, "Keep your mouth shut about this."

SYLVIE HELD ON TO THE DOOR HANDLE as the jeep bumped along a dirt track toward the fringes of the camp. She was afraid of being alone with the big man, worried that she had made a mistake by trusting him. But she had no choice.

"You don't have to be afraid of me," he told her, as though guessing her thoughts. "My name is Fiston. I'm Congolese, like you." That proved nothing—the man who raped her was also Congolese. When she said nothing in reply, he remarked, "Olivier is a good man. Kayembe likes him."

Sylvie found her voice. "What does he do for Kayembe?"

"Best not to ask too many questions like that," Fiston advised her.

They reached the gates of Nyarugusu. Congolese weren't supposed to leave the camp without permission, but the Tanzanian guard waved Fiston through as if he knew him.

"Where are we going?" she asked, glancing behind her as the distance grew between the jeep and the camp gates. For years she had longed for escape from Nyarugusu, but now that she was outside, she felt afraid.

"Not too far now," Fiston told her.

The jeep continued across a stretch of empty savannah until they entered a scrubby forest. Without warning, Fiston veered the jeep off the road and wove it in between sparse trees, with Sylvie bracing herself against the bumpy ride—wondering if this had all been a ruse. She was completely at Fiston's mercy. She was relieved when, after several minutes, a camp of army tents came into view. Fighters milled about, wearing combinations of camouflage shirts and pants. A ragtag army.

"Is one of them your little brother?" asked Fiston as he pulled the jeep to a stop.

He was pointing to a group of boys of various heights and ages playing target practice with knives against the trunk of a eucalyptus tree. Sylvie spotted Pascal on the fringes of the group, waiting for his turn to throw.

"That's him!" replied Sylvie.

She climbed out of the jeep and headed toward Pascal, just as Jean-Yves stepped forward with his family's machete. His aim was true, but his throw weak. The machete bounced off the tree to the ground. Pascal laughed along with the older boys as Jean-Yves ran to fetch it.

"My turn!" shouted Pascal.

He stepped up, taking careful aim with the knife he had taken from the hut that morning, but Sylvie reached him before he had a chance to throw.

"Pascal!" His face fell when he saw her. She seized hold of his arm, ready to drag him home. "How dare you run off like that!" she scolded.

"Are you going to let a girl boss you?" taunted the tallest of the boys.

The others laughed, Jean-Yves the loudest. Embarrassed, Pascal shook loose from Sylvie's grip.

"I go where I want to!" he declared.

Sylvie knew that if she wanted him to come with

her, she mustn't humiliate him any further. "Come home now and see Mama," she pleaded more gently. "You had us worried."

"Go away!" he told her. Pascal waved the cooking knife in the air, swaggering like a soldier. "Go, I said!"

"You heard him!" Jean-Yves joined in, brandishing his family's machete toward Sylvie's face. "Go, or I'll give you another cut!"

For a moment, Sylvie was too stunned to speak. Jean-Yves was no older than Pascal, but he seemed vicious, like a wild animal.

"Hey!" Fiston marched toward them with unexpected speed, given his size. Pascal and Jean-Yves were suddenly just boys again, shrinking in fear. "Watch your mouths! And you," he said, wagging his finger at Pascal, "you're lucky to have a sister who cares about you."

Sylvie was beginning to believe she had misjudged Fiston. "Will you take us back to the camp?" she asked him.

"But don't you want to see Olivier first? Come," he said, walking away without waiting for her reply.

"You wait here," Sylvie told Pascal. "You're coming home with me."

"I'm staying with Jean-Yves!" he protested.

"Then he's coming, too."

In truth, now that she had found Pascal, Sylvie had no interest in seeing Olivier, who had traded her away to Kayembe as easily as farmer would trade a goat. But she followed Fiston across the clearing where men were gathered around a cook fire, roasting bushmeat. Sylvie's mouth watered at the smell of it.

"Fiston has got a girlfriend," one of them teased.

"There's enough of me for three girlfriends to share," joked Fiston, spreading his broad hands over his belly. "But not this one," he told them. "She belongs to the boss."

The men went silent. Sylvie noticed how their gazes fell to the ground, away from her, and she realized, *They're afraid!*

Fiston led her to an area behind the army tents where a dozen vehicles were parked. Men and boys were shoveling black nuggets of ore from the back of a small truck into a larger one. Sylvie knew what the stuff was from Papa showing her when she was little. It was coltan—the same coltan that made soldiers rich, but so many others miserable. *Kayembe is bringing it from North Kivu*, she realized. *From home.* As they drew closer, Sylvie recognized Olivier, shoveling alongside the others.

"Olivier!" Fiston called to him. "You have a visitor!"

Olivier at first looked shocked when he saw Sylvie, then angry. "What are you doing here?"

"Looking for Pascal. He ran away."

"He's fine," he replied irritably. "He hitched a ride here this morning."

"I know," she said. "I'm taking him home."

"Your sister was very worried," contributed Fiston. "A man looks after his family, Olivier, and doesn't make them worry."

"Of course, Fiston," Olivier responded with respect.

"Thank you for bringing her."

"Be the man your father was," he advised.

"You knew him?" asked Sylvie.

"Everybody knew him," replied Fiston. For a moment, it seemed he had more to say, but he thought better of it. "I'm getting some food," he told Sylvie. "Let me know when you're ready to go back."

Sylvie waited until Fiston was a safe distance away before turning on Olivier and hissing, "How dare you?"

"How dare I what?!"

"Promise Kayembe I would marry him! How can you work for that man, when he's helping the Mai-Mai, who killed Papa?"

"Keep your voice down!" Olivier told her with a nervous glance toward the camp. He led her away from the trucks and the men.

"Papa would be ashamed of you," she told him.

Her words wounded him, as she had intended, but he lashed back. "Papa was too soft! He couldn't protect us," he said. "Only Kayembe can protect us."

"I won't marry him!"

"Yes, you will, Sylvie. Kayembe will make us rich. He'll give us a future."

Sylvie shook her head, revolted by the idea of growing rich by causing even more suffering for the people back home. "Where did that coltan come from?" she demanded, nodding toward the trucks. "Who did he steal it from? Who is he selling it to?"

"Keep quiet!"

"How many people did he kill because of it?" Olivier

looked away. Sylvie studied him. There was hardly anything of her brother left in his hardened face. "Have *you* killed for coltan, Olivier?"

His eyes locked onto hers. "No!"

"But you will." He had no reply. "We're going to Canada," she said, more determined than ever.

"You're crazy," Olivier scoffed. "You think those foreign doctors care about what happens to us, just because you're their pet?"

"There are people in Canada who want to help us. You can stay here if you want to, but the rest of us are leaving!"

Olivier's brow furrowed with worry, as though he saw his plans unraveling. "No you're not! We're going home to North Kivu, where we belong."

"You can't stop me."

"But Kayembe will," he told her. "Don't be stupid, Sylvie! He's strong because people are afraid of him. If you make him look weak, he'll kill you. He'll kill all of us. Mama, the children. All of us." Sylvie turned away, not wanting to hear any more, but Olivier was unrelenting. "You're wrong about Kayembe," he said. "He's a patriot. He's getting his coltan from our people, the small miners."

"He's with the Mai-Mai! They're like all the other fighters—they don't care about the people."

"He's only helping the Mai-Mai until the Rwandans have been chased out of the Kivus. Then we can all leave Nyarugusu and go home."

"He's greedy like all of them, Olivier."

"You don't know anything!" he shouted angrily, throwing up his hands. By reflex, Sylvie cowered, afraid he would hit her. Seeing her fear, Olivier seemed suddenly ashamed. His shoulders slumped, and a confusion of emotions played over his face—helplessness, sadness. And something else, something Sylvie was unable to name. He was the one who had seen their father die. Was he seeing it again now, in his mind? "You don't know what people are capable of, Sylvie," he said, pleading with her to hear him. "I do."

Searching his face, Sylvie tried to understand what he *wasn't* saying. A monstrous thought took shape. "Olivier," she said, barely above a whisper, "did Kayembe kill Papa?"

Olivier squeezed his eyes shut. When he opened them again, it was clear that a door had closed. He would give nothing more away.

"Be glad Kayembe wants you, Sylvie," he told her flatly. "It's the only way, for all of us."

He wasn't being stubborn now. He was simply stating the facts as he saw them. Sylvie didn't bother to argue. Secretly, she knew he could well be right. There was no guarantee Marie and Alain could get the whole family out—that was only wishful thinking. Marrying Kayembe might be the sacrifice she had to make to save the family, no matter what other life might be waiting for them, far away in Canada.

LAIPING WAS GETTING USED TO WORKING the night shift and sleeping through the day—although the daytime heat sometimes kept her awake, sticky with sweat. On Saturday, her shift worked overtime, with the promise of a day off on Sunday. But at the end of the Saturday shift, the supervisors decided they were falling too far behind on the new product, and told them they would have to work overtime on Sunday as well, if the company was to meet the American launch date.

She hadn't forgotten her promise to Min to find out when Kai's meeting was going to be held. She'd been thinking hard about how to get in touch with him, apart from going to the Internet café and hoping to run into him. But with working overtime all weekend, she didn't even have time to do that.

By Monday, Laiping had worked eight days of eleven-hour shifts, without a day off. She was so tired that she went for long periods in factory working like a brainless robot, so when on Tuesday evening following marching exercises Mr. Wu approached her, she was nervous.

"You, come with me," he said. His expression was grim, and frightened Laiping.

"Why?" she asked.

"Don't ask questions. Just do as you're told!" he barked.

Mr. Wu led Laiping down the wide staircase. When they reached the ground floor, they turned down a long narrow corridor where the factory offices were located.

"Mr. Wu, can you please tell me where we're going?" she asked politely.

"You'll find out soon enough. We're almost there."

At last he stopped at a door marked, *Lau Ceon-Cau, Assistant Manager, Human Resources.* Mr. Wu knocked on the door.

"Come in," came a woman's voice.

Mr. Wu opened the door and indicated Laiping should enter. Inside, a woman of about Laiping's mother's age, wearing a gray business suit and black-rimmed glasses, sat behind a desk. Laiping recognized her as the lady who had spoken to them on their first day at the Training Center. Her smile had been as wide as her whole face then, but today she looked stern and angry.

"Please come in, Mr. Wu," she said, and now Laiping recognized her voice, too. She was the loudspeaker lady!

Mr. Wu bowed his head slightly and told her, "This is the worker you asked to see."

"Sit down please," instructed the loudspeaker lady. Her voice was tight with displeasure—not at all like the friendly tone she used to encourage the workers during morning exercises. Laiping took a seat in a chair facing the desk.

"I will leave you then," said Mr. Wu with another bow.

"I am Miss Lau," the loudspeaker lady told Laiping once Mr. Wu had closed the door behind him.

"Hello, Miss," replied Laiping, trying to hide the terror she felt.

The fluorescent tubes overhead cast a harsh light that gave Miss Lau a ghostly look. She picked up a small container from her desk that had a number on it: 12-298153—Laiping's employee number. Laiping recognized it as one of the containers where she placed the finished circuit boards, after soldering on the capacitors. Miss Lau took tweezers and lifted a circuit board out of the box.

"Is this your work?" she asked.

Laiping swallowed. "I guess so."

"You guess so? Look at it."

Laiping leaned over the desk to take a closer look at the circuit board, which Miss Lau had placed on the blotter. She felt her cheeks flush when she saw that one of the two capacitors had broken off. Laiping had no memory of producing such inferior work. Then again, she had so often snapped awake from half-sleep while on the night shift—perhaps the mistake had slipped by her.

"I'm not sure it's mine," she stammered.

Lightning quick, Miss Lau picked up a ruler from the desk and—*thwap!*—struck Laiping on the side of her head with it.

"Let me assure you, it *is* yours," she stated. She pulled several more circuit boards out of the container, each one flawed in its own way. "And this one, and this one, and these. Let me assure you of something else: if you wish to continue working here, such carelessness will not be tolerated!"

Laiping wanted to tell Miss Lau that a dozen flawed circuit boards out of the thousands she had made was not so bad. She wanted to tell her that mistakes must be expected if the supervisors insisted on working the employees to the point of exhaustion. But she stayed silent as she suffered a tongue-lashing about her laziness and ingratitude.

"Mr. Chen is taking a chance on ignorant girls like you by bringing you from your miserable villages and letting you work here," said Miss Lau, the overhead lights glaring off her glasses so that Laiping couldn't see her eyes. "He's giving you the opportunity for a better life. It is your duty to repay him by working your hardest and your best, every minute of every day."

"Yes, Miss Lau," replied Laiping, bowing her head.

"As punishment, you will not work in the factory tonight and you will not be paid."

"Yes, Miss Lau."

Miss Lau reached for a small bound book that was resting on top of a file organizer. She handed the book to Laiping.

"Instead, you will spend tonight's shift copying out *The Sayings of Steve Chen.*" Laiping saw that this was the title of the small book. "Perhaps through his wisdom you will understand the dedication it takes to be successful and prosperous."

"Yes, Miss Lau," repeated Laiping humbly, but inside, she burned with the sense that she was being treated unfairly. She had worked so hard to please Steve Chen—she didn't deserve to be punished! She thought of what Kai had said about him getting rich by treating the workers like slaves. If she was supposed to think of Steve Chen as a father, he was a mean one. She remembered the video Kai showed her on his smartphone, of the Americans protesting Steve Chen outside a store, and took comfort from the fact that she wasn't the only one who knew the truth about him.

These thoughts raged inside Laiping's head as she followed Miss Lau down the corridor, the loudspeaker lady's heels click-clicking against linoleum, to a small room with one table and one chair and no windows. On the table there was a pad of cheap paper and a pencil. Laiping looked up and saw a surveillance camera pointed at the table from a corner of the ceiling.

"I'm leaving for the day," explained Miss Lau. "Another supervisor will come and check on you later."

"What if I need the washroom?" asked Laiping.

"You'll have to hold it. Cheer up, Laiping," she told her, suddenly smiling her broad, tight smile. "You still have your job. This will help you to remember to be more careful in the future."

"Thank you, Miss Lau."

"You're welcome," she said, the smile unfaltering, and exited.

Laiping opened *The Sayings of Steve Chen* and began copying characters and phrases:

Efficiency leads first to Productivity, then to Prosperity.
The ability to solve problems is the best way of judging a manager.

The ability to obey instructions is the best way of judging a worker.

Laiping found the sayings of Steve Chen boring, but she had liked combining tiny strokes on the page to make characters from the time she first learned to write at school. She took her time and made sure that her penmanship was neat and pleasing, just to prove that she *was* a careful worker. She kept at it steadily for several hours, enjoying the solitude—even though she was aware the entire time that she was being spied on by the security camera. Finally, a different manager came into the room, a man in a gray suit and striped tie. He took the pages that Laiping had copied and studied them. At last he nodded, she hoped in approval.

"What have you learned?" he asked Laiping.

Laiping was caught. She had been focusing so hard on drawing the characters that she hadn't paid much attention to the sayings themselves. But one of the posters she stared at every night during marching exercises bubbled up from her memory to save her.

"That if I don't work hard today, I can work hard finding another job tomorrow," she said.

"Very good. I've been watching you," he told her, nodding toward the camera. "I can see that you know how to work hard. After the meal break, you may go back to your job and receive half a day's pay."

"Thank you, sir," said Laiping, glowing at his praise. But at the same time, she kicked herself for being so eager to please, like a running dog. She was beginning to notice a pattern in the factory—one day they praised, the next they found fault. She wondered if the bosses were intentionally trying to keep the workers off balance.

LAIPING ATE MORE HEARTILY at the midnight meal than she had all week, even though it was the same dish of rice, vegetables, and pork. Her coworker Bohai spotted her and joined her. Laiping wondered if he ever bothered to shower, because his hair was greasier than ever, and he smelled of old sweat. He hunched over his bowl shoveling food with his chopsticks, talking with his mouth full.

"So what happened?" he wanted to know, a little too eagerly. "Where did they take you?"

Nosy! thought Laiping. "It's none of your business," she said.

"Did they make you write a confession?" asked Bohai.

"A what?"

"That's how they punish people in metal processing. You have to write a letter to Steve Chen, telling him you're a lazy good-for-nothing and begging him to give you a second chance—then they'll let you keep your job."

"How do you know?" she asked. "Were you punished?"

"Not me!" he huffed. "I was one of the best workers. That's why they chose me to work on the new product."

Arrogant, too, thought Laiping. She knew the type from her village—a young prince, an only son spoiled by parents and grandparents, raised to believe he deserves to have everything handed to him. She filled her mouth with rice and greens, hoping he would take the hint and stop talking. It worked—Bohai gave up on conversation and focused on wolfing down his own food. But between the sight of his flaky scalp as he bent over his bowl, and the thought of returning to the monotony of the line, Laiping had suddenly lost her appetite. She could already feel the ache in her shoulders and neck. Part of her missed the peaceful solitude of the little room, and writing out the sayings of Steve Chen.

"Are you going to finish that?" asked Bohai, eyeing the remaining food in her bowl.

"Help yourself," she replied.

Without registering her sarcasm, Bohai took Laiping's bowl and greedily ate her leftovers. She wondered whether he was lying, if the reason he knew about having to write confessions to Steve Chen is because he *had* been punished. And if so, she wondered what he had been punished for.

ON WEDNESDAY EVENING following marching exercises, Miss Lau, the loudspeaker lady, made a special announcement.

"Despite generously giving you overtime, production is falling behind. The reputation of the company is at stake if we fail to meet the product launch date! Therefore, as of now we are increasing the production quota per shift." The workers received this news in silence, no one so much as daring to steal an anxious glance at her neighbor. "You will have to work harder if you want to continue to work here," warned the voice of Miss Lau. "Are you willing to work harder?"

"Yes!" called out the workers, as one.

"I hope so!" she scolded them. "Let us all strive to make Mr. Chen proud of us!"

Laiping took her place beside Bohai and pulled on mask and gloves. She told herself there was nothing to be worried about—by now, she was an expert at soldering capacitors. She would just work a little faster, that was all, and pay greater attention to what she was doing.

For the first half of the shift, her concentration was perfect, her rhythm effortless as she fixed capacitors onto circuit boards. When Mr. Wu reached Laiping on his ceaseless stroll up and down the aisle, he nodded his approval. By the time the meal-break whistle sounded, Laiping's container of finished circuit boards held several hundred. She felt proud of herself, but Bohai was in a bad mood.

"This isn't fair," complained the young prince. "They can't expect us to work this fast for twelve hours straight."

"You can always go back to the metal processing shop," replied Laiping without sympathy, pulling off her latex gloves.

She headed toward the exit with the other workers, hoping to avoid Bohai's company, but something made her look back—a half-formed suspicion that was starting to take shape—and she saw Bohai drop something into her "completed" bin. By the time she strode back to him, he was walking away from the work bench.

"What did you do?" she demanded.

"What are you talking about?"

"Did you switch circuit boards with me?"

"No!" he replied with a sneer, backing away.

Laiping stepped toward him, refusing to let him get away. "You did, didn't you?"

"Listen," he said, leaning close so that only Laiping could hear, "my uncle is a Party boss, so you better not start making crazy accusations against me, or you'll be sorry."

He hurried away without giving her time to reply. Laiping looked into her bin and found several botched circuit boards that Bohai had ruined with too much solder. Workers with carts were coming down the aisles, collecting the containers of completed boards.

"What are you waiting for?" yelled Mr. Wu when he saw Laiping still at her work station. "You better not be late coming back from the break!"

Laiping was on the verge of telling him what had been happening—that Bohai had been letting her take the blame for his poor workmanship. But she remembered the blow of the ruler she'd received from Miss Lau when she questioned whether the bad boards could have been hers. This was the fifth rule she had learned since starting work in the factory: *Never talk back to a supervisor.* Besides, if Bohai's uncle really was a Communist Party boss, he could make trouble not just for Laiping, but for her family, too. The Party ran everything, from the government in Beijing to the village councils.

"I'm going, Mr. Wu," she said—and quickly dropped the defective boards back into Bohai's container.

On Thursday evening, Laiping arrived early for her shift to ask Mr. Wu for permission to move to a different place on the line. She didn't tell him the reason.

"What does it matter where you sit?" he barked. "If I make a change for you, then everyone will want to change!"

Laiping thanked him anyway, and took her place beside Bohai. From then on, she and Bohai didn't speak. And Laiping watched Bohai like a hawk.

FISTON SANG while the jeep bumped over the dirt road on the way back into Nyarugusu, a lullaby about rowing on the river that Sylvie remembered Mama singing to her when she was small, back when Mama was happy. *Olele, olele, the current is very strong!* Fiston's voice was surprisingly sweet, coming from such a rough man. Riding in the front seat with the cooking knife in her lap while Pascal sulked in the back, Sylvie would have found his song comforting if she hadn't been so filled with worries.

"I know you won't tell me what Olivier is doing for Mr. Kayembe," Sylvie said to Fiston after they had passed back through the camp gates, "but can you at least say if what he's doing is dangerous?"

Fiston shifted in the driver's seat, taking a moment to consider his answer. "Olivier is with experienced fighters," he replied at last, "but in the Kivus, everything is dangerous. The Chinese want to buy coltan, and the Canadians want to sell it to them. Mr. Kayembe is in the middle between them trying to do business, but so are the Mai-Mai and the Rwandans, and other rebels."

"The Canadians?" repeated Sylvie, startled. "What do they have to do with it?"

"They own a lot of the big mining companies," he replied. "Sometimes the foreigners have need of a militia to do their dirty work for them."

"What kind of dirty work?"

Fiston kept his eyes on the road and honked several times at refugees who were ambling along. "Get out of the way! Do you want to get hit?"

"You mean like when the Mai-Mai killed my father," Sylvie said, watching for his reaction.

Fiston shot her a warning glance. "You're a smart girl, *Mademoiselle* Sylvie," he said. "You know it isn't wise to ask too many questions." Abruptly, he changed his tone and became carefree and joking once again. "Where shall your chariot take you? You live in Zone 3, no?"

Sylvie thought for a moment. "Would you take us to the Zone 3 clinic?"

"At your service, *mademoiselle*."

Sylvie rode the rest of the way wondering if it could be true what Fiston said, that Canadians were somehow involved with the misery that had befallen her family, and thousands of other Congolese. She remembered Marie telling her something about her friend Alain's website keeping tabs on mining companies in the Congo, but she hadn't told her that those companies were Canadian.

When they reached the clinic, Fiston gave Pascal a grave look. "You listen to your sister and go home with her, or you will have Fiston to deal with."

"Yes," whispered Pascal, in awe of Fiston, but Sylvie could see he was still pouting over being pulled away from his new friends.

"Thank you," Sylvie told Fiston.

He dipped his head and drove off, the jeep kicking up dust in its wake. Sylvie turned to Pascal.

"Go home. Give this back to Mama," she told him, handing him the cooking knife. "Tell her I will be there soon."

"Where are you going?"

"Never mind that. Go right home, or I will tell Fiston!"

Reluctantly, Pascal headed away, scuffing his bare feet through the red earth. Sylvie watched him long enough to be certain that he was obeying, then she went into the clinic to find Doctor Marie. She wanted to hear from her if it was true that Canada was involved in the fighting back home.

"She is with a patient. You will have to wait," said Neema, at the admitting table. She took in Sylvie's impatience. "What is so important?"

"I need to talk to her, that's all," Sylvie replied. She had no intention of sharing more.

"Is it true what they're saying, that Kayembe wants you?" Neema asked. When Sylvie didn't reply, she added, "You know he recently took a wife in North Kivu, don't you?" She hadn't known this, but it didn't surprise her. A man like Kayembe wouldn't care that taking many wives was considered backward by modern people. "Sure he's rich, but you'd better watch out," advised Neema. "You will be his second wife, under the thumb of his first one."

It was on the tip of Sylvie's tongue to tell her she would rather die than marry Kayembe, but Olivier's words rang in her ears. *He'd kill all of us. Mama, the children. All of us.*

Sylvie took a seat on one of the rough wooden benches in the small waiting area, beside a man moaning with a toothache. She waited for half an hour, watching patients come and go. A rash, a sprained ankle. One young man on crutches, his pant leg pinned under the stump of his right leg, complained to Neema he was having trouble breathing. Doctor Van de Velde came out to the waiting area to check on him, making Sylvie nervous. She hadn't forgotten how angry the head doctor had been when the young American, Martin, had let her come inside the foreign workers' compound. But Doctor Van de Velde ignored Sylvie, listening intently through his stethoscope to the man's lungs, round gold-rimmed glasses perched on top of his large nose like a tiny bicycle.

"I can find nothing wrong," the Belgian told the man in his strangely accented French. "How have you been sleeping?"

"Not well," replied the man.

"Nightmares?" The man nodded. "Are you Congolese? From the DRC?" The man nodded again. "You came from the Kivus recently?"

"Yes. Someone killed a Mai-Mai soldier in our village," the man explained. "So they came and butchered thirty people, maybe more." His kept his voice flat while he told his story, as though his emotions were all used up.

"They pulled us from our homes," he said, "women and children, too."

He winced, as though he was seeing them in his mind. Sylvie could see them, too. She could hear their screams.

"They cut us with machetes," he went on, "even the babies."

Sylvie's heart pounded painfully as she saw the soldier's machete raised over her face. There was no escaping memories. They stayed close, like unhappy spirits, demanding attention.

"You saw this?" asked Doctor Van de Velde. His face was blank, without feeling, his skin ashen against his white lab coat—not rosy, like some Europeans.

How can he be so heartless? thought Sylvie. *How can he be a doctor and not care?*

The man nodded and bowed his head, admitting in shame, "I pretended I was dead, and hid under the bodies."

Now Sylvie understood why he couldn't breathe— because he survived when his friends and family died. She felt guilty, too, sometimes, because she lived and Papa died.

"Your shortness of breath is most likely related to post-traumatic stress," Doctor Van de Velde told him.

"Is there medicine for it?" the man wanted to know.

"There is, but we don't have any right now. There are counselors who can help, other refugees who've been through the same things you have." The man looked disappointed. Doctor Van de Velde at first looked angry, but when he spoke, Sylvie could see he was trying to be helpful. "When you feel a panic attack coming on," he suggested, "try some simple exercises to regulate your breathing."

He demonstrated, drawing in a deep breath and releasing it slowly. Sylvie tried, breathing in and then out. But the man wasn't interested. Taking hold of the crutches, he struggled up from his wooden bench.

"What use is breathing?" he said. He wouldn't look Doctor Van de Velde in the eye.

"I'm sorry," the doctor told him. "I wish there was more I could do to help."

The man shook his head. "There is no help for us. When the mines are open, there is work, but then the fighting comes back, too. The people suffer, and the warlords get rich."

Like Kayembe, thought Sylvie.

She and the doctor watched the young man lumber slowly out of the clinic, planting his crutches on the ground and swinging his good leg between them. Sylvie glanced to Doctor Van de Velde, and saw that he was not without feelings after all. He looked like he wanted to yell at someone. He looked helpless. How many times had he heard the same story? For millions of people, since before Sylvie was born, it had been the same, over and over again.

"Are you here to work?" the Belgian asked, at last acknowledging Sylvie's presence. He was stern, even when he was trying to be friendly.

"No. I'm waiting for Doctor Marie."

"Anything I can help you with?"

There was, in fact. "Is Canada bad?" Sylvie asked abruptly.

He got a puzzled half-smile. "No, Canada is not bad. Why?"

"Someone told me the big mining companies in the Kivus are owned by Canadians. Is it true?"

"Yes, it's true," answered Marie. Sylvie and Doctor Van de Velde turned to see her coming into the waiting area, pulling surgical gloves from her hands. She looked tired. "A lot of the companies are Canadian-owned."

"But...you said people in Canada want to help us," said Sylvie, struggling to make sense of it.

"There are many people in lots of countries who want to help, Sylvie," remarked Doctor Van de Velde. "Take my country. A long time ago, a Belgian king declared he owned all of the Congo and everything in it! Now, some of us are trying to make up for that arrogance."

"Most people have no idea what the mining companies are doing over here," added Marie. "That's why Alain and his group started their website."

"Why don't you tell them what's happening, Sylvie?" said Doctor Van de Velde with a shrug. "Marie, this website your boyfriend started, it's a good start. But how about a video, telling people exactly what's going on, from Sylvie's perspective?"

From the look on Doctor Marie's face, Sylvie could tell she liked the idea. "Sylvie, what do you think?" she asked.

More people staring at me, is what she thought. But if it would help to change things... "What would I say?" she asked.

"You could start by telling people what happened to you," suggested Marie. "I mean, the parts you're comfortable talking about," she hastened to add.

Sylvie thought about it. "We need a movie camera, don't we?" she asked.

Marie fished her mobile phone out of her pocket, tapped the screen with her finger, and suddenly it was a video camera. "*Voilà!*"

"It's ironic, isn't it, that there's coltan in that thing," commented Doctor Van de Velde.

Sylvie thought he had missed the point. "Coltan is just a rock. " she said. "It's the fighters who hurt people."

The two doctors exchanged a look.

"Sylvie," Doctor Van de Velde told her, "I think you know exactly what to say."

AT FIRST IT SEEMED STRANGE to Sylvie to be speaking to a mobile phone. Marie held it up in front of her as they sat together in the clinic waiting area, after the staff and patients had gone. Sylvie tried to convince herself that she was simply telling the story to Marie. Still, it was hard to know where to begin.

"How old were you when your village was attacked, Sylvie?" prompted Marie.

"I was ten."

"When did you first see the soldiers?"

"I was in our house, playing with Pascal, my little brother. We heard a truck outside. The next thing I knew, soldiers were breaking the door down."

"Then what happened?" asked Marie.

Sylvie saw the soldier in her mind, felt his weight on top of her. Smelled his heavy stink of diesel and sweat. She wanted to tell Marie about it, wanted to let go of the festering memory, but her mouth refused to form the words.

Marie turned the camera off and let the phone rest in her lap. "Do you want me to stop recording?"

"No," she replied in a whisper.

"If you say something, and you decide you don't want it to be in the video, I can erase it," Marie told her.

Sylvie nodded. Marie lifted the camera-phone up, and they tried again. "The soldier pushed me down…" Sylvie began. Her heart raced. She couldn't speak.

Marie saw her difficulty and said it for her, "He raped you?" She said it in a calm way that made Sylvie realize she had guessed it a long time ago. Sylvie gave a short nod. Marie kept the camera-phone steady. "Have you ever told anyone about this before?"

"The Congolese don't talk about things like that," she told Marie.

"But talking about it can help," Marie said, choosing her words carefully. "It's what psychotherapists do with their patients. It can help people to be able to remember traumatic events without reliving them."

"Reliving them," said Sylvie, grasping her meaning, "like in nightmares, and panic attacks?"

"Exactly. Should we keep going?"

Sylvie hesitated before replying, "Yes."

"What else do you remember?"

"I woke up in a truck," she said. "I couldn't see because there was a bandage over my face, but then I pulled it up a little." She lifted an imaginary bandage. "The first thing I saw was Pascal, sleeping, and that made me happy because he was safe. Then Mama told me it was my own fault that the soldier cut my face, because I was so stubborn."

"She said that to you?"

Sylvie nodded. She could tell that Marie was struggling not to let anger show.

"Then my other brother, Olivier, said, 'Papa is dead.' Just like that."

Sylvie stopped. She was remembering Olivier in the truck, sitting apart, sullen—his words so cold and hard, twisting in her like a knife.

"What did you feel in that moment?" asked Marie, her voice thick with emotion now. "I felt…" What *had* she felt? Until this moment, she hadn't realized. Now, she was sick with shame as it came to her. "I hated him," she said. "I hated Olivier, because he was the one who told me about Papa. Because of the way he told me," That was why she had let her heart turn against him, finding defect in everything he did. Mama had been right all along—he stayed away because of her bad temper. Sylvie looked past the camera-phone, searching Marie's eyes. "He was only nine," Sylvie said, tears streaming freely. "It wasn't his fault."

Marie turned the camera off. "But, Sylvie," she told her, her own cheeks wet with tears, "you were only ten." Marie was quiet for a moment as she ran her thumbs under her eyes, wiping them clear. "Maybe this wasn't such a good idea, after all," she said, turning back to Sylvie. "It's good you're talking about these things, but it's too personal for a video." Sylvie watched as Marie tapped the phone's screen a couple of times. "There!" she said, forcing a smile. "Erased, all gone. It isn't your responsibility to be the poster child for coltan."

Poster child? Sylvie didn't understand what Marie was talking about, but it didn't matter. She was busy thinking about Olivier, and how she could make it up to him. *I can get him away from here, to a better life!* she thought. *If only I can convince Mama to go.*

"Marie," she said, "we have to make the video."

"No, Sylvie. It's too hard on you."

"But we won't make it about me," she said. "We'll make it about all of us. My family."

Marie studied her for a moment. "Will they agree?"

That was the question. Sylvie couldn't be sure if they would. But she was sure of this—that unless she could persuade her mother to go with her to Canada, Olivier would never leave. And if Olivier stayed, how long would he go on living?

FIONA

AT THE BEGINNING OF THE SUMMER, Fiona found a job
working part-time at the food concession at Kitsilano
Beach, dishing ice cream bars, fries, and burgers for
swimmers and sailboarders. Kits Beach had the most
California vibe of all the Vancouver beaches. It was where
the under-thirty crowd made the scene, showing off hot
bodies in skimpy swimwear. Fiona wasn't into competitive
tanning, but it was nice to be near the water, and she liked
her boss, Cathy. Still, by the middle of July she was having
a hard time even looking at a hot dog, and she missed her
friends—all of them, it seemed, were either away at camp,
or vacationing with their families.

　　She missed her cell phone, too—more than ever.
Without it, it was so much harder to stay in touch with
Lacey and Megan and Brit. She'd been hoping that her dad
would relent and help her get a new one without making
her wait for her birthday, but no. Mr. Learn-Your-Lesson
was holding fast.

　　"You're making money now," he told her when Fiona
raised the issue at a Sunday barbeque in early August.

Fiona had taken the bus over the Lions Gate Bridge to her dad's place in West Van. "You should be able to pay for a basic phone in no time."

"Nobody has a basic one anymore," Fiona replied. "I need Internet."

"A smartphone is a luxury, not a necessity. Surely you could live without Friendjam 24/7," he remarked, flipping salmon steaks over a stainless steel grill that was the size of a small car. Looking around at the kidney-shaped pool and the set of outdoor furniture that was nicer than the stuff in her mom's living room, Fiona rolled her eyes. Her dad wasn't exactly denying himself his share of luxuries.

"Dad, seriously. You're talking social death."

"She's right, Dave," Joanne chimed in as she came through French doors out onto the patio. Joanne was blonde and perky—pretty much the opposite of Fiona's mom. Out of loyalty to her mom, Fiona had tried for a long time to dislike Joanne, but resistance had proved futile. She was younger than Fiona's parents. She *got* things. "Phone's are everything to kids today," she told Fiona's dad. "Besides, it's a safety issue. I wouldn't let Brandon or Katie leave the house without theirs."

They all looked over to Brandon and Katie, who were sitting in lounge chairs by the pool. Brandon, who was eleven, was playing Angry Birds on a tablet, and six-year-old Katie had her mom's touch screen laptop open, using a paint program to trace a picture with her finger.

"It's a beautiful summer day, and look at these guys, glued to little screens," remarked Fiona's dad.

"Hey, Brandon," Fiona said, rallying his support, "Dad's taking your cell phone away."

"No way!" he howled, looking up from his game.

"Fiona's just teasing," said Joanne.

"Dad, please?" pleaded Fiona. "Just give me my birthday present a few weeks early."

"The answer is no, kiddo."

His tone told her there was no point in pushing it any further.

"Fine. So I'll be a social outcast for the rest of the summer," grumbled Fiona.

She headed to the pool, stripping off the cover-up she was wearing over her swimsuit.

"Hey, dinner's almost ready!" her dad called to her.

"I know." *And I don't care.*

She was about to dive in when Katie's drawing caught her eye. She was tracing a balloon face with big round eyes.

"That's really good," Fiona told her, even though it wasn't.

Katie put her finger above the right eye, and drew a diagonal line to the left cheek.

"What's that?" Fiona asked.

"What's what?" Joanne came over to look. "Katie, that's wonderful!" she exclaimed, her voice rising by an octave. In Joanne's eyes, Brandon and Katie were mini-geniuses. Fiona loved them and everything, but really—it could be a bit much.

"It's that girl," Katie explained.

"What girl?" Joanne asked.

"That girl, on your favorites."

She clicked the mouse and a blog spot came up on screen, featuring a photograph of a black girl with a scar across her face.

"Katie!" scolded Joanne, "I don't want you looking through my favorites, okay? Pictures like that aren't appropriate for kids."

"Like what?" asked Fiona's dad from his post at the grill. Joanne carried the laptop over for him to see. "Oh, not her!" he groaned. "The media has been after me all week because of her. Why do you have her on your favorites?"

"Somebody in my book club sent the link. Her story is heartbreaking."

Fiona went over to take a look. Under the girl's photo was a caption. *Help Sylvie!* "What's her deal?" she asked. "Help her with what?"

"She lives in a refugee camp somewhere in Africa. They're trying to bring her to Canada," explained Joanne.

Fiona turned to her dad. "What's she got to do with you?"

"Nothing. That's the point. Our company's operations in the Congo are completely ethical. There's so much misinformation on the Internet. Another reason you don't need unlimited access to it," he added, pointing his barbeque fork at Fiona.

"But what happened to her face?"

"Can we drop it, please?"

"Yeah, what happened to her face, Mommy?" echoed Katie.

"I don't know, honey," replied Joanne, closing the site

with a click of the mouse. She handed the laptop back to Katie, "but I'm sure she's okay now."

Katie turned her attention back to her drawing. Joanne gestured to Fiona with a "don't go there!" look. If her dad hadn't been such a hard-ass about getting her a smartphone, she could have been googling the site right now.

"Come and get it, everybody!" declared her dad, dishing the salmon steaks onto a platter.

Fiona pulled her cover-up over her head, accepting that her swim—along with her smartphone—would have to wait.

WHEN FIONA'S DAD dropped her back home later that night, Fiona discovered that her mom wasn't yet home from her weekend camping trip with friends. Spared the usual debrief that followed a visit at her dad's, Fiona booted up her laptop and checked her Friendjam account. A bunch of people had posted since she last checked yesterday. Megan wouldn't be back from camp until next week. Lacey complained about being held captive at her family's cabin for another two. And Ryan had updated his photo. He must have been working out since they broke up, because he wasn't looking so ridiculously skinny anymore. In fact, he was actually looking pretty buff. But Fiona didn't care—she would never forgive him for basically calling her a slut.

Fiona remembered Katie's drawing and typed a few keywords into the search box. Congo…mining…Sylvie. Up popped a page on a website—*Help Sylvie!*—with the girl's photo. The website was raising money to bring her to

Canada. *Enough with the guilt*, thought Fiona. *I don't even have enough money to buy a phone.* But there was something captivating about Sylvie's picture. The page said nothing about how she'd gotten the long scar across her face. She was staring into the camera with a strange look. Kind of angry, kind of scared. *What am I doing here?* her eyes seemed to ask. Fiona saw there was a video, and clicked the icon.

Sylvie was walking along a red dirt path, passing mud huts and scrubby trees, looking over her shoulder to address the camera. She was speaking French, which Fiona didn't understand. There were English subtitles, but they were so blurry that Fiona could barely read them.

The girl led the camera toward one of the huts. There was a little girl in a hand-me-down dress, about Katie's age, seated on the ground outside, playing with a wooden doll, and a pouting boy a little younger than Brandon standing in the doorway. The image went dark when the camera followed the girl inside the hut, but an angry woman could be heard, shouting something, and the girl shouted back. A corner of Fiona's mouth lifted in a knowing expression. *Must be her mother*, she thought. Then a shrunken-looking woman came out of the hut into the light, blinking, feebly waving away the camera with her hands. Sylvie came back into frame again and the woman started yelling at her in some African language. *Definitely her mother*, thought Fiona.

She was so wrapped up in the video that a sudden knock at the door made her jump.

"Hi! Can I come in?" *Speak of the devil.* Fiona's mom barged in without waiting for a reply. "Just got back!" She planted a kiss on Fiona's forehead. She reeked of campfire smoke and her curly hair was wildly frizzy around her freckled face. "How was your weekend? Oh, *her!*" she exclaimed in the same breath, seeing Sylvie on the screen. She sat down on the edge of the bed in her grimy camping clothes and she was off, talking a mile a minute about victims of war. *More guilt*, thought Fiona.

"Did you send money to this website?" she asked when her mom paused for breath.

"Of course I sent money."

"Mom, you can barely make the rent!" said Fiona. It wasn't exactly a secret that her mom didn't make much from the magazine articles she wrote.

Her mother folded her arms across her chest. "I'll find a way to pay the rent, Fiona," she replied.

Fiona didn't want to fight. She turned back to the laptop and exited the video, flipping to Friendjam and pretending to read posts. For several moments neither of them spoke.

"Okay," said Fiona's mom finally, her voice tight as she got up from the bed. "I can take a hint. I'll see you in the morning."

"Mom," Fiona said as her mother reached the door. She turned back. "What does this Sylvie have to do with Dad...I mean, with his job?"

"Why do you ask?"

"Dad said something about being bugged by reporters because of her."

Fiona's mom opened her mouth to reply, then she seemed to think twice.

"I don't know," she replied, in an obvious lie that was meant to say, *It would be wrong of me to speak against your father.* "Goodnight, my love," she said. "Sleep well."

She closed the door behind her. Fiona was left to wonder, as she so often did, why her parents ever got married in the first place.

ON MONDAY, Fiona started her shift at the food concession at eleven. It was slow at first—the hot bodies of Kits Beach liked to sleep in on Monday mornings. Fiona kept busy cleaning the ketchup and mustard dispensers, all the while adding up in her mind how many more paychecks it would take before she could afford a smartphone.

"Hey, Fiona."

Fiona looked up from daydreaming to find Ryan standing at the order window. He was going shirtless, presumably to show off the baby abs he'd acquired over the summer.

"Hi," she said back, maintaining her cool. He was the last person she wanted to see.

"How's it going?" he asked.

"Good. You?"

"Good. Just got back from camp. I was a junior counselor this year."

"Cool. What can I get for you?"

"Make it a large fish and chips," he said, scanning the menu board.

Fiona rang his order into the cash register. "Anything to drink?"

"Coke."

"Got it."

"Is something wrong?" asked Ryan.

"Why would anything be wrong?"

He was scowling. Fiona got it—he was pissed that she was being so unfriendly. She wished he would take the hint and go away—this was *so* awkward!—but he just stood there, shaking his head.

"You could at least talk to me."

"I *am* talking to you."

"Why are you being such a bitch?"

"I'm not!" Fiona spat back. "I'm just doing my job."

Cathy lumbered out from the kitchen at the back, stiff with arthritis. "Everything okay here?" She was old enough to be Fiona's grandmother, and she was just as protective as one."Fine," replied Fiona evenly. "Could I get a large fish and chips?"

"Coming up," said Cathy, giving Ryan a warning look as she headed for the deep fryer.

Ryan handed Fiona a twenty. She gave him his change and poured his soft drink.

"We'll call your order when it comes up," Fiona told him, avoiding his eyes as she set the drink down on the counter.

"Why did you break up with me?" he blurted suddenly.

Fiona looked up at him, surprised to see a hurt look on his face. "You called me a slut, Ryan," she told him.

"No, I didn't!" he shot back. He seemed flustered, and confused.

"That's what you were thinking."

"I tried calling you. You never bothered to call me back."

That was true. Fiona's mother had given her the message, but Fiona had been too angry to talk to him, and had managed to steer clear of him at school until the summer break.

"So? I was busy," Fiona replied, lamely.

His face pinched with anger. "Just forget it," he said bitterly, and strode away.

"What about your food?" Fiona called after him, but he kept walking without turning back.

Now she felt bad. She should have at least returned his phone call. But at that point, she had wanted nothing to do with him. *Is it so wrong*, she thought, *to want to forget about last year's mistakes—including Ryan?* She was sorry that Ryan's feelings were hurt, but she refused to feel guilty. Guilt was what had made her take that stupid boob shot in the first place, when she was trying to make it up to Ryan for getting sick at Jeff's party. And she was willing to admit that maybe—just maybe—the real reason she broke it off was that the thought of him made her cringe about what a dumb move it had been to send him that selfie.

From now on, I'm going to be smarter than that, she decided.

All she wanted was a fresh start in grade ten. Maybe, eventually, she'd be able to explain it all to Ryan. Maybe they could even be friends. But for now, she decided, she was going to concentrate on reinventing Fiona.

AT THE END of Laiping's seventh week in Shenzhen, she went to the row of bank machines outside the American-style restaurant and lined up along with the hundreds of other workers waiting to receive their paychecks. When it was her turn to put her card in the slot, she discovered with relief that the company had at last put money in her account. It was only two weeks' pay plus overtime—the company was still withholding her first month's earnings—and deductions had been made for the dormitory and the cafeteria meals. That left her with a little less than 600 yuan, from which she still owed Min 110, and she had to send at least some of the remaining yuan home to her parents.

"You're a good daughter," her mother said when Laiping talked to her later that morning over the computer at the Internet café. "When can you send the money?"

"Right away," Laiping promised.

Laiping was exhausted from last night's shift and needed sleep, but before going back to the dorm, she went to a financial services kiosk and stood in line for almost another hour—which gave her plenty of time to consider just how good a daughter she was. A good daughter would send all of her money home, but that would mean waiting for her next paycheck to buy a mobile—another two weeks. Laiping decided that she could be a good daughter and be good to herself, too. She sent 250 yuan home to her parents, and kept nearly that much for herself, hoping it would be enough to pay for a basic phone.

When she reached the dorm, Laiping fell into a heavy sleep. Fen shook her awake far too soon.

"Let's go, lazy!" she said, adding "*Okay?*" in English to show off how much she'd learned from her book.

Laiping was off for the rest of the day, and she and Fen had made plans to go into the city in the afternoon to shop. They walked to the subway station where Laiping had first arrived nearly two months ago, and boarded a train for the main shopping district. The subway car was crowded and they had to stand up, holding onto hand straps as the train jostled along. Laiping looked around at the girls in their pretty tops and short skirts and wished that she could afford to buy some new clothes to replace her jeans and T-shirt, but she knew she barely had enough money for a phone.

They got off the train and climbed up to street level, where Laiping finally got her first real look at the city. It was just as Min described it—block after block of shiny new buildings rising up to the sky, enough apartments for hundreds of thousands of people. Laiping wondered who could possibly afford to live there—and if she ever would. The sidewalks were jammed with smartly dressed girls and guys—it seemed that no one in Shenzhen was old! Shop after shop was bursting with all sorts of things to buy, from shoes and handbags to TVs and cameras. Laiping had never seen so many brand new things in one place. She wanted them all! Fen was shopping for clothes, and she called everything she saw *cute!*, practicing her English again.

"Look at them," she said to Laiping, pointing to a couple of stylish girls in frilly tops and sleek skirts walking along together with their heads bowed over their mobile phones. "I bet they're office workers," she said enviously. From that point forward, Fen pulled Laiping into every dress shop they passed until she found a similar top and a skirt and bought them. *"Address to success!"* she said in English, then translated for Laiping's benefit, "That means, dress for success!"

Everywhere they looked, there were shops and street vendors selling mobile phones. The ones the street vendors were selling were cheaper.

"That's because they're stolen," said Fen.

Stolen or not, Laiping could only afford the street vendors' mobiles. She bought the cheapest one, for 175 yuan, and a phone card for fifty yuan, leaving her just enough for subway fare back to campus.

It was evening now, and the restaurants and clubs they passed were full of laughter and loud music. Laiping wished they could go in and join the fun, but neither she nor Fen had any money left. At any rate, the legal drinking age was eighteen, and their fake IDs said they were only sixteen. They had to content themselves with swaying to the music out on the sidewalk, and with people-watching.

As Laiping and Fen rode the subway back to the

factory campus, the fatigue and frustration of the past weeks faded away. For the first time, Laiping felt she'd had a taste of city life—and she loved it. *All the hard work has been worth it*, she realized, happy at the thought of her very own mobile, resting in her pocket.

IT WAS NEAR MIDNIGHT when Laiping and Fen entered their dorm room.

"It's almost curfew!" snapped Big Sister Choilai, who was sitting on the edge of her bunk, painting her toenails. "Better keep the noise down, unless you want a fine."

"You're the one making noise," Fen talked back.

"Watch yourself, Fen," replied Choilai. "Your type always thinks they're destined for better things."

"If you mean I plan to make more of myself than an ordinary worker after being here for as long as you have, you're right."

Choilai scowled. Laiping started climbing up to her bunk so Choilai wouldn't see the smile on her face.

"Laiping," said Choilai, "Your cousin was here looking for you."

"What did she want?"

"How should I know what she wants? Something about your father."

Laiping's blood ran cold. "What about him?"

"I'm not your answering service!"

"Quiet down!" came a sleepy voice from one of the bunks down the row.

Clutching her new mobile, Laiping barreled up the ladder to her bunk and punched Min's mother's number into the keypad, even though she knew she would be waking her up.

"Auntie," she said, trying to keep her voice low. "Is something wrong?"

"It's your father, Laiping. He had a heart attack this afternoon." Laiping felt her own heart miss a beat. "He's in the village clinic, recovering," Auntie quickly added. "Your mother is with him."

"Will he be all right?" she questioned her anxiously.

"They say he needs an operation, but the doctors at the village clinic are no good—they bought their diplomas on a street corner!" clucked Auntie. "Your father should be going to Heyuan, to a city hospital."

"How much will that cost?" asked Laiping, reeling at the thought of poor Baba, and Mama, too. They must be so frightened. She wished she could be there with them.

"Thousands of yuan," replied Auntie.

"Auntie, tell my mother I will send the money!" she said, although she had no idea how.

"You are a good daughter, Laiping. Not like Min, who never calls."

But Laiping didn't feel like a good daughter. She was overwhelmed with guilt—she shouldn't have bought the phone! Still, she was owed almost a thousand yuan in back pay. If only they would give it to her, there would be no problem. She slept fitfully that night, knowing that her father's life depended on the mercy of the company.

OLDER COUSIN MIN had warned Laiping not to call the company's Help Hotline, which had been set up after the suicides. It was supposed to be private, a counseling service that workers could turn to when they had problems—but people said the calls were recorded and that any information a caller gave found its way to the bosses. When she woke up in the morning, Laiping decided out of desperation to risk it, and dialed the line on her new mobile.

"Are you feeling depressed?" came the sympathetic voice of a young woman.

"No," replied Laiping.

"Are you having thoughts of harming yourself?"

"No!"

"Are you missing your family back home?"

"Well, yes," Laiping admitted.

"You should get out of your room more often," advised the young woman. "Go to the movies or go for a swim. The company provides lots of different kinds of entertainment. Have you heard about the karaoke competition?"

"I just need to find out how to get my back pay."

"Oh," said the young woman, sounding annoyed. "In that case, why are you calling us? You should go see Human Resources!"

Laiping knew only one person in Human Resources—Miss Lau. An hour before her shift was due to start, she entered the factory building and made her way down the management corridor to Miss Lau's office. Timidly, she knocked. When there was no answer, she knocked again—a little louder this time. After a moment, Miss Lau opened the door.

"Yes?" she asked, wearing the same gray suit, and a humorless smile.

"Hello, Miss," croaked Laiping, her throat suddenly dry. She was regretting her boldness in coming here.

"What is it?"

"I'm Laiping. Remember?"

"I meet many Laipings."

"I…I need help," Laiping faltered. In a rush, she explained about her sick father and her back pay. It was on the tip of Laiping's tongue to point out that it wasn't legal for the company to withhold the money she was owed, but she didn't want to seem like a troublemaker—not when she needed Miss Lau to be on her side.

"This is highly irregular," said Miss Lau.

"But my father is ill," Laiping explained again. "I need the money now, to pay for the hospital." Miss Lau's jaw tightened. She shook her head. "Please," implored Laiping, tears budding in her eyes. Miss Lau seemed to soften slightly. Laiping thought about what Fen would do in this situation to get her way—she would lie. "The doctors say if my father doesn't have the surgery immediately, he will die!" she exclaimed.

Miss Lau let out a sigh. "Come with me," she told Laiping.

Not daring to ask where they were going, Laiping followed Miss Lau back down the corridor from which she had just come. They veered off down an adjoining corridor and pushed through a glass door, into a large office in which many nicely dressed men and women sat at computers, typing.

"Miss Jang," she said to a pretty young woman who had her hair up in a smart style, "please show this girl how to fill out Form G-32."

"Yes, Miss Lau."

Miss Lau turned to Laiping. "Miss Jang will help you apply to payroll for special consideration."

Laiping was overjoyed. "Thank you! Thank you so much!"

"You see?" said Miss Lau, smiling her stiff smile. "At this company, we look after each other with a loving heart."

With that, Miss Lau turned and left the office at a smart pace. Miss Jang smiled at Laiping—warmly, not the coiled-snake smile of Miss Lau. She took a form from a cubbyhole beside her desk.

"Write your name and employee number here," she said, "and down here, the reason why you need the money." Laiping couldn't stop thanking her. "It's okay," laughed Miss Jang. "It's my job!" She leaned closer, as though letting Laiping in on a carefully guarded secret. "Just be sure to make it sound like a real emergency!"

Without warning, Laiping burst into tears, alarming Miss Jang.

"Don't cry!" she told her, half comforting, half insisting.

"I miss my mama and baba," confided Laiping in a choked whisper. Suddenly she was overwhelmed with longing to see them.

"It's all right," said Miss Jang, looking concerned. "I'm sure everything will be all right."

Miss Jang showed Laiping to a counter where she could fill out Form G-32, then went back to her desk. Laiping cheered herself up by thinking about the money she would soon be able to send home. Perhaps she would go home herself soon—but that would require applying for permission to take leave, which was unlikely to be granted with the push for the launch of the new smartphone. *One thing at a time*, Laiping decided. First she must persuade the company to release her money.

After handing the form back to Miss Jang and thanking her again, Laiping climbed the wide staircase to the fourth floor for her shift. She lifted her knees higher than usual during marching exercises, and worked with extra concentration—ignoring Bohai at her side—so grateful was she to Miss Lau and Miss Jang, and to Steve Chen. Yes, the work was long and hard and some of the rules seemed unfair. Yes, there were a few bad eggs, like Bohai. But she saw now that, just as troublemakers were punished, loyalty would be repaid. She worked diligently all night—*circuit board-capacitor-solder-capacitor-solder; circuit board-capacitor-solder-capacitor-solder*—counting her good fortune to be employed by a company so full of loving hearts.

MAMA MADE SYLVIE'S LIFE UNBEARABLE after Marie shot the video, complaining to Lucie and Pascal—as though Sylvie wasn't sitting right there on the dirt floor mixing dough to fry—that their sister had no pride, letting a foreigner take pictures of them so that the whole world could see their miserable state.

"Sylvie wants everyone to laugh at how we live, like animals," she told them. "When Papa finds us, he will give her the beating she deserves."

Sylvie tried several times to explain that when these foreigners saw the video, they would want to help them get out of Nyarugusu, but Mama turned away and pretended not to hear. Finally, Sylvie bit her tongue as she went about her daily chores, concentrating on making sure that the children were clean and fed, and that Pascal went with her to school each day.

In class, Sylvie found it hard to pay attention. The math teacher, Charles—a Congolese from South Kivu—understood less algebra than she did, and spent most of his time pestering the high-school girls to give him love in exchange for him giving them passing grades. Sylvie he left alone, for which she was grateful. *You're lucky you'll never have a husband*, Mama had told her. She was beginning to believe she *was* lucky, in many ways.

Marie had been right when she said to Sylvie that telling her story would make her feel better. She was having fewer nightmares, and her stomach didn't tighten every time someone stared at her scar. She held her head high and thought about what the future might hold, about becoming a doctor. Maybe even the kind of doctor who helped people like her.

"You mean you want to be a psychiatrist, or a psychologist," said Marie, when Sylvie shared her dream during her shift after school on Thursday.

"Yes," said Sylvie. But there was more. All week, a new idea had been taking shape. "Once I'm a doctor," she told Marie, "I'm coming back to the Congo, to help the people, the way you do."

Marie looked up and smiled. "That's a wonderful plan, Sylvie," she replied. She didn't look up from the patient's chart she was reading. She didn't even smile. Sylvie was a little wounded—*she doesn't believe me*, she thought. Then again, maybe she was just tired. There were so many patients in Nyarugusu, and so few doctors.

"Are you all right?" asked Sylvie.

"Yes, fine," Marie said, but her smile was fleeting.

"What have you heard from Alain?"

"The video is getting hundreds of hits. Maybe not so many donations yet, but it's been less that a week," she replied.

Marie's expression clouded slightly, as though she

wanted to say something more, but then thought better of it. Sylvie kept silent and watched her as she bent her head over a medical chart. Patience, she knew, was one advantage that refugees had; they were used to waiting. Finally, Marie relented and met Sylvie's steady gaze.

"It helps to talk," Sylvie reminded her.

Marie laughed. "Are you going to be *my* psychologist, Sylvie?"

"If there's something wrong, you can tell me."

"Everything's fine," she said. Then, growing serious, she chose her next words carefully. "It's better if we don't mention the video and the website around the camp, that's all. Now, don't you have bedpans to clean?"

"Do psychologists clean bedpans?" Sylvie asked.

"Never."

"Then that is definitely what I want to be."

Sylvie carried a stack of bedpans to the sink at the back of the clinic and, pulling on rubber gloves, scrubbed them with disinfectant. She wondered what had changed, to suddenly make Marie so secretive. What did she know that she wasn't sharing? *Maybe she knows we won't be able to go to Canada, after all!* Her chest began to tighten at the thought, but she forced herself to breathe slowly, to control her heart rate, the way Doctor Van de Velde showed the man in the waiting area. Soon, she felt a little better. *Patience*, she reminded herself. That was her advantage.

ON FRIDAY in the afternoon, after Sylvie gave the third grade a lesson in basic arithmetic, she took the worn atlas down from the small shelf of books that had been donated to the school and studied the world map. She found it impossible to imagine that Canada was real, and not simply a large pink rectangle on the page, surrounded by white for ice and blue for ocean. She found the Congo in the middle of Africa—also pink, but a fraction of Canada's size, and in its way just as unreal. She had been a child of ten when she last saw the hills of Kivu; Nyarugusu was the place where she had done most of her growing up. As she put the atlas away, she felt a twinge of longing for the place her father had loved so well. She had only a few pictures of it in her mind—their tidy house, the long low concrete block school on the edge of the village with one entrance for boys and another for girls. She realized there was a way to remember more, by asking the one person who dwelled almost entirely in memory—Mama.

When Sylvie came into the dark of the hut with Pascal after school, she found Mama sitting in the shaft of sunlight provided by the doorway, braiding Lucie's hair.

"What did you learn today?" she asked Pascal, ignoring Sylvie.

"Nothing," replied Pascal, his lower lip thrust out in a pout that was becoming his permanent expression.

"You have to want to learn," Sylvie told him. "It's up to you." She lifted the lid from the cooking pot sitting on the ground. Porridge from breakfast was congealed in the bottom. "Are you hungry?" she asked Pascal, handing him the pot. He took it from her and dug his fingers into the gooey meal, eagerly gulping it down. Sylvie sat on the dirt floor and, taking the pot from him, dipped two fingers into the porridge to stave off her own hunger.

"Mama," she said, swallowing the gluey lump, "I was trying to remember. Back in the village, what was the name of your friend, the one who used to come for chai?"

Mama seemed thrown for a moment, then she answered stiffly—making it clear she had still not forgiven Sylvie for the video—"I had many friends. Mrs. Bemba came most often. Also Mrs. Muamba, but she was a gossip."

"I must be thinking of Mrs. Bemba. I wonder what became of her, after the village burned."

Mama tapped Lucie's head and gave her a little shove to let her know the braiding was done. "I wouldn't know," she replied curtly. It was one thing to talk about the village—quite another to mention the fire. It brought to mind too many horrors. Yet after a moment, Mama surprised Sylvie by adding, "Her husband had family in Kinshasha. They probably went there. Us, we had no family to go to."

There was silence in the hut for a moment, so rare was it for the children to hear about their family's history. Even pouting Pascal looked curious.

"Why didn't we have family?" asked Lucie.

"Because Papa and I fell in love and married outside our tribes, and our families disowned us."

Mama said this with a quiet pride, a stubborn defiance. Sylvie was stunned to learn that her mother had been so brave—brave enough to sacrifice everything for Papa. It seemed unbelievable, looking at her today.

"Didn't you miss them?" asked Lucie with a worried frown.

"I had Patrice. And then I had my own babies,"

replied Mama, her voice unusually lucid, as though remembering her strength back then was giving her strength now.

A picture rose in Sylvie's mind, as clear as a movie on a screen. "Papa used to put music on the player and dance with you," she said, hearing the lively music and seeing the broad smiles on her parents' faces—her father so handsome, her mother soft and round—as they moved together in perfect rhythm around the living room. Pascal was barely walking and Lucie hadn't been born yet, but Sylvie and Olivier hopped and shimmied in pure joy, trying to copy them. What was it that Papa had called the dance? "The rumba," she pronounced. "That was the dance. Do you remember, Mama?"

Suddenly, without warning, Mama began to sob. Her thin shoulders heaved as deep waves of pain seemed to well up from inside her, all the pain of the past five years. Lucie began to cry, too, but Sylvie just stared, unable to move. What had she done? For so long she had despised her mother for living in her own world—for refusing to face reality. Now she willed her to go back to her delusions, where Papa was alive and at any moment would arrive to rescue them—anything to stop the raw outpouring of her grief.

Upset, Pascal went to Mama and took her hand. "Don't worry, Papa is coming!" he said, lying to comfort her.

Mama took a deep, rattling breath and became calmer, as though the storm of emotion had cleared her mind. "Papa is never coming, Pascal," Mama said as she stroked his head. "Papa has gone to the other side."

Sylvie's heart broke for her. Tears streaming, she went to her mother and put her arms around her. She felt her stiffen, and then gradually relax. Slowly, a bony hand reached out to cup Sylvie's. Pascal was weeping softly into Mama's neck. Lucie climbed into her lap and pressed her wet face into her mother's sunken chest. For several minutes, the four of them held together as one, clinging to each other. *Talking about it makes it better.* Feeling her family close around her, the truth of that came back to Sylvie.

THE NEXT DAY was Saturday. Sylvie had just returned from the communal tubs and was getting Pascal to help her stretch the damp laundry against the thatch walls of the hut to dry when Lucie came running from where she'd been playing with some other children in the cluster's common area.

"Soldiers are coming!" she called out in warning.

Sylvie looked up to see several of Kayembe's men approaching, holding machine guns across their chests, their expressions set and stern. Sylvie recognized Fiston among them. At the center of the parade was Kayembe, wearing a military uniform and striding along like the all-powerful king of Nyarugusu—the air around him crackling with ill omen. A tiny woman, gnarled with age, shuffled behind him trying to keep up. She was Fazila, a *mkunga*—a midwife. And behind her was Olivier, an AK-47 positioned across his chest, just like the other soldiers. He kept his gaze blank and forward, as though he had no connection to this place, or to his brother and sisters.

"*Mademoiselle* Sylvie," pronounced Kayembe with a sweeping bow. "Beautiful as ever, I see."

Sylvie said nothing. From the corner of her eye, she saw Mama come to the opening of the hut. She stopped short when she saw Kayembe, eyes wide as though she was beholding a ghost—or a devil. Kayembe included her in his greetings.

"Sifa! How lovely to see you again. It's been too many years. How I regret that I never had the opportunity to offer you my sympathies when Patrice died. Such a loss to our country." His words were kind, but his manner was dangerous. Mama's face was filled with rage, and fear. "Soon we leave for what was once our village," continued Kayembe, not expecting Mama to reply, "to take back what is ours—to make it ready for our people to return. I wish to take Sylvie with me, as my wife."

Sylvie's stomach lurched. Her heart was pounding. She gave Mama an urgent look, willing her to be brave, the way she was when she defied her own family to marry Papa.

"She is too young," said Mama feebly. "My husband wanted her to finish school first."

"By marrying her," replied Kayembe, "I pay tribute to your late husband."

And you benefit from his good reputation, thought Sylvie. His motives were clear to her now. *You think people will trust you if you marry his daughter.*

"His eldest son has given his consent to the marriage," added the warlord reverently, implying that proper etiquette had been observed.

Mama and Sylvie glanced to each other, then looked helplessly down the line of soldiers to Olivier, whose eyes stayed forward, unflinching—uncaring.

"You may know Fazila," said Kayembe, sweeping his hand toward the old woman. "She has come to check Sylvie, before the wedding."

Now Sylvie understood why Fazila was here—to poke and prod her. "No!" she blurted.

"My dear, I do not expect you to be intact. How many girls are virgins, after what we've all been through? But I must know you are not too damaged to bear children."

"I never said I would marry you," Sylvie told him flatly, although her heart was hammering so hard, she was afraid he would hear it.

Kayembe turned his head slightly, signaling to Olivier, who stepped forward to the front of the group. He locked eyes with his sister.

"You will do as he says, Sylvie," he told her, tightening his grip on the automatic rifle. Sylvie wondered, *If Kayembe ordered him to shoot me, would he do it?*

"Mama?" she said, turning a pleading look to her, hoping somehow she could save her. But Mama had disappeared inside herself, leaning into the wall of hut for support. Pascal and Lucie stood like small statues, frozen with fear. Sylvie looked to Fiston, who has been so kind, but his expression was hard, his eyes wilfully unseeing. Sylvie knew she was alone. Her mind raced. If Fazila declared her fit to have babies, then there would be no stopping a wedding. She needed time to think of an escape. Turning to Kayembe, keeping her head high and her voice even, she told him,

"I will agree to be checked, but only by the doctors at the clinic."

A threatening scowl spread over Kayembe's face. He puffed himself up like an angry god summoning thunder. "The clinic!" he roared, making the air vibrate. "More foreign devils!" Sylvie felt her knees go weak, and Lucie began to cry. "You think I don't know about your video," he ranted, "about your plan? I warned that doctor what would happen if she persisted in this brainwashing." Sylvie remembered Marie's nervousness, her warning to stay quiet about the video. So Kayembe had been making threats against her! "You are Congolese! You will stay with your own people. You and you," he commanded, pointing to Fiston and one other man. "Go to the clinic. Burn it down, and everyone who's inside!"

Without hesitation, Fiston and the other soldier marched away.

"No!" Sylvie shouted.

She dashed toward them—hoping somehow to stop them—but she took only a pace or two before Kayembe grabbed her violently by the arm, spinning her face-to-face with him so that her nostrils were hit by the sour stench of his breath. The scuffle caused Fiston and the other man to turn back, cocking their weapons by reflex.

"From now on," Kayembe informed Sylvie with menacing calm, "you will obey me, as a wife should."

"Leave the clinic alone! Please!" Sylvie pleaded with him, keenly aware of the automatic rifles pointing toward her and her family.

He tightened his grip to bring her even closer to his

face, lifting his chin so that he was looking down his broad nose at her.

"I will give you a choice. Either I burn the clinic, or I burn your family's hut."

His eyes were cold and heartless. Looking into them, Sylvie saw that there was no limit to the evil he was willing to commit to prove his power.

"Please," she said, forcing her gaze to stay steady, "don't make me choose. Fazila can examine me. Just leave the clinic alone, and my family."

"Kayembe does not make false threats," he told her.

"Do this for me, and I'll marry you," she choked out.

Kayembe studied her for a long moment, holding her arm so tight she feared it would break. Then, abruptly, his mood shifted, and a pleasant smile chased away the thunderous frown. He loosened his grip, his manner becoming almost gentle.

"Your wish is my command, *Mademoiselle* Sylvie," he said. "Consider this my wedding gift to you." Turning to Fiston and the other soldier, he nodded to them to get back into formation. "The clinic is saved, for another day!" he announced to the entire group, as though this was cause for celebration.

Rubbing the burning skin of her arm, Sylvie glanced at Olivier, wondering if he cared how close his family had just come to disaster. His eyes remained fixed forward, but she thought she detected a trace of emotion in his face. Anger, perhaps? Disgust? But a moment later the look was gone. There was nothing of her brother left in him.

INSIDE THE HUT, Sylvie lay on her back, legs spread apart while Fazila examined her privates. She put her ear to Sylvie's belly, listening for what Sylvie didn't know, and pushed her fist into her gut until it hurt. Then she forced her hand up inside Sylvie, making her wince with pain. Finally, Fazila labored up from her knees and went outside to report back to Kayembe, without speaking to Sylvie.

"She is undamaged," she heard her tell him.

She didn't hear what Kayembe said in response, but she pictured him grunting in satisfaction. She knew there was no way out. To save her family, to save the clinic and the doctors—especially Marie—she had to marry Kayembe. There was no hope left for a different future. Sylvie lay on the dirt floor, her limbs like rubber, unable to move—her heart oddly calm. She had a single thought in her head, which was strangely soothing: *This is what it must feel like to die.*

AFTER FIONA finished refilling the ketchup and mustard dispensers at the beach concession on Friday evening, and downing one of Cathy's special salmon burgers, she raced home to do her hair and change. Lacey had arrived back from her family's cabin the day before and, as compensation for depriving her of a life for a whole month, her parents were letting her have a few friends over. Fiona couldn't wait.

Getting ready for the party in her room, Fiona pulled a newly purchased black smock top over mid-calf skinny jeans. She was experimenting with a more sophisticated look—no more skimpy tops and three-inch zippers. She pulled her unruly curls into a sleek knot and took it easy applying makeup, foregoing last year's heavy eyeliner in favor of a more natural look—mascara, blush, and a light lipstick. Standing back from the full-length mirror, she was pleased by what she saw—a fresh Fiona for a new start.

After the long, boring summer, everything was starting to happen again. In just one more week, school started, and two weeks after that, it would be her fifteenth birthday. At last she'd have her smartphone! The latest version wasn't even in the stores yet, and people would be lining up for it as soon as it was. But her dad knew somebody who had an in and could get one for her. He'd promised.

"You look really nice, honey," said her mom, peering over her glasses from the kitchen table, where she was working at her computer.

"Don't sound so surprised," remarked Fiona.

"Not surprised. *Impressed*," she corrected. "Have fun. Back by midnight, right? And call my cell if you need to be picked up. No walking home alone."

"Check, check, and check," replied Fiona, heading out the door.

There was a crisp nip of fall in the air as Fiona made the short walk to Lacey's house. The last low rays of the sun turned her figure into a willowy shadow trailing her along the sidewalk, boosting Fiona's confidence in her new look. As she rounded the corner and Lacey's front walk came into view, she saw Megan and Brit out front and picked up her pace, but they both had their cell phones out, cutting up over something, and didn't see her approaching.

"Omigod!" shrieked Megan, loud enough for the whole neighborhood to hear.

"*So* embarrassing!" remarked Brit. "I would *die!*"

"Hey, guys. What's up?" asked Fiona with a curious smile as she reached them.

Megan and Brit looked up, like deer caught in headlights.

"Omigod. Fiona," said Megan, oozing sympathy.

"Fee, we weren't laughing at you. Honest," Brit assured her.

"Why would you be laughing at me?" asked Fiona, baffled.

An awkward look passed between Megan and Brit. Brit gave Fiona an ominous look.

"Have you checked Friendjam lately?"

"Not since last night."

"So you don't know?"

"Know what?"

Brit handed her cell phone to Fiona carefully, as though it could explode at any moment. Fiona looked at the phone in the palm of her hand, and the world stopped—or, at least, Fiona's world. On the tiny screen, Fiona puckered her lips in a pouty, sexy pose, her pajama top pulled up—the boob shot, the one she had thought was just a bad memory. Fiona felt her stomach lurch.

"How many people have seen this?" she asked in a choked whisper.

"That depends," replied Megan. "How many people are on Friendjam?"

It took Fiona a moment to understand. Then, squeezing the phone's screen image down with her thumb and finger, she saw that the photo had been posted to a Friendjam page. The "share picture with all friends" button flashed at the bottom of the page, like a tiny blinking death star.

"Who sent this?!" she blurted, her mind flooding with questions. Where did it come from? She'd deleted the photo off Ryan's phone. He must have made a copy! She knew he was mad at her, but posting the boob shot was beyond nasty. She looked up the walk to Lacey's house and saw her friends in the front window, talking and partying. Had they all seen her naked? Stupid, useless tears burned in her eyes. *I'm such an idiot for trusting him!* she thought, biting her lower lip to try to make it stop quivering.

"Don't worry about it, Fee," Brit told her, seeing her about to cry. "I mean, everybody was doing it last year."

"*I* wasn't," Megan pointed out with a sharp glance at Brit. "Were you?"

"No," admitted Brit. "But lots of people were."

"You mean sluts," said Fiona.

"No!" insisted Brit, a second too late and a tad too emphatically.

Lacey came running down the walk from the house, having spotted Fiona through the window. She looked gorgeous in a turquoise dress and high-heeled sandals, but the sophisticated effect was spoiled by her snorts of hysterical laughter. She grabbed hold of Fiona's arm.

"Holy crap! Can you believe that douche?"

"Does everybody know?" asked Fiona, suspecting the answer, but still hoping.

On cue, Rick Yee appeared on the front stoop from inside the house.

"Hey, Fiona," he hollered, "give us a show!"

Just in case Fiona missed his meaning, he hauled up his own shirt to reveal his bare chest. Fiona wished she could disappear.

"C'mon, Fee," said Lacey, low so only Fiona could hear. There was a sort of imploring desperation in her eyes. "You gotta laugh it off."

For a moment, Fiona tried to reframe. So what if all

of her friends, male and female, had now seen her naked? It wasn't the end of the world. She could see Lacey's point—if she laughed it off, everybody else would, too. In a way, it *was* funny. But then her heart sank. What if her parents found out? She wished she could be the type of girl who didn't care, but she wasn't—and she *did*.

"I have to go," she told Lacey.

She fled back down the sidewalk. Lacey charged after her, teetering on her high heels.

"Fiona, wait!"

Fiona turned back, tears streaming down her face.

"I've never been so humiliated in my life!" she cried. "Why would he do that to me?"

"Because Ryan's a jerk! If people see you're upset, he wins," Lacey pleaded with her. "C'mon back. It's a party!"

Fiona shook her head. "Tell everybody I had to go because I'm sick, okay?"

"Like that's going to fool anybody."

"Then tell them what you want," Fiona said.

She hurried away, faintly hoping that if she could just get to her room and pull the covers over her head, when she woke up in the morning Friendjam would never have been invented, and she and Ryan never would have met.

FIONA REACHED HOME just as her mother was leaving to meet friends for dinner.

"Why are you home so early?" she asked, alarmed by Fiona's tear-stained face. "What happened?"

"Nothing," replied Fiona, sniffling.

"Then why are you so upset?" She put down her bag

and took off her jacket. Fiona knew that look on her face, ready to take on the world to defend her little girl. *This is a job for Supermom!* she used to joke when Fiona was little and came home crying over something mean another kid had said at school. Only this time there was nothing Supermom could do to help.

"I'm okay. Just go," pleaded Fiona. But the more Fiona insisted that she wanted to be by herself, the more determined her mom was to stay.

"I wouldn't have a good time, knowing you're here crying in your pillow," she said.

Finally, Fiona snapped, yelling at her, "Just leave me alone!"

Her mother looked really hurt, which made Fiona feel all the more wretched.

"What happened to my beautiful little girl?" her mom asked.

"I'm sorry. Just go," she said miserably. "I'll be fine."

Her mother gave her a lingering look of concern. Shaking her head, she went out the door without evening saying goodbye. Fiona retreated to her room and flopped onto the bed, hot tears soaking the pillow, just as her mom had predicted. As she lay there replaying the night over and over in her mind, humiliation turned to shame at taking the picture in the first place. Shame turned to surreal disbelief that this could actually be happening to her. And, finally, surreal disbelief turned mercifully into sleep.

FIONA WOKE UP EARLY on Saturday morning to sunshine streaming through her window. Drifting up from sleep, she felt cozy and safe—until the memory of the night before began to seep in. Opening her eyes, she saw that she was still lying on top of the covers, wearing her party outfit, but there was a blanket over her. Her mom must have come in to check on her.

Fiona sat up. Everything was less frightening in the daylight. *Morning has more wisdom than night.* She remembered the line from a Russian fairy tale her mother used to read to her. *Right*, she thought, *you've had your cry. Time to get over yourself.* She got up, showered, washed her hair. By the time she came out of the bathroom, her mom was up, reading the paper over coffee at the kitchen table.

"Good morning," said her mother, using a tone that invited meaningful discussion.

"Hi," replied Fiona, pouring cereal into a bowl. "Sorry about last night."

"Do you want to discuss it?"

"No."

Hell no. Fiona had talked herself into believing that eventually her friends would forget about the boob shot. But if her parents ever found out, they'd make a huge deal about sexting and the dangers of the Internet. Maybe even try to take her laptop away. Definitely there'd be no new smartphone.

"Okay," nodded her mom reluctantly. "But you know I'm always here if you want to talk, right?"

"I know. Thanks."

"Want to hang out today? I'm going to the farmers' market."

"Can't. I'm working at eleven. Then I'm going to

Dad's tonight," Fiona reminded her.

"Right," she replied with a tight smile. She turned back to her newspaper, and asked a little too casually, "How's he handling the heat, by the way?"

"What heat?"

"Over their operations in the DRC."

"The what?"

"Fiona," she said, the frustration clear in her voice, "I thought you were following this. You know, the girl in the video, Sylvie. About the fighting over coltan."

"What?"

"Coltan. It's used in electronics. Millions of people in the Congo have died because of it."

"I don't know what you're talking about," she said, and headed toward her room with her bowl of cereal.

"Where are you going? Can't we at least have breakfast together?"

Not if you're going to rant at me, thought Fiona. But she said, "I downloaded this show I want to watch."

Mom pursed her lips, her I'm-so-disappointed-in-you look. "On your laptop."

"Yeah."

"Does that not strike you as a little ironic in light of this conversation?"

"I just want to watch my show."

"So go."

Gawd, thought Fiona.

"I hate it when you roll your eyes at me like that," said her mother.

"You use a laptop, Mom. Everybody does."

"The point is we should be able to buy laptops and cell phones that are manufactured without causing endless human suffering."

"Omigod, Mom! This is exactly why nobody likes you!"

It came out a lot harsher than Fiona intended. Her mom looked wounded for a brief moment, then her jaw tightened.

"I just want you to be a thinking person, Fiona."

"Okay. I *think* I'll go to my room."

"Fine. Be a smart-ass," she replied, burying her face in the newspaper.

Fiona carried her cereal bowl to her room, seething. It felt like her mother was *constantly* disappointed with her for not being out there saving the world. But she had enough trouble dealing with her own problems. If only her mother knew.

Wait—rewind, realized Fiona. *On second thought, thank God she doesn't know!*

ASIA

LAIPING HELD OFF UNTIL THURSDAY before going back to Miss Jang's office to inquire about her overtime pay.

"You must be patient," said Miss Jang. "These things take time."

"Please, can you find out how long it will be until I get the money?" asked Laiping.

Miss Jang smiled. "Yes, of course. I will try."

But Laiping heard nothing. On Saturday she received another paycheck— her first month's wages had still not been paid.

"Where is my money?" Laiping asked Miss Jang before her shift on Sunday.

"Do you know how many employees the company has?" replied Miss Jang, no longer smiling. "Hundreds of thousands."

"But you said you marked my form 'urgent'."

Miss Jang pursed her lips—and suddenly Laiping understood. No such notation was ever made. Miss Jang had lied to her.

"I want to fill out another form," said Laiping.

"You're not allowed," replied Miss Jang.

"It's my money," implored Laiping. "My family needs it now."

"You think you're so special? You must wait your turn like everyone else."

On Monday morning after work, Laiping called her auntie, who fetched Mama to the phone. Baba was back home, but the doctors said he had to stay quiet in bed.

"He's on the list for surgery," her mother told her. "When will you send the money?"

Laiping was beginning to feel that all Mama ever thought about was the money. "Soon," she promised, wishing she could talk to Baba and tell him how tired and lonely she was. But she could already hear Mama scolding—*Don't upset your poor sick father with such nonsense!*— and kept her feelings to herself.

Laiping didn't sleep well following her Sunday night shift. The dorm room was too hot and humid. The air was close with the curtain drawn across her bunk, but the sun was too bright if she left the curtain open. When she did nod off, she dreamed that she was soldering capacitors at her work station in her pajamas and that Mr. Wu was yelling at her for forgetting to wear gloves and a mask. She woke up late in the afternoon, groggy and disoriented, to the sound of Big Sister Choilai calling her name.

"Laiping! Wake up! Your cousin is here to see you!"

Laiping wondered, *Why didn't Min just phone me?* She checked her mobile, which she kept beside her pillow while she slept, and discovered that the battery had died. Doubly anxious now between her dream and Min's unexpected arrival, Laiping maneuvered quickly in her bunk to pull off her pajamas and put on jeans and a top. She found Min waiting for her in the common room and took in her worried expression.

"What's wrong?" asked Laiping with alarm.

"It's your father," she said, tears budding in her eyes. Laiping went light-headed. She gripped Min's arm, fearing the worst. Min saw the shock on Laiping's face and quickly added, "He's alive! But Uncle ignored the doctors' advice. He went out to plow, and he collapsed. Here," said Min, handing Laiping her own mobile. "Call my mother. She will tell you."

Laiping's fingers were trembling so much that Min had to take the mobile back and punch the speed dial for her.

"It was another heart attack, a bad one this time," Auntie said when she came on the line. "He's been taken to the district hospital in Heyuan. He must have the surgery soon."

"I'm coming home!" Laiping said into the phone, choking on tears.

Hearing this, Min leaned into other ear, warning, "If you leave without permission, they will never give you your pay!"

"There's nothing you can do here, Laiping," Auntie was saying at the same time. "The best thing you can do for your baba is stay there and work."

Min took the phone and spoke to her mother for a moment before hanging up.

"She says she'll call if there's any more news," Min reported to Laiping.

Laiping's whole body was trembling. Min put her arms around her waist and held her tight, her head coming up to Laiping's chin.

"What if he dies? What if I never see him again?" sobbed Laiping.

"Don't say that!" Min told her. "Don't even think that! What you need is to eat something, and stay strong!" Min sounded just like their grandmother, which gave Laiping a little comfort.

LAIPING WENT WITH MIN to the cafeteria and picked at her vegetables and rice, eating little. After dinner she went to the factory for her shift, turning a single thought over in her mind all night, so that by morning it was sharp and clear and hard. *Baba will live if I get the money I'm owed to pay for the surgery.* In the morning when she finished work, she went down the wide staircase with the other workers. But on the main floor, instead of going outside she veered off to the corridor where the managers' offices were located. At Miss Lau's door, she knocked. Miss Lau opened the door, and—recognizing Laiping this time—frowned.

"Yes, what is it?"

"My father had a second heart attack yesterday," Laiping told her. "Please, Miss Lau, I need my money—today."

"I'm sorry about your father. Is he…?"

"He's in the hospital."

Miss Lau nodded as she took this in. "Come. Sit down," she said, standing aside to let Laiping enter.

Laiping took the same chair she'd sat in the last time she was in Miss Lau's office, when she was unfairly punished for Bohai's poor workmanship. Miss Lau seated herself behind the large desk and found Laiping's file in a tall stack. She opened it and read through it while Laiping waited. Laiping could see her G-32 form at the top of the papers inside the file. When she finished reading, Miss Lau folded her hands together and leaned forward.

"We have reviewed your request. The decision has been made that we cannot make an exception for you."

Laiping's mouth fell open in shock. Her first thought was that she hadn't heard correctly—there had to be a mistake. After all this time waiting!

"That can't be right!" she exclaimed.

Miss Lau showed no emotion. "You told Miss Jang that you were homesick," she stated.

"No, I didn't," Laiping replied in confusion.

"She was very clear about it," said Miss Lau, picking up the G-32 form to show her. Laiping could see that someone—Miss Jang?—had written notes on it. "She says you told her you miss your mother and father." Miss Lau put the form back into Laiping's file. "If we give you this money, what is to prevent you from quitting and going home?"

"I won't! I promise!"

But Miss Lau looked doubtful.

"Many migrant workers are homesick when they first arrive. You need time to fit in and feel that you belong here. Mr. Chen understands this. That's why he made this rule."

"But—"

"There will be no further discussion! Mr. Chen is paying you much more than other factories pay, in other parts of China. If you're a good worker, you will have future paychecks to send home."

Laiping wanted to tell her that by the time she received her next paycheck, her father might be dead. But she could see the look on Miss Lau's face—the same look that Mr. Wu got if a worker questioned him. *The ability to obey instructions is the best way of judging a worker.*

Miss Lau smiled her tight smile, dismissing Laiping. "I'm happy to hear that your father is recovering."

INSTEAD OF GOING BACK to the dorm to sleep, Laiping went directly to the Internet café where she'd last seen Kai, even though the chances of finding him there on a Tuesday morning were slim.

"Do you know a boy named Kai?" Laiping asked one of the servers behind the counter.

"I know twenty boys named Kai!" she replied.

Laiping's palms were moist with anxiety—Kai now seemed like her only hope, even though she had only the vaguest idea of how he might help her get her money. But she had run out of places to turn for help.

An idea sprang to her mind. She remembered the first place she met Kai and hurried to the employment office building. When she got there, she saw that the line of job-seekers was even longer than the day she and Fen, who was then Yiyin, were hired. Hundreds of people were waiting for their chance to go inside the building and apply for work. *It's true what the bosses say*, she thought. There would always be somebody else willing to take their place. So maybe she shouldn't have been thinking about making trouble. But how could she not, when her father's life was at stake?

Laiping walked down the line, scanning the crowd. There were girls in baggy jeans and T-shirts who looked like they had just come out from the countryside, and others in short skirts and fashionable tops, bent over mobile phones—like the girls downtown Fen said were office workers—but there was no sign of Kai. She glanced back over her shoulder and saw a security guard near the building's entrance eyeing her suspiciously. Realizing she couldn't remain there loitering, she rounded the corner of the building and went to the end of the line, as though she was one of the new applicants. She waited for fifteen minutes, watching for Kai to appear and listening to the nervous chatter of the girls and guys in line around her, sounding so much like she and Fen had on their first day—frightened but excited, worried about whether the employment office would deem them company material. Was it only eight weeks ago? It felt like a lifetime had gone by since then.

Suddenly, Laiping was weary—so weary she thought she could fall asleep right there in line, standing up. So weary, her arms and legs felt like lead. She let her eyelids drop like weights, just for a second or two. She snapped awake, uncertain if she had actually gone to sleep, or for how long, although the line hadn't moved. Then something caught her gaze—a crumpled paper caught in the tall weeds growing along the wall of the building. She picked it up and unfolded it. It was yellow, not pink like the paper Kai had handed her eight weeks ago, but the message was the same: *Know Your Rights!* There was an email address.

Hiding the paper from those around her, Laiping slipped it into her jeans pocket. She stepped out of the line and walked quickly away, being careful not to look back. She kept her eyes forward all the way to the Internet café, imagining as she cut through the crowd of hundreds waiting for busses along the main boulevard that any one of them could be a company spy—afraid of what would happen to her if they found out she was carrying the yellow paper. At the café, she waited for her turn on one of the computers.

"*I need to know my rights*," she typed. "*Please contact me.*"

She included her cell phone number in the email and signed her name. Then she worried all the way back to her dorm that the email address was a trap set by the company to catch troublemakers, and that she had given herself away. As she reached the building, she glanced at the nets surrounding the dorm. She tried imagine what it was like for those people—how frightening it would be to jump from the roof, and how horribly desperate they must have felt. Then a realization came to her, an idea so fully formed that it hardened immediately into resolve: *Once I get my money, I'm quitting and I'm going home.*

EXHAUSTED, Laiping went back to the dorm to catch a few hours of sleep before her next shift. But she couldn't sleep. Her senses were full of longing to be back home in her own bed, listening to Baba snore behind the thin wall. She imagined the sound of oxen lowing softly in the village pen, and of a rooster crowing—smelled the tangy aroma of the fields outside the open window. But she must have at last drifted off, because she was jolted awake by the ringing of her mobile. She grabbed it from under her pillow and fumbled to answer it.

"Mama?" she said, dopey with sleep.

"Laiping?" came a man's voice. Laiping was filled with dread, certain that someone must be calling from the hospital with news about Baba. But the voice continued lightly, "It's Kai. You were looking for me?"

"Where have you been?!" replied Laiping.

"Away."

"I need your help," she told him. "Can we meet?"

"Not at the usual place," he said.

An hour later, Laiping was sitting with Kai at a small table in a near-empty bubble tea shop, located in a small strip mall clear across the factory campus. Kai hadn't wanted to meet at the Internet café—especially after learning that Laiping had sent her email from there.

"You can't be too careful," he said. "The company has spies everywhere."

"I've been looking for you there," Laiping told him.

"I've been traveling, to Dongguan and Guangzhou," he replied, naming other factory cities in the Pearl River Delta, "meeting with workers, to see how conditions compare, and what can be done."

"That's dangerous, isn't it?"

"Of course it's dangerous! There are work camps full of people whose only crime is trying to change things. If somebody dares to speak out about being worked to death, or about corrupt officials taking all the money for themselves, the next thing they know, police are busting down their door in the middle of the night."

Laiping shivered and thought of Fen's father, the troublemaker. Perhaps that was where he was, in a work camp somewhere.

"I thought…" she began, then hesitated about saying what was on her mind. Kai was discussing such important things, and she didn't want to appear to be shallow, or selfish.

"What?"

"I was afraid you were mad at me," she said, "because I didn't want to go to your meeting."

"I was rude last time," he told her, his voice softening. He reached across the table and took her hand, like a boyfriend would. Laiping felt a thrill run through her. "You're so new here," he said, "it takes a while to understand why we have to fight back."

"I understand now."

"What do you mean?"

"I applied for my back pay because my father is ill—"

"I'm sorry to hear that."

"They refuse to give me my money. Is there anything I can do?"

"To be honest," he said with a shrug, "no. The company has the power to do what they want."

Laiping's heart sank. Kai squeezed her hand.

"Come to our meeting the day after tomorrow," he said. "Talking with others at least makes you feel you're doing something."

Laiping nodded. "My cousin might want to come, too," she added. "People on her line are getting sick."

Kai looked her in the eye—measuring, assessing. "If I tell you where the meeting is, you can't tell anybody else. It's too risky. We could be arrested."

Without meaning to, Laiping pulled back slightly. Kai saw her uncertainty, and dropped her hand.

"Do you want things to change, or not?"

She answered without hesitation, "I want things to change." And she wanted him to take her hand again.

Kai nodded and smiled. He did a quick shoulder-check to make sure no one was watching, then he told her, "Give me your mobile."

Laiping fished in her bag for her phone and handed it over. Kai typed an address into her date book.

"Come to this address on Friday morning," he said, and handed the phone back to her.

"I'll be there," promised Laiping.

When they left the tea shop, he held her hand as far as the bus stop on the main boulevard. When they paused to say goodbye, she wondered if he'd kiss her right there in public the way some couples did—even though such displays were frowned upon by the older generation—but he turned away from her and quickly lost himself in the crowds along the sidewalk. Laiping watched him until she lost track of which bobbing head was his, already counting the hours until she'd see him again.

THE MORNING AFTER Kayembe brought Fazila to examine Sylvie, Olivier came striding into the cluster of huts carrying something large and pink in his arms. At first glance, Sylvie—outside squatting over the cook fire as she stirred the porridge—thought how strange it was that he was holding a flamingo, like the ones they'd seen years ago when they crossed Lake Tanganyika from the Congo. As he came closer, however, she saw that it wasn't a flamingo at all. It was a frilly, European-style dress, something an actress on TV might wear.

Kayembe and his men were leaving tomorrow for North Kivu, and he had insisted that the marriage take place before they go—just in case Sylvie had any ideas about running. He forbade her from going to the clinic to talk to Doctor Marie. Sylvie would have defied him and gone anyway, but she was worried about what Kayembe might do to Marie and the clinic as punishment.

"Here," Olivier commanded, holding the dress out to her. She could see the strap of his AK-47 across his chest, and the gun barrel behind his right shoulder. "Put this on. It's for the wedding." Stubbornly, Sylvie stayed squatting and continued to stir the pot. "Sylvie!" he told her. "Mr. Kayembe sent this for you. Put it on and come with me."

"I'm making breakfast," she told him, refusing to meet his eyes—bracing herself for more of his bullying.

But Olivier surprised her by crossing his ankles and plopping down onto the dusty ground across the fire from her, still holding the dress. Sylvie glanced at him. He gave her a look that was almost shy. "You need to put it on," he said. "I'm to bring you to the church at noon."

"Is that all he's offering for my bride price?" asked Sylvie resentfully. Back home, the groom had to give the girl's family so many goats, so many cows, pots and pans—all of which could amount to a lot of money. Kayembe was wealthy enough to afford any bride price, but nobody, least of all Olivier, was about to negotiate with him.

"Why are you so ungrateful?" Olivier shot back. "Who do you think you are, to turn up your nose to any man, let alone Mr. Kayembe? I'll tell you who you are—an ugly girl that nobody wants!"

Sylvie wished with all her heart that nobody wanted her—most of all Kayembe—but before she could tell Olivier this, Pascal came out from the hut, rubbing sleep from his eyes.

"What's going on?" he asked.

"Sylvie is getting married today," Olivier told him. "This is the dress she's going to wear."

Pascal wrinkled his nose at the strange dress. "Will you still live with us, Sylvie?" was all he really wanted to know.

Since yesterday, Sylvie had been practicing hard at

feeling nothing. It was the only way she could bear to take another breath, knowing the future that awaited her. But Pascal's question made a familiar panic rise in her stomach. Tonight, she supposed, she must stay with Kayembe. The thought of him touching her sickened her—she could feel the weight of the soldier who raped her; she smelled his diesel smell.

"Don't be stupid, Pascal," Olivier answered for her. "From now on, Sylvie is going to be Hervé Kayembe's woman. She'll be important," he added.

Sylvie wondered if Olivier really believed that she would become anything other than Kayembe's slave, or if he was simply trying to convince her to go with him willingly. She gave the porridge a final stir and knocked the spoon on the side of the pot. "Tell Mama and Lucie breakfast is ready," she told Pascal. After Pascal went into the hut, she spoke softly to Olivier. "I will go with you," she said, "but you must promise me something first."

"What's that?"

"That you will look after the family. That you will put them first, before Kayembe. Before anyone. Swear that you'll do it, Olivier. Swear it so that Papa's spirit can hear you."

Olivier eyed her nervously. Sylvie wasn't sure if he was spooked more by the mention of the spirit world, or of Papa. After a moment, his expression became solemn. "I swear," he said, and Sylvie believed him. Maybe there was something of her brother left inside him after all.

Standing up from the fire, Sylvie took the dress from Olivier and held it up against her. It had straps—no sleeves—and the top part had wires in it to shape a woman's bosom. Sylvie supposed that some girls might think it was pretty, but the fact that Kayembe had chosen it for her made it hideous. From Olivier's dubious expression, it seemed he agreed.

"We don't have to leave right away," he told her. "You can eat breakfast first."

"I'm not hungry," she replied.

As she carried the dress into the hut to change, she told herself that when Kayembe touched her after the wedding, she would go inside of herself, the way Mama did when she didn't want to face the truth about Papa. Then it would be only her body that Kayembe took. She would never give him her true being, the self that from now on she would keep locked away so down deep that Kayembe would never reach her.

OLIVIER INFORMED THEM that Mama, Pascal, and Lucie were not invited to the wedding, but no one protested. In spite of Sylvie's fancy dress, even little Lucie seemed to understand that there was nothing to celebrate, and, since Kayembe's visit, Mama had withdrawn to the place in her mind where she believed that Papa was still alive. "Patrice won't approve," she said when she saw Sylvie in the long pink dress, forgetting all about the firm grasp she'd held on reality just two nights before, when she'd told Pascal that Papa was gone to the other side. "We must wait for your father to come."

By mid-morning, Sylvie could delay no longer. She set out with Olivier, tripping over the billowing skirt as she walked toward the far side of the old marketplace, where they were to meet Kayembe at a small church. The bodice was too big for her—it cut into her underarms and the straps kept slipping. Olivier slowed his pace to match hers as she fumbled to lift the hem of the dress out of the red dust, her plastic thongs slapping against the soles of her feet. He, too, seemed in no hurry. She wondered where his thoughts were leading him, and decided to take a risk to find out.

"Olivier," she said. "Why do we never talk about Papa?"

Olivier gave her a startled look, then let out a short laugh. "Mama talks about him all the time."

"But *we* never do."

"There's nothing to say," he shrugged. He fell into a brooding silence.

Sylvie thought, *No, there is too much to say.* She'd always been afraid to ask what he saw at the school the day Papa was killed, but somehow today she felt brave enough to hear it.

"Tell me about how he died," she said, after a few more paces.

"You know how he died. He was shot."

"By the Mai-Mai?"

"You know it was the Mai-Mai."

"Did you see it?

Olivier looked away sharply and didn't reply. *That's it,* Sylvia thought. *He's closed the door.* Then he surprised her.

"Yes."

"What did you see?"

"Stop this."

"You'll feel better if you tell me," she said, because it was true, and because she needed to know—needed to lock the picture of Papa's last moments inside her, deep down with her true self. "Where was he? Where were you?"

"I was outside, playing football with the junior boys."

"And Papa?"

"Inside with the older grades. Teaching French, I think. They were reciting poetry."

Sylvie could see him—Papa at the head of the class, his shirt and tie, his dark-rimmed glasses, his hand waving to mark the rhythm of the poem.

"How did they come, the soldiers?" asked Sylvie. "In a truck?"

Olivier shook his head. "Out of nowhere, they were all around, walking through the grass, coming from all directions."

"What did you do?"

"I yelled for Papa, and I ran into the school to tell him."

"What happened next?"

"Papa told the kids to get out of the school, but the soldiers were already coming in both doors." Sylvie pictured it, the single room of the cinder block schoolhouse, the two doors, one at either end of one long wall. "The doors were blocked. Some kids tried to climb out a back window. They shot them." Sylvie pictured this, too. Probably her friends were among the dead. She wondered which ones.

Olivier kept talking, as though a dam had burst and his memories were spilling out. "Papa gathered the kids behind him, with his arms out, like this." He held his arms out straight from his body. "He asked the commander what he wanted. The commander said they came for him, because he was making trouble with the miners."

"What did Papa say?"

"I can't remember."

But Sylvie could imagine what Papa told the commander, that it was his moral duty to help protect the miners and their families against soldiers like him. Did he know about the foreign mining companies, driving the Congolese off their plots? Did he know the Mai-Mai were working for them? He must have.

"Then what happened?" she asked.

"They made us go outside, all of us. Papa said not to worry, they wouldn't hurt us if we did what they said. But everyone was crying."

She saw Papa, herding the children out through the doors into the playing field, comforting them, when he must have known he was about to die.

"Did he die quickly?"

"Stop asking so many questions," he said.

They walked on for several paces. Olivier kept his head turned away from her. *He's crying*, she realized. Then, abruptly, he stopped walking and turned to her. His eyes were a little wild, as though he didn't know where to look, and he was breathing heavily. Tears streaked his face and sweat dotted his forehead. He was remembering, reliving— Sylvie recognized the signs. She touched his arm.

"What is it?" she asked. "What are you seeing?"

"I didn't have a choice!" he cried, suddenly a child again. "Papa said so!"

"About what?"

She saw him struggling to speak, but the words seemed to choke him. She stepped closer so that she was looking up into his wet face and gripped his arms with her hands.

"Olivier, whatever it is, you have to say it," she told him. "You have to get it out."

Under her steady gaze, Olivier's eyes became ghostly calm.

"It was me, Sylvie," he said at last, in barely more than a whisper. "I shot him. They put the rifle in my hands, and they made me shoot him, or they said they would shoot me."

The odd thing was that Sylvie wasn't really shocked, or even surprised. She should have guessed that Olivier bore a scar far worse than hers—from his moods, from the way he used words to wound her. From what she knew about the Mai-Mai, and their inhuman cruelty. Of course Papa would have told him he had no choice—because Papa wouldn't have wanted him to live his whole life under a cloud of guilt.

Olivier put his face in his hands and began to sob. Sylvie squeezed his arms to let him know that she didn't hate him, that somehow the truth had made them brother and sister again. They stood like that in the middle of the path for what seemed like a long time, with passing people casting curious looks at the boy soldier, weeping, and the scarred girl in the frilly pink dress that was too big for her. But Sylvie didn't care if they stared. Her mind was clear, and she was strong. She knew what they had to do.

INSTEAD OF CONTINUING ON to the church, where Kayembe was waiting for them, Sylvie and Olivier went to the clinic. The waiting area was crowded with mothers holding crying babies in their laps. A man was sleeping sitting upright on one of the wooden benches, crutches propped beside him. Neema, at the admitting desk, laughed out loud when she saw Sylvie's dress.

"Do you think you are a movie star now?" she said, "just because of that video?"

Olivier threw Sylvie a doubtful look. "These are your *friends*?" he asked.

"Where is Doctor Marie?" demanded Sylvie, ignoring Neema's laughter. "It's urgent!"

At the commotion, Doctor Van de Velde came out from the back, holding his stethoscope. "I can't hear myself think!" he said crossly. He gave Sylvie a baffled look, taking in her dress. Then he saw the rifle over Olivier's shoulder. "Hey, no weapons in here!" he barked.

"This is my brother," explained Sylvie. Then she told Olivier, "Give them the rifle!"

Olivier hesitated, reluctant to give it up, but he let the strap of his AK-47 slide off his shoulder and handed the gun over to Doctor Van de Velde, who dangled it by the strap, as though it was a bomb about to go off. Marie came out from the back with a patient and took in the bizarre scene—Sylvie's pink frills, Doctor Van de Velde holding the AK-47 at arm's length.

"What on earth is going on?" she asked.

The words tumbled out of Sylvie, about the wedding —about Kayembe's threat to burn the clinic down. Marie listened with anger, Doctor Van de Velde and Neema with alarm.

"You're not marrying that monster, Sylvie!" exclaimed Marie.

"No, she's not," said Olivier, speaking for the first time. "That's why we're here. We need your protection."

Sylvie smiled at him, so happy to have her brother returned to her. But at the mention of trouble, one by one the patients in the waiting area—including the man with the crutches, who was now wide awake—stood up and left. Neema looked like she wanted to join them, but she stayed.

"He's threatened you, too, hasn't he?" Sylvie asked Marie.

Marie gave a quick nod, avoiding Doctor Van de Velde's hawk-like gaze. But she couldn't escape his anger.

"Do you mean to tell me that tin-plated thug has been making threats against this clinic?" he bellowed. "Why didn't you say something?!"

Sheepishly, Marie explained. "Everybody said Kayembe was leaving for Kivu. I hoped Sylvie would be gone for Canada before he came back."

"We have to hurry," warned Olivier. "Kayembe is expecting us soon."

"Hurry to do what, exactly?" asked the Belgian.

"To clear the clinic!" Sylvie told him. "When Kayembe realizes we're not coming, he'll attack!"

Doctor Van de Velde shook his head vigorously from side to side. "This is not our problem. We can't put our facilities at risk for the sake of one family!"

Marie turned on the head doctor, sheepish no longer.

"Is this how we're measuring people's lives now, Bernard?" she said, waving her hand around at the now empty clinic. "In concrete blocks and tin roofs?"

The Belgian shot Sylvie and Olivier an embarrassed look. "Of course not," he replied, "but if they destroy this clinic, what's to prevent them from going after the other ones, and even the hospital?"

Olivier spoke up. "That's exactly the problem. Kayembe counts on everyone being afraid of what he will do to them, so he does whatever he wants. Somebody has to stand up to him." Sylvie was proud of him. He sounded just like Papa.

"You know he's right, Bernard," pleaded Marie. "Somebody has to take a stand. Otherwise, what are we doing here?"

Doctor Van de Velde wavered for a moment. At last persuaded, he crossed to the admitting desk and, putting down the AK-47, picked up a satellite phone and dialed.

"It's Doctor Van de Velde," he said. "We need increased security at the Zone 3 clinic immediately, secondarily at all medical facilities and the foreign workers' compound."

Olivier stepped forward and whispered to the doctor, "Not the camp guards! Kayembe owns most of them!"

It took Doctor Van de Velde a second to process this, then he rang off immediately.

"Call the Tanzanian police," suggested Marie. "Call the Canadian embassy in Dar es Salaam, too. Call all the embassies."

Doctor Van de Velde thought for a moment. "We have

to keep our people in one place. Neema, go to the compound and tell everyone to stay there." She nodded anxiously and started away. "Wait!" he said. When she turned back, he thrust a portable defibrillator into her arms. "Take whatever we can carry!"

Marie told Sylvie, "Help me gather things from the back."

Sylvie started to follow Marie, but stopped when she saw Olivier grab the AK-47 from the desk. He slipped toward the door. "Where are you going?" she called to him.

"To get Mama and the children. I'll meet you at the foreign workers' compound."

"Don't take them there!" countermanded Doctor Van de Velde, his ear to the sat phone as he waited for a connection. "Sylvie, okay, she's staff. But the general population isn't allowed inside."

"But Kayembe will kill them!" protested Sylvie. "He'll burn down the hut!"

"If we let one family in, they'll all want in."

Olivier gave Sylvie a searching look. "You said they would help us."

"Please!" pleaded Sylvie. "Not everyone is at risk. Only my family."

"If we don't allow them inside, then I'm not going either," said Marie. She had come out from the back, her arms full of equipment. Neema turned a scathing glare on Sylvie, as though this was all her fault. But the Belgian took in Marie's determination, and relented.

"There's no time to argue about this," he said, and turned to Olivier. "Go, then. Get your family—but only *your* family." Olivier nodded and headed out the door. "And bring that rifle back with you!" Doctor Van de Velde yelled after him.

Marie saw Sylvie's anxious look. "Don't worry," she told her. "They'll be safe soon."

Sylvie wished she could believe her. "Here, take these," said Marie, loading Sylvie's arms with tubing and monitors.

Doctor Van de Velde at last got through to the Tanzanian authorities. "We are expecting an attack," he shouted into the sat phone. "Please hurry!

BY THE END OF THE WEEK, Fiona had more or less succeeded in putting the whole sexting episode behind her—aided greatly by a call from Lacey telling her that everybody at the party felt really bad about what had happened, and the way they reacted. Rick even wanted to find Ryan and kick his ass, although Lacey thought that was mostly just talk. Lacey put a message out on Friendjam, telling anybody who had received the photo to delete it immediately, so hopefully that was the end of it.

"Ignore it," was Lacey's advice. "Stay off of Friendjam for a few days, and just forget about it."

Fiona briefly considered texting Ryan to tell him what a low-life scumbag he was, but she decided that would give him too much satisfaction. Lacey was right—the mature response was to rise above the whole thing and pretend it never happened.

It was Labor Day weekend and the beach was packed. A breeze off English Bay hinted at the end of summer, cooling down the open kitchen at the back of the food stand and putting Cathy in a good mood as she worked over the deep fryer.

"I'm going to miss you around here, kiddo," Cathy told her, "but you must be looking forward to getting back to school."

"I am," agreed Fiona as she set up the coffee machine for a fresh batch. She wouldn't have said so after her humiliation at Lacey's party, but now that her world hadn't actually ended, she was once again excited about grade ten, and about moving past last year's mistakes—namely Ryan.

Cathy threw a nod toward the order window. "We got customers."

Fiona turned to see a gaggle of three boys, doubled over with laughter, as though they were trying to outdo each other telling dirty jokes. From their scrawny frames and zit-pocked complexions, she pegged them as grade eights.

"Can I get you something?" asked Fiona, going to the window.

"Yeah," said the boldest of the three. "How about a feel?"

Fiona stared at him in confusion for half a second. Then she saw the cell phone in his hand.

"You're Fiona, right?" he said.

Fiona's head was suddenly light. "Get lost," she said, knowing she had gone every shade of red.

"C'mon!" shouted the shortest of the trio. "Show us your tits!"

Cathy was at the window in a flash.

"Get out of here!" she yelled. "Don't you let me see you back here again!"

The three boys took off at a run, laughing even harder.

Cathy turned to Fiona. "What the hell was that about?"

It was on the tip of Fiona's tongue to say "nothing," but instead she burst into tears.

"I did something really stupid," she said. "I took this picture of myself…"

She trailed off, unable to say the words. Fiona couldn't look Cathy in the eye, but Cathy must have understood, because the next thing Fiona knew she was being folded into a grandmotherly hug.

"Honey," she said, "everybody makes mistakes when they're young."

Fiona's mind raced. How did those walking pimples get hold of the photo? She imagined it loose on the Internet—forever!

"What am I going to do?" choked Fiona between sobs. "My life is ruined!"

"Kiddo, your life has barely even started," Cathy replied, matter-of-factly.

But her words were no comfort. How could somebody Cathy's age possibly understand how unforgiving cyber-space could be? But Fiona knew, and she also knew what was going to happen next. *I'll be the joke of Vancouver, of the whole country. Of the whole world!*

Customers were lining up at the order window, and Cathy eyed them, no doubt thinking about how this was going to be one of the busiest afternoons of the year.

"Can you pull yourself together?" she asked, then smiled as Fiona gave a quick nod. "Attagirl. Go wash your face," she said, "and don't let the bastards get you down!"

FIONA MANAGED TO GET THROUGH to closing time, but she wondered with each hot dog and ice cream bar she served whether the customer had seen the picture—imagined that every group of teens trading laughs as they waited in line was laughing at her. After work, she sat at the back of the bus on the way to her dad's, keeping her face turned to the window in case anyone recognized her, and her backpack on the seat beside her to discourage anybody from sitting down.

Never had Fiona been so grateful to climb the hill into her dad's neighborhood, where nobody except her family knew her. But when she entered the house, a strange stillness greeted her. Katie was likely in bed already, but where was everyone else? She wondered for a moment if she'd gotten the night wrong, but—no—it was definitely her night at Dad's.

"Hello?" she called.

"Back here," came her father's voice in reply.

Fiona headed to the large open kitchen at the back of the house, where she found her dad and Joanne seated at the glassed-in table that overlooked the backyard pool, apparently waiting for her.

"Hi," her dad said, mustering a smile.

He tried to look her in the eye, but he couldn't quite seem to manage it.

"What's wrong?" asked Fiona, her mind rapidly processing various scenarios of disaster. Brandon and Katie must be okay, she figured, or Joanne wouldn't be so calm.

"Sit down, honey," her dad told her.

"You're scaring me," she said.

"Nothing's wrong," he replied. Joanne threw him an *oh really?* look, prompting him to add, "We just need to talk."

Fiona sat down at the table, looking from one to the other.

"Are you hungry?" asked Joanne, but her manner was cold—lacking her usual determination to be the world's best stepmom.

"I ate at work," said Fiona.

Joanne looked to Fiona's dad, as if to say, *get on with it.*

"I don't think I was supposed to receive this," he began. "Talia from the softball team must have me in her address book and sent it to me by mistake."

Flustered and embarrassed, her father took his smartphone out of his pocket and handed it to her. With a sickened feeling, she glanced at the screen long enough to register a few words from Talia's email below the photo—"stupid dumb slut!" Fiona passed the phone back to him, wanting to die right there, right then.

"We're surprised, to say the least," Joanne piped in. "What if Brandon or Katie saw that?"

"Joanne, let me handle this," said her dad. Fiona had never heard him use such an angry tone with Joanne before.

"Saw what?"

They all turned to see Brandon standing at the top of the basement stairs, emerging from the rec room below with his friend Tommy.

"Nothing," said Joanne with forced pleasantness. "Go downstairs and play Ping-Pong or something. I'll bring you down a snack in a minute."

Brandon and Tommy exchanged a look, like they knew they were missing out on something juicy, and reluctantly headed back to the rec room. Fiona's dad waited until they were out of earshot before saying, "Fiona, you know we're on your side no matter what. But obviously there's stuff going on in your life that we don't know about."

"I made a mistake," said Fiona, her voice small.

"I'm really struggling to understand why you would take a picture like that in the first place," said her father, "let alone why you would send it to all your friends."

"I didn't!" protested Fiona. "I sent it to one person I *thought* was my friend."

"Who?"

"Ryan, when we were going out."

Fiona saw her dad struggling to process this. His little girl…

"Have you…been intimate with this guy?"

"No!" replied Fiona, shocked that he could even think that. "We only dated for a few weeks, and we broke up months ago."

"And this guy sent this picture around?" said her dad, reddening with anger.

"Great company you keep," remarked Joanne.

Fiona's father snapped, "She's my daughter—let me deal with this."

"Fine," Joanne bit back. She went to the counter and started pulling together a snack for the boys. Fiona glanced at her dad, but he seemed fixated on his balled fists resting on the table. He stayed silent until Joanne had disappeared down the stairs with a plate of cheese and crackers. His next words sent shock waves through Fiona.

"I'm going to need a phone number for Ryan's parents."

"Dad, no! Just leave it."

"I just want to talk to his parents."

"No! Let me handle it."

"Fiona, how are you going to handle it?" he said, letting his exasperation show. "This guy took advantage of you, and now he's damaged your reputation, possibly permanently. That picture is out there. I mean, ten years from now, future employers are going to google your name and find it."

Fiona felt her stomach rise with renewed dread. "Thanks for the pep talk."

"I'm just telling it like it is. Ryan has to take responsibility for what he's done."

"What you mean is, *I* have to take responsibility."

He paused. Then, "Yes. That too." He took a deep breath and sat up straighter. "Okay, so you want to handle it. What's the plan?"

"I don't know. I'm afraid of making it worse." She felt tears stinging in her eyes.

"Does your mom know?"

"No."

"We should go talk about it with her, together."

He pushed his chair back and got to his feet.

"No!" That was the last thing Fiona needed, her parents squaring off like pit bulls, with her as the bone in the middle. "I'll tell her," she promised.

He sighed. "We should go now, Fiona. Your mother should know what's going on."

"Tomorrow, okay? I'm really tired. I just want to go to bed."

He hesitated, like he didn't know what to say. From the painfully awkward look on his face, Fiona started to get it.

"What? Am I not allowed to stay here?"

"I'm sorry, honey. Joanne's really upset," he said, lifting his hands as if to say he knew it was crazy, but it was out of his control. "I'm going to drive you back to your mom's."

FIONA AND HER DAD drove in silence as they headed back across the bridge. She was glad it was dark out, so he couldn't see how miserable she felt. As they crossed into the city, she watched twentysomethings walking in couples and in groups, and wondered if when she was that age the photo would still be out there circulating on the web, haunting her.

"Don't worry about Joanne," her dad told her as they got near her mom's place. "She'll get over it." But the way he said it, it didn't sound as though Joanne would "get over it" any time soon.

"What about my birthday?" Fiona asked uncertainly. It was just a couple of weeks away. They were supposed to have had a family party around the pool.

"I'll call you, okay? We'll figure something out."

When he stopped the car outside of the apartment, he reached out his broad hand and cupped the back of her head, pulling her forward so they bumped foreheads.

"Listen," he said. "I love you, no matter what. You'll always be my girl."

Will I? she thought. *Because it feels like you don't even know who I am.* But she said,

"I love you, too."

She collected her things and opened the car door. As she climbed out, he leaned over to tell her, "Tell your mom."

"I will."

"I'll call you."

Famous last words. He drove away, leaving Fiona with the distinct impression that her own father had broken up with her.

FIONA CAUGHT ONE LUCKY BREAK—when she came into the apartment, she heard the shower running. She slipped down the hall to her bedroom, hoping to avoid a confessional with her mom for at least one night, but just as she closed her door, the shower stopped and she heard her mother shout out in alarm, "Who's there?"

"It's just me," she called back.

"What happened?" her mom asked, pulling on her robe as she opened the bathroom door, wet hair dripping around her anxious face. "Why aren't you at your dad's?" Fiona's chin started to quiver. She could feel tears coming. "Honey? What's wrong?" her mom asked, taking her in her arms.

"I made a big mistake, Mom," Fiona choked out.

Her mom held her away from her by the shoulders and gave her a reassuring look. "Fiona, nothing can be so bad that we can't get through it. Are you pregnant?" she asked calmly.

"No!" What was it with her parents? Did they think she was some kind of sex fiend?

"I had to ask," she said. She seemed relieved. "C'mon," she told her, steering Fiona toward the kitchen. "I'll make tea and you can tell me all about it."

Once they were seated at the kitchen table with mugs of steaming tea, Fiona told her mom everything. She was surprisingly cool about the boob shot—"Everyone does things in a relationship they regret later," she said, "Unfortunately, with the Internet the consequences are bigger than they used to be"—but she was furious when Fiona told her about Joanne's reaction. "As though you haven't been punished enough!"

After she'd calmed down a little, she told her, "Fiona, taking that photo wasn't the smartest thing you've ever done, but what you do with your body is your business and nobody else's. There's going to be fallout, though, and you're going to have to have a strategy to deal with it."

Fiona knew what her mom was worried about—there had been several stories in the news in the past year about girls who were cyberbullied so badly after pictures of them got passed around the web that they wound up committing suicide.

"I'll be okay," she said. But would she? Did those other girls think they could handle the heat, until they couldn't anymore?

"The main thing is to know who your friends are,"

said her mom, getting up from the table and carrying their empty mugs to the sink. "Don't allow anybody to turn you into a victim." She came back to the table and kissed Fiona on the forehead. "I'm here for you, honey. And I'm sure your dad is, too. Just don't get me started on Joanne again."

Fiona put her arms around her mother and hugged her tight. "I'm sorry I'm so mean to you."

"You can't help it," she said, stroking Fiona's hair. Fiona looked up at her. One corner of her mother's mouth was lifted in a wry smile. "Sadly, sometimes 'mean' is what teenagers do best."

ON THE FIRST DAY OF SCHOOL, Fiona sat in the auditorium with the other grade tens waiting to get their homeroom assignments. She had planned to wear a denim mini with a loose cami. Instead, she wore jeans and a long T-shirt to achieve maximum coverage, even though the day promised to be sweltering. The auditorium was loud with excited chatter and joking. Fiona was on alert for glances and whispers, trying to determine whether she was the center of gossip, or—dare she hope?—if the photo had been forgotten. Lacey and Rick were seated on either side of her as protection, both having vowed to stay glued to her today, just in case anything ugly happened. A loud burst of laughter drew Fiona's attention to the back row. She turned to see Ryan's friend, Jeff, sitting with another jock, Max.

"Sweet rack!" Jeff proclaimed.

"Wonder what her ass looks like," mused Max.

Max caught Fiona looking at them and, grinning,

made a gross pumping motion against his crotch. Fiona turned her eyes forward and sunk down into her chair.

"Smarten up, douche bag!" Lacey snarled at Max.

"Omigod," moaned Fiona. "The whole football team has seen it."

"Fee, if you let this get to you, Ryan wins," Lacey reminded her.

Vice-Principal Bains walked onto the stage and read off class lists. Fiona was disappointed she wouldn't be in the same homeroom as Lacey, but at least she was in with Megan and Brit. After he was done, VP Bains dismissed the grade tens and told them their first full day would be tomorrow. Fiona filed out of the auditorium with Lacey and Rick, keeping her head down. Then she heard her name.

"Fiona?"

Fiona looked up to see Ryan just outside the auditorium door. Fiona wanted to spit in his face, but before she could do or say anything, Rick stepped toward him.

"Get lost!" he told Ryan, all macho—even though Rick was half a head shorter and, since Ryan had beefed up over the summer, about twice as scrawny.

"I just want to talk," Ryan said to Fiona, ignoring Rick. He was acting nice, like when they were dating.

"She's got nothing to say to you," Lacey replied.

Lacey and Rick marched Fiona away, flanking her like her own personal bodyguards. She appreciated their loyalty, but after overhearing Jeff and Max, she was starting to realize that she couldn't count on her friends to protect her forever, any more than she could avoid fallout from the photo. It was better to know what people were saying about her than to imagine something possibly worse. When she got home, she fired up her laptop and went onto Friend-jam, bracing herself.

On the first page alone, Fiona had been tagged in the boob shot a half-dozen times. She scanned messages from people she didn't even know, containing words like *whore*, *skank*, and *stupid bitch*. Oddly, it was the word *stupid* that hurt most of all. Nobody had ever called Fiona stupid before—not that they'd called her a *whore* or a *skank*—but she knew she was neither of those things. Now she felt like she had to prove to strangers she was smart. What was she supposed to do—post her GPA? *Don't give them the satisfaction!* her instincts warned her. *Don't even acknowledge them!* There was only one way for her to fight back, and that was to shut down her Friendjam account. With a few clicks of the mouse it was done—Fiona had severed ties with cyberspace. Now all she had to worry about was saving her reputation in the *real* world.

ASIA

AFTER MEETING KAI at the bubble tea shop, Laiping rode the crowded bus back across the company campus, worrying that she would be late for her shift. The bus seemed to take forever, with a dozen people getting on and off at every stop. By the time they arrived near Building 4, she had no time to get dinner at the cafeteria, or to return to the dorm to drop off her mobile, which workers were not allowed to take into the factory. She saw Fen coming down the stairs from the factory floor while she was going up, and she cut across the stream of workers.

"Put this under my pillow for me?" she asked, handing her the mobile phone.

"Sure," replied Fen. "How are you?"

But there was no time for Laiping to reply before each was swept away by the crowd.

Laiping hadn't eaten since the morning, and her stomach rumbled in complaint. She was also short on sleep, but nervous energy propelled her through her shift.

"Slow down!" hissed Bohai from his station beside her.

"Mind your own business," she hissed back.

When they broke at midnight, Mr. Wu praised her.

"See how quickly Laiping has worked, and how well," he said, holding up a couple of finished circuit boards from her full bin for all to see. "What's the matter with the rest of you donkey-brains? You must work faster!"

She ate ravenously at the meal break, and in the morning after her shift was over went back to the cafeteria for breakfast before returning to the dorm, where she slept soundly until six in the evening. When she woke up, Laiping thought about trying to reach her mother, but her phone battery was low. Fen must have used it—without her permission! Still, she was secretly relieved not to have to make the call. If her father was worse, she'd rather not know. She wanted to hold onto this good feeling she had. Finally, she was taking her future into her own hands. Somehow, with Kai's help, she would find a way to make the company give her the money she was owed.

But on Wednesday evening, Laiping broke her promise to Kai. When she met Min in the cafeteria before her shift, she noticed that her cousin's cough was worse, and her chopsticks trembled when she lifted food to her mouth. Min's transfer to another department, away from the toxic cleaner, still hadn't come through.

"There's a meeting tomorrow," Laiping told her, keeping her voice low. "I'm going to tell them about what that screen cleaner is doing to you."

"Don't you dare!"

"But you said the workers on your line want to talk to Kai," replied Laiping.

"The guy who was saying that the loudest got fired! And then they made the rest of us stay for an hour after our shift, writing letters of apology to Steve Chen."

"They can't treat us like this," Laiping told Min. "It's not fair."

"Keep your voice down! You sound like you've been brainwashed by that guy!"

"I'm not brainwashed," Laiping replied hotly.

"Fen told me you've been seeing him."

"How would she know?" asked Laiping in a huff. Then she remembered the low battery. "She's been snooping in my mobile!" If Fen had looked in the address book, she would have found Kai's number.

"She's worried about you, and so am I. She told me to tell you to stay away from him."

Suddenly, Laiping wished she hadn't told Min about Kai, or the meeting. They may have been cousins, but Kai was right—you had to be careful about who you trusted.

"I won't go then," she lied. "Forget I said anything."

"Don't worry, I will," replied Min.

Laiping glanced over to the nearest security guard, standing sentry by the wall. Her eyes were forward. She hadn't heard anything—Laiping was sure of it.

AT THE FACTORY, Laiping made a point of staying to the far right of the crowded staircase as she climbed up, knowing that Fen would be on the left coming down. She was angry at her for nosing around in her mobile, and for talking to Min behind her back. Fen gave her a friendly wave, but Laiping noticed that she was making no effort to come over—so maybe Fen was avoiding Laiping just as much as Laiping was avoiding her.

Laiping continued up to the factory floor and took her place in formation for marching exercises, just has she had done almost daily for the past eight weeks. Tonight, though, everything seemed different. Miss Lau's cheery voice over the loudspeaker irritated her—her kind tone a reminder of her unkindness. When they took their work stations, Laiping discovered that Bohai had been replaced by somebody else, a girl who didn't bother speaking to Laiping. She wondered if Bohai was being punished, and almost felt sorry for him.

Mr. Wu strutted up and down the aisle as usual, praising a worker here, ridiculing another there, like a self-important general. *Circuit board-capacitor-solder-capacitor-solder; circuit board-capacitor-solder-capacitor-solder.* Laiping thought: *We aren't soldiers. We aren't robots, either. We deserve better.*

IN THE MORNING AFTER HER SHIFT, Laiping followed the flow of workers down the stairs. She looked for Fen going up and spotted her, but Fen didn't look her way—giving Laiping an unsettled feeling. Outside, she averted her eyes as she passed the security guard, afraid that somehow he would read what was in her mind.

The address Kai had given her was a fast food restaurant on the far side of campus. He said the meeting was at 9:00 a.m.—it was 8:30 now. On the main boulevard, Laiping got in line for a bus to take her there, but with the shift changes, two busses came and went, too crowded for Laiping to get on board. Laiping's anxiety grew. If she was late for the meeting, Kai might think she wasn't serious enough to join his group—or to be his girlfriend. When the third bus came, Laiping pushed her way on board. The passengers were packed like tinned fish, smelling of sweat and bad breath.

They stopped frequently on the way across campus and were delayed while people got on and off the bus. Laiping dug her fingernails into her palms, willing it to go faster. They were almost at Laiping's destination at the end of the route when the bus lurched to a halt. She craned her neck to see out the window. The street and sidewalk were jammed with people, pushing and shoving. She could hear shouting from nearby, then screams.

"Open the doors! Let us off the bus!" someone called to the driver.

"No!" she yelled back. Then she used the loudspeaker. "We have encountered an emergency," she announced. Laiping couldn't see the driver, but she sounded young, and nervous. "Please be patient until it is safe to proceed."

Laiping squeezed by other passengers to get a better view out the window, and saw a phalanx of police in visors and riot gear protecting the bus from the surging crowd. Beyond the police she saw people fighting—a thug thrashing his baton at a young man who was cowering at the blows. Another man hauled a youth out of a shop and punched him, bloodying his nose. To her horror, Laiping saw that the youth with the bloody nose was Kai. She wanted to cry out: *Somebody stop them!* But the police kept their backs turned to the fighting, making no effort to intervene. She watched helplessly as Kai and his friends were bundled into an unmarked van.

A whistle blew. Outside the bus, the police were ordering the crowd of onlookers to move along.

"Show's over!" they shouted. "Get going!"

One of the police waved the bus forward to its stop, where at last the doors opened and Laiping and the other passengers poured out. On the sidewalk, Laiping fought the crowd to reach the van. People bumped against her as they streamed by in the opposite direction, keeping their heads low and hurrying for safety.

"Keep moving!" commanded a policeman close by.

Laiping managed to reach the van, just at the moment when Kai turned his face, bloodied and cowed, to the window. He saw her, too, and his eyes filled with hatred. It took Laiping a long moment to understand. Then she realized, *He blames me for this! He thinks I gave him away!* Her next thought was, *Fen.*

"It wasn't me!" Laiping shouted to him through the glass.

But the van carrying Kai was pulling away, forcing the crowd to part around it. Laiping called out, "Let them go! They didn't do anything! Where are you taking them?"

"Get going!" a policeman yelled at her.

The van was gaining speed as it reached the edge of the crowd.

"Stop the van!" cried Laiping, to anyone who would listen. "Workers have rights!" A few people stopped and turned to her. Laiping couldn't be sure if they were on her side, or if they thought she had mental problems, but at least they were listening. "Why are they being arrested?" she demanded. "They didn't do anything wrong!

Stop the van and let them go free!"

In the next instant, somebody grabbed her by the hair and yanked her backward so hard that she landed on the pavement on her back, the wind knocked out of her. She looked up to catch a glimpse of three policemen staring down at her through their visors, just as one of them drove his boot into her side. Another hauled her up by her arm, then all three of them began landing their fists on her face and body. Laiping was too shocked to feel pain, and then the beating was over. The police turned their attention back to dispersing the crowd, leaving Laiping curled up like a baby in the middle of the road. No one came near her. No one dared.

After a few seconds, Laiping forced herself to her knees, and then to her feet. The van carrying Kai and the others was nowhere in sight. She staggered forward, testing her legs. There was a sharp pain in her side where the boot landed, but nothing seemed broken. She wiped her nose with the back of her hand and examined a smear of blood. A policeman approached her and gave her shoulder a hard shove.

"Get going," he said. "Consider yourself lucky we're not taking you in."

In a daze, Laiping limped to the bus stop and lined up behind some girls. They kept their backs to her, as though they were afraid the police might think they knew her. No one spoke.

Laiping was able to squeeze onto the first bus that came along, so maybe she *was* lucky. Luckier than Kai, at least.

AFRICA

ARMS FULL of what supplies they could carry—bandages, syringes, medicines stuffed hastily into plastic sacks—Sylvie and Marie made their way through the camp to the foreign workers compound, taking a back route to avoid the main roads where Kayembe's men might spot them. Neema had left ahead of them, but Doctor Van de Velde stayed behind to collect more equipment. Sylvie had changed out of Kayembe's pink frilly dress into the only other clothing available, a set of green surgical scrubs.

"What's your hurry?" asked a teenaged boy who was passing by. Sylvie realized he was Jean-Yves's brother, Luc, and that they were near the brothers' hut.

"Tell people to stay away from the clinic!" Marie warned him.

Sylvie nudged Marie along with her shoulder. "Careful," she told her. "That family is with Kayembe."

The peacekeeper at the wooden gate of the compound, a soldier with the African Union, was nervous, holding his weapon poised across his chest. When he saw them approach, he opened the gate quickly and hurried them inside.

"Did Neema arrive?" asked Marie.

"The nurse? She's inside. What's this about an attack?"

"Doctor Van de Velde has called for help," Marie told the worried guard. "This girl's family is coming," she added. "They have permission to come into the compound."

But to Sylvie, the fence of thorn branches surrounding the compound was a ridiculous defense—easily destroyed with gasoline and matches. The soldier seemed to think so, too, because he licked his lips and asked, "What help is coming? The police or the army? How many?"

"I don't know," admitted Marie.

As soon as they entered, Martin, the young American, rushed up to them. He looked as frightened as the guard.

"What's going on? Neema said there's trouble."

"It's the local warlord, he's after Sylvie and her family," Marie explained.

Sylvie saw Martin's glance shift to her, as though he was thinking, *Then why are we letting her in here?*

"I need the sat phone," Marie told him, heading for the communications hut.

Sylvie followed her inside and watched as she punched a long string of numbers into the phone, from a list taped to the desk. Sylvie glanced at the list and saw that she was calling the Canadian embassy in the Tanzanian capital of Dar es Salaam, two days journey to the east, on the Indian Ocean. She wondered how help could possibly arrive in time from so far away.

"This is Doctor Marie Pierre," she said when she connected. "I am a Canadian citizen working for the UN High Commission for Refugees at Nyarugusu Camp. I am in need of protection." Marie waited while her call was passed onto someone else, then explained again who she was and why she needed protection. "I must tell you there are Congolese refugees in my care whose lives are at risk," she told the embassy official. Sylvie watched her frown. "But that's exactly the point," Marie said with frustration. "This family isn't safe in the DRC, or Tanzania!" She argued some more with whoever was on the other end of the line, then rang off angrily.

"What is it?" asked Sylvie.

Marie gave her a bold smile. "Don't worry," she said. "When Olivier gets here with your family, we're leaving for Dar es Salaam. Once we're inside the embassy, we'll be safe."

"But will they let us in?" asked Sylvie.

"They have to," she replied, which wasn't the reassurance Sylvie was looking for.

AN HOUR WENT BY. Sylvie and Marie waited anxiously by the gate for Olivier, Mama, and the children. Doctor Van de Velde hadn't appeared yet, either. The very air around them seemed tense, like the tingle before a lightning storm, and outside the thorn fence, the camp was too quiet. Sylvie wanted to go out to look for Olivier and her family, but Marie told her that if anyone reported to Kayembe that she was here inside the compound, then everyone would be in danger.

"But he must already know," Sylvie pointed out. "Luc saw us, remember?"

Just as this truth dawned on Marie's face, a single rifle

shot splintered the air, then the rapid-fire of an automatic weapon.

Martin ran out from one of the tents. "Where's it coming from?"

"The clinic, I think," replied Marie.

Neema and the other nurses and aid workers started to gather, fear in everyone's eyes.

"Where are the police?" shrieked Neema. "Who is going to protect us?"

"Look!" said Martin, pointing.

They all turned to see a wisp of black smoke rising into the sky, from the direction of the clinic.

"Doctor Van de Velde!" exclaimed Neema.

"They won't hurt him," Marie told her. "They have no reason to hurt him." But she sounded like she was trying to convince herself.

Suddenly, Neema took hold of Sylvie's arm. "It's you they want!" She half pushed, half pulled Sylvie toward the gate. "Go! Get out!"

Marie grabbed hold of Neema—"Leave her alone!"— and all at once the entire group was bickering and shouting, some wanting Sylvie to stay and others all for sending her straight to Kayembe.

"Kayembe wants me dead, too!" Marie shouted. "Does that mean I should go out there?"

A piercing whistle silenced them. It was Martin, four fingers in his mouth.

"Stop it!" he yelled in his fumbling French. "Stop it right now! Sylvie is staying here, and so is Marie!"

But Sylvie's gratitude turned quickly to despair when

she looked back to see that the wisp of smoke in the distance had turned into leaping orange flames. The clinic was burning. There were more gunshots, coming closer. *They're right*, she realized. *I have brought this upon them.* While the others stared in disbelief at the fire, she dashed for the gate and threw off the wooden bar that kept it locked. Marie reached her just as she pushed the gate open.

"Sylvie!"

The rattled peacekeeper swung his gun at them, ready to shoot.

"No!" Marie cried out, pushing the barrel away with trembling fingers.

"Marie, go back inside," pleaded Sylvie. "I have to find my family."

Tearfully, Marie told her, "Sylvie, they may already be dead."

Sylvie looked into Marie's eyes, and went numb. She was right. Of course she was right. Too much time had gone by—Kayembe had caught them by now. Mama, Pascal, Lucie. Olivier. Sylvie felt her limbs go weak. Her legs wouldn't move. Her heart pounded—so hard it felt like it might burst through her chest. She wished it would, and then at last all the pain would be over.

Sylvie heard the rattle of a heavy truck turning into the lane behind her. She saw Marie's eyes go wide with dread. The peacekeeper lifted his gun and took aim. *A truck full of soldiers*, thought Sylvie. Would they kill them all here, or would they take her to Kayembe to give him the satisfaction of doing it himself?

Then, a strange smile crossed Marie's face. "My

God," she said in wonder.

Sylvie turned slowly. The truck was large, like the ones Kayembe's men used to carry coltan. Seated in the cab were Olivier and Doctor Van De Velde. She blinked twice to make sure that what she was seeing was real, and broke into a grin. Yes, Fiston was driving! As the truck creaked to a stop, the Belgian leaped out.

"You two," he said to Marie and Sylvie. "Quickly! Get in the back!"

Fiston leaned out the driver's window.

"It is my pleasure to take you as far as Dar es Salaam, *mesdemoiselles*," he said. "After that, Fiston must seek new work—preferably outside the reach of my previous employer."

"Hurry! Get in!" shouted Olivier, jumping down from the passenger side, cradling the AK-47 at the ready. "The others are in the back."

Marie turned to Doctor Van de Velde. "You can't stay, either. They'll come to the compound."

"Go!" he said. "We'll be all right. The army is almost here. I spoke to them an hour ago."

Marie threw her arms around his neck. "I'll see you soon!" she said, and hurried to the back of the truck.

Sylvie lingered for a moment. "When I become a doctor," she promised him, "I'm coming back."

"By the time you are a doctor, Sylvie," he told her, "I pray to all that is holy that this place will no longer be needed."

Olivier held open the canvas flap at the back of the truck. "Let's go!" he shouted, glancing urgently down the lane behind them. "They're not far behind!"

Inside, Pascal and Lucie were taking turns to see who could throw the scraps of coltan nuggets that littered the floor the furthest, oblivious to the danger they were in. Marie was seated beside Mama, who gripped her hand anxiously.

"Where are we going?" Mama fretted when she saw Sylvie. "How will Patrice find us?"

Sylvie took her mother's other hand. "We're going someplace safe," she told her.

But no sooner had she spoken the words than a new burst of gunfire rang out—much closer than before. Pascal and Lucie stopped their game. Sylvie slid over and peeked through the canvas to see a jeep rounding a corner into the lane, still a good distance behind them but approaching fast. There was a machine gun mounted on top, and one of Kayembe's men was firing it wildly into the air.

The UN peacekeeper gaped. Olivier stood his ground at the rear of the truck, gun raised, poised to shoot. Fiston joined him from the driver's side of the truck, removing the safety from his automatic rifle as he ran.

"Can we outrun them?" Olivier asked him.

"With our weight? Not a chance." Fiston saw Sylvie looking out the canvas. "Tell everyone to get down!"

Sylvie did as she was told, making Pascal and Lucie flatten themselves against the bed of the truck, while Marie helped Mama. She heard shots ring out from Olivier and Fiston, and then the rat-a-tat of the jeep's machine gun, coming closer. *Papa*, she prayed silently, *be with Olivier now. Help him to save us.*

WHEN MIN SAW LAIPING'S INJURIES, she insisted on taking her to the campus clinic, where a doctor told her one of her ribs was cracked, and cleaned out the cuts under her left eye and at the corner of her mouth. Laiping noticed the doctor did not ask how her injuries happened.

"That could have been you," Min said, when Laiping told her abut Kai being taken away in the van. "This isn't our village. You can't trust anybody."

But Laiping had already learned this lesson. Lesson Number…she had lost count.

Laiping got a note from the clinic allowing her to miss her shift in the factory for one night. She went back to the dorm and lay flat on her bunk—the only position in which the cracked rib didn't hurt—and waited for Fen to come back in the evening. Fen's shock when she saw Laiping's bruises seemed real, but she was less convincing when she denied knowing anything about the police and the meeting.

"You found the address in my mobile. You gave it to the company," Laiping accused her.

"Don't be crazy. Why would I do that?"

Laiping was prepared for Fen to lie—she'd known she was a liar since the first day they met. "Because you're a company spy," she told her.

"*Ai ya!* You must have mental problems," she replied hotly. "Troublemakers always get punished. That's just the way it is."

"Including your father?" asked Laiping.

"Don't talk about my father! Everything bad that happened to my family happened because of him."

That was the last time Laiping and Fen spoke. A few days after Kai's arrest, Fen was promoted to a job as an office clerk in another building. Laiping heard her boasting to some of the girls in their dorm room that she was hired because the boss was impressed by her knowledge of English. But Laiping knew exactly how she got the job.

You can't trust anybody.

Laiping tried phoning Kai's number, but a recording told her it was no longer in service. She used a pay phone to do this, just in case the company tried to trace the call back to her mobile. The thought of another beating made her careful about drawing attention to herself. She wondered where Kai was. Maybe he had been fired, like the man on Min's line who complained too loudly about the chemical they were forced to use. Or maybe he was in one of the work camps he'd told her about, where they send people simply for wanting things to change.

LAIPING WENT BACK TO WORK on Friday night, her side aching from the cracked rib. Mr. Wu yelled at her when she couldn't keep up her usual pace on the production line. From the corner of her eye, she could see the girl who'd replaced Bohai smirking, but she kept her head bowed over her work, ignoring her. No one asked what happened to her face, and she noticed in the dorm and in the factory that people seemed to avoid talking to her.

On Sunday, Laiping had the day off. She phoned Auntie and learned that the hospital had sent her father back home to the village to wait for the surgery. Laiping asked if she could speak to him, and Auntie took the phone over to her parents' house, where he was confined to bed. When Laiping heard his voice, she burst into tears.

"Baba, I want to come home!" she cried.

"What's wrong, Laiping? What's happened?" he asked with concern. In the background, she could hear her mother asking the same questions, and her father telling her to be quiet—he couldn't hear Laiping.

"I don't like it here," Laiping told him. She wanted to explain about Kai and the beating, but she was afraid it would be bad for his heart.

"You must give it a chance," he told her.

"You don't know what it's like, Baba! They work us so hard, and everyone's so mean."

"Let me talk to her!" she heard her mother saying, and pictured her grabbing the phone out of his hands. "Laiping," she said when she came on the line, her voice hard and scolding, "what are you thinking, upsetting Baba like this when he's just out of the hospital?"

"I didn't mean to upset him," said Laiping, wiping her eyes.

"What's this about you coming home?"

"I've made up my mind. As soon as they give me my back pay, I'm quitting."

There was a hesitation, then, "Laiping, you can't quit."

"I'll make sure I get the money for the surgery first."

"You have to keep your job."

"Mama, I hate it here!"

"Think, Laiping! Your father can't work anymore, and I have to look after him. How will we live if you don't have a job?"

"We'll run the farm, you and me!"

"You're being foolish! The farm barely feeds us as it is! Besides, we can't do the heavy work."

Laiping tried to picture herself behind the plow, the blade catching in the mud, the ox balking. She remembered the suffocating heat of the fields, and the sticky sweat. Was factory life really so much worse than that? The sickness in her soul when she thought about the monotonous nights at her work station, of the endless fatigue, of the bullying supervisors—of Kai's bloodied face, and her own—told her it was.

"Mama," she said, "it's too hard here."

"Bitter first, sweet after, Laiping. A good daughter obeys her parents. You must stay and learn to tolerate the work."

A deadening weight took hold of Laiping. It started in her stomach and moved out through every nerve in her body—extinguishing hope as it went, leaving her limbs heavy and her mind dull. There was no point in struggling against it.

"Yes, Mama," she replied.

After she said goodbye, Laiping lay down on her bunk. She stayed there for hours, too self-conscious to go out because of the bruises on her face, too sleepless to drive away visions of her future in the factory, stretching before her in endless repetition, day after day after day.

But the very next night in the factory, something exciting happened.

"Tonight we will have special visitors, and a great honor," Miss Lau announced over the loudspeaker. "Mr. Chen has given his permission for a film crew all the way from America to come in to shoot video of our factory."

Laiping remembered the video of protesting Americans Kai had shown her and wondered if that was why the film crew was coming, to see the conditions in the factory for themselves. For once, she was glad for the bruises on her face—maybe she would have the chance to tell the *gweilo* how it happened. But when Laiping went to take her station following marching exercises, Mr. Wu stopped her.

"You're being transferred," he told her.

Laiping was sent with a group of a hundred or so workers to a different building, where they were given white smocks instead of blue, and where instead of soldering capacitors to circuit boards, they checked the finished product to make sure that the smartphones worked. Laiping noticed that most of the workers who were moved were very young, perhaps underage. She thought, *How clever of Steve Chen to let the American cameras see only what the company wants them to see.* She remembered Kai's words: *There are things you need to know.* But if the company had its way, the world would never know. Just like Laiping would never know what happened to Kai.

"Smile!" said the young girl next to her on the assembly line.

She pointed a smartphone at Laiping. There was a clicking sound.

"This one works," the girl said, checking the photo she'd taken.

She showed it to her. Laiping barely recognized the girl in the white smock and cap as herself. That girl could be anybody. Not happy, or unhappy. Not a city girl, or a country girl. Except for the purple-gray bruise around her eye, she was just a factory girl, like a hundred thousand others.

AFRICA

SYLVIE LAY FLAT against the bed of the truck, holding Pascal and Lucie close to her. Beyond the canvas flap covering the back, the rapid fire of the machine gun grew louder as the jeep closed in on them, answered by shots from Olivier and Fiston. The truck's engine was still running—Sylvie could feel the vibrations through the floor, and she tasted diesel fumes along with the tang of fear. She looked over to where Marie lay with her arm over Mama, their eyes meeting in shared terror.

The canvas flap flew up—Doctor Van de Velde held it open for them. "Get out of there!" he shouted. "You're sitting ducks!"

Behind him, Sylvie could see Olivier and Fiston shooting their guns. The UN peacekeeper stood with them, firing his rifle at the approaching jeep. Sylvie started to move toward the Belgian, but suddenly he arched his back, his face widening in surprise as a bullet hit his shoulder.

"Bernard!" Marie shrieked, inching forward on her stomach.

Together, she and Sylvie managed to pull Doctor Van de Velde into the truck. A cry of pain from the peacekeeper rang out; Sylvie saw him go down just as the flap fell shut.

"Olivier, get in and drive!" they heard Fiston yell.

"You said we can't outrun them!" came Olivier's reply.

"We can't outshoot them, either. Go!"

Abruptly, the shooting stopped. Sylvie heard the jeep rumbling closer, and the squeal of its brakes. She prayed for the truck to move, but the engine continued to idle. Marie, cradling Doctor Van de Velde, gave her a desperate look, while Lucie and Pascal huddled in terror with Mama behind them.

"What's happening?" mouthed Marie.

Sylvie lifted a corner of the canvas and saw Fiston with his hands in the air, his rifle on the ground. The scrawny fighter, the one Fiston called Arsène, was at the wheel of the jeep.

The man behind the machine gun kept the barrel aimed at Fiston as Arsène climbed out of the jeep and walked stealthily down the driver's side of the truck, tightly gripping his AK-47. As he came back into Sylvie's view, he dipped down, sweeping the barrel of his gun under the truck.

"Where did Olivier run to?" he said, relaxing a little as he turned to Fiston. "Decided to save himself, did he?" Arsène kicked the rifle out of Fiston's reach, taunting, "How much did they pay you, Fiston, to throw your life away?"

"Not enough," said Fiston, trying to joke with him. But Sylvie could see he was sweating. "Let us go, Arsène. I'll make it worth your while."

For a moment, Arsène seemed to consider Fiston's

offer. Then he nodded to the man in the jeep. There was a burst of machine gun fire, and Fiston fell to the ground. Sylvie recoiled into the truck, sickened. In the next instant, Arsène threw back the canvas. He was pointing his AK-47 at them now, and the soldier in the jeep was directing the machine gun toward the truck, too. Sylvie heard Mama let out a cry, but she didn't dare turn to her.

Arsène looked them over, as though deciding who should die first. "You," he said, waving his gun at Marie. "Get down here." Marie didn't move. Arsène fired into the air, making all of them jump. Lucie was sobbing. "Now!" he commanded. He began undoing his belt.

Sylvie watched helplessly as Marie slid across the floor of the truck toward Arsène. When she got near enough, he grabbed hold of her ankle and pulled her the rest of the way, so that she went sprawling onto the ground. Laying the AK-47 in the dust, he got down on his knees and opened his pants, while the soldier in the jeep kept the machine gun trained on Sylvie and the others. Marie began crying. Doctor Van de Velde, bleeding and weak, looked away in horror.

Suddenly, there came a shot. The man behind the machine gun toppled. Arsène, caught off guard, grabbed for his AK-47, but when he looked up, Olivier had him locked in the sights of his own automatic rifle.

"No!" Arsène pleaded for his life, his pants down around his knees. Olivier waited while Marie, trembling, crawled out from under him, his aim unwavering. Sylvie jumped down from the truck to help her. "Please!" begged Arsène, "just go! I won't stop you!"

But Olivier had no mercy. As soon as Marie was clear he fired, bullets riddling Arsène's chest until he lay in the dust, wide-eyed and unseeing. Marie sobbed uncontrollably in Sylvie's arms. Holding her tight, Sylvie looked up into her brother's face. There was no emotion in his eyes, no remorse—not even relief.

"There'll be more coming," he told her coldly. "Get her in the truck, and let's go."

THEY REACHED THE CAMP GATES ahead of Kayembe's men, in time to meet an arriving convoy of Tanzanian soldiers. By then, Marie had fashioned a bandage for Doctor Van de Velde from his bloodied shirt. The wound wasn't life-threatening—the Belgian opted to let the Tanzanians take him to the camp hospital to have it seen to, but he insisted that Marie go on to Dar es Salaam with Sylvie and her family.

"Your time here is done," he said in his blunt fashion. "You've become a liability."

Marie didn't argue with him.

FOR THREE DAYS they drove across grasslands and high country, morning and night. Olivier taught Marie how to handle the truck so that she could spell him off at the wheel. They worried the whole way that Kayembe might follow them, but they found out later from Doctor Van de Velde that the Tanzanian troops succeeded in driving Kayembe and his forces out of Nyarugusu. The Zone 3 clinic burned to the ground, but the other clinics and the hospital were saved. According to the Belgian, now the

UN was arguing with the Tanzanians about rebuilding the clinic that burned, since the Tanzanians would have been just as happy to shut the entire camp down.

Sylvie shed tears for Fiston, who had given his life trying to save them. He had known her father, and, like him, he died a good man—even if circumstances had made him choose to work for Kayembe. She prayed that his sacrifice had allowed his spirit to cross over, and that it wasn't still trapped in Nyarugusu.

When they reached Dar es Salaam, Marie had to argue with the staff at the Canadian embassy about letting them inside. At last she managed to convince the embassy officials that the family's lives were in danger from Kayembe and his men. Marie explained to Sylvie that the embassy was considered Canadian territory, and as long as the family stayed inside, they'd be safe from attack. But as wonderful as the embassy was—Mama was delighted with the indoor toilet, and Pascal and Lucie quickly became spoiled watching the TV that the staff provided in their living quarters—it soon began to feel to Sylvie like another refugee camp. Until the Canadian government, oceans away, decided what to do with them, they couldn't even go outside the embassy grounds for fear they wouldn't be allowed back in.

On the tenth day after they arrived in Dar es Salaam, Marie left them to fly to Montreal. She planned to do what she could from there to persuade her government that the family would never be safe from Kayembe, not so long as they remained in central Africa, and to let them come to Canada.

Before she left, Marie warned Sylvie not to tell anyone about Olivier shooting Arsène. If the Canadians found out he had killed someone, they might never let him into the country. As far as anyone was to know, Olivier was just a fourteen-year-old boy. But, watching him roam the embassy like a caged animal, Sylvie worried for him. She had seen the look on his face when he shot Arsène. How would he ever adjust to life in a place like Canada, where there were laws to be obeyed?

"It's so boring here," he complained at the beginning of their third week at the embassy. "There's nothing to do."

"Here," said Sylvie, handing him a book about Canada, "learn something about where we're going."

"If we ever get there."

"We'll get there. Marie says thirty thousand people have signed the petition. She won't let us down."

Sylvie taught herself to type on an old computer the embassy staff let her use—a skill that Marie told her, when they spoke on Skype, she would need once they finally arrived in Montreal and she started school. For the first time in her life, Sylvie had daily access to the Internet. She visited Alain's website frequently, and was heartened by the comments people wrote there—complete strangers wishing Sylvie and her family well and urging their government to let them into the country.

Encouraged by Marie and Alain, Sylvie began to post on the site, too. People had many questions for her about her family, and about their lives in North Kivu and in Nyarugusu. At first she was shy, but when other Congolese started sharing their stories about the murder, rape, and torture that went on there, she found the courage to tell her own story—how she and Mama were raped, and how the soldier cut her face with the machete.

"Please do not feel sorry for me," she wrote. "I am one of the lucky ones."

And she saw that she was. Soon, forty thousand people had signed the petition, then fifty thousand. Sylvie counted the hours and the days until the Canadian government, thousands of miles away, would decide their fate. Surely it wouldn't be long before they agreed to let them come.

FIONA HAD ONLY BEEN in Vice-Principal Bains's office once before, when she was on the planning committee for last year's Artravaganza Night, the school's annual art show. She was a star student then. Seated in front of him now, she felt like some kind of criminal.

"Fiona, something has come to my attention," he began ominously.

From the way he was avoiding looking at her, Fiona could guess what that something was. For the last two weeks, since the start of school, everything had been about the boob shot—from finding a hard copy of it taped to her locker on the first day of classes, to being snubbed by Megan and Brit when she saw them in homeroom. Fiona found out from Lacey—who was no longer speaking to Megan and Brit—that they'd been going around saying horrible things about her, calling her a slut, a skank, a whore. It seemed that, to them, she'd gone from being the girl they'd known all their lives to some completely different person, defined only by that picture. She thanked her lucky stars for Lacey and Rick, who had stuck by her, constantly reassuring her that, sooner or later, the whole mess would blow over—even if, right now, it just blowed.

"First, you should know that I have *not* seen this picture of you that's going around," said Mr. Bains, leaning back in his chair as though he was trying to keep as much distance between them as he could manage. Everybody was used to the turban Mr. Bains wore with his usual chinos and open shirt, but right now, to Fiona, it seemed intimidating. She didn't want to imagine what Sikhs thought about girls who took nude photos of themselves. "I promise you I will never look at it," he continued. Fiona struggled for something to say. She sat like a lump, gaze fixed on the floor. But from the corner of her eye, she saw him shrug helplessly. "To be honest, we've never had to deal with something like this at our school before."

Fiona thought, *You mean you've never found out about it before!* Because she couldn't have been the only one.

"The implications are very serious," he continued. "Technically, that photo is child pornography, and distributing it is a crime." *Seriously?* "Anybody caught viewing it or sending it around could be arrested." His gaze became intense. "Fiona, this is very important. Did anyone force you to pose for that picture?"

"No!" she exclaimed.

"Look, I know you're a good kid. I'm just trying to understand what happened, and whether I should be calling the police."

"Don't call the police," she half insisted, half pleaded. "Mr. Bains, please. I made a mistake, and I'm dealing with it."

He studied her for a moment. "Fiona, if you took that photo of yourself and then sent it to somebody, *you* could be charged with distributing child porn."

What? "It's my private business," she said, growing angry.

"It isn't private anymore," he pointed out. "Do your parents know about it?"

"Yes."

"What action are they taking?"

"They don't think it's such a big deal," she said, which was at least true of her mom. "They're letting me handle it."

He clicked his pen open and closed a couple of times, looking unconvinced. "Don't fool yourself," he said. "This isn't going away. There's counseling available—you don't have to face this alone."

He was being really nice, but Fiona found herself repeating something her mother had said to her. "If I act like a victim, then I become a victim."

"I still have to report it to the police," he said. "Maybe they can shut this thing down."

"Please don't. There's nothing they can do."

They both knew it was true—trying to stop a picture from circulating on the Internet was like trying to catch a shadow.

Mr. Bains chewed his lip. "So what's your plan? How are you going to deal with it?"

"One asshole at a time," she told him, at which he raised an eyebrow. "Sorry," she apologized. But as she got up to leave, an idea started to form, and she realized she might just have come up with the solution—somehow, she had to make all those people who were tearing her down see her for herself again. See her as Fiona.

WHEN SHE GOT HOME, Fiona found her mom at work at the kitchen table, surrounded by stacks of research. The TV was on in the living room, which was unusual, since her mom didn't watch much TV. But ever since the news broke about that African girl being holed up in a Canadian embassy someplace, she'd been glued to it.

"How was school?" she asked, without looking up from the article she was writing.

"Okay, unless you count Mr. Bains accusing me of being child pornographer."

Her mom stopped typing and looked up. "*What?*"

"He found out about the photo," she said. "He says he has to tell the cops, that I could be charged with distributing porn."

"Oh, honey. That's ridiculous." She got up to take her in her arms, and Fiona let her. She needed a hug. "What's going to happen to Ryan?" her mom asked. "He's the one who sent it around."

"They don't know it was him, and I'm not telling them."

Her mom stood back and studied her with surprise. "Why are you protecting him?"

"You're the one who said not to be a victim!"

"But I didn't mean he should get away with it," she replied.

"Why can't everybody just drop it?" Fiona snapped at

her. "I said I would handle it!"

"Okay, okay," said her mom, backing off.

Fiona flopped down on the living room sofa. A half-hour ago in Mr. Bains office, her plan had seemed clear—one by one, she was going to talk to all the jerks who'd been putting her down to let them know how much the things they said about her hurt. Now she wondered how she would ever find the guts to do that. Everything was muddled again.

On the TV, a young black woman was being interviewed from her home in Montreal. *Dr. Marie Pierre*, it said on the screen. "Sylvie and her family face persecution and quite possibly death in the DRC *and* in Tanzania, unless Canada accepts them," she said. Her English was perfect. "We owe them a new life. Canadian mining companies have a history of supporting the militias against the people, so we've been part of the problem. This is a chance to help."

"That poor girl and her family," remarked Fiona's mom. "They're trapped inside the embassy in Tanzania until the government agrees to recognize their refugee claim."

Fiona watched as the now famous photo came up on the TV screen, the one where Sylvie was looking into the camera with deep, frightened eyes—eyes that make you shudder to think what they'd seen. But who was she, really? *She's been defined by a picture, too*, Fiona realized. She'd become known by the scar on her face, but the scar was just an idea of a girl, just like the boob shot was an idea of Fiona.

But who was the girl? Those eyes—what were they saying? Fiona thought that maybe she understood. They were saying, *See me for who I really am.*

FIONA'S BIRTHDAY was the next day, Saturday. Her dad made a plan to take her out to lunch with Brandon and Katie, and then to the Vancouver Aquarium—one of Fiona's favorite places. Joanne didn't join them. Fiona didn't ask why, and her dad didn't bring it up.

After they finished eating, the restaurant servers brought a cake to the table and sang "Happy Birthday." Then came the moment Fiona had been waiting for all summer.

"Surprise!" said her dad, handing her his present.

Fiona tore off the gift wrap to find the very latest smartphone. The official launch date wasn't until tomorrow, but Fiona's dad *had* managed to get this one early, just as he'd promised. It was slim and light, with twice the speed of the previous version.

"Thanks, Dad," she said, throwing her arms around his neck.

"You're welcome. Careful with this one, right?"

He had to say it.

"Don't worry," she replied, acknowledging his multiple meanings. "Believe me, I've learned my lesson."

AFTER LUNCH, they drove to Stanley Park and checked out the penguin exhibit and then the sea otters, where Fiona and Katie put their faces up to the glass to watch the otters dive and roll. Even though she was now officially fifteen,

Fiona felt like a kid again, and she was loving it. But after a while, Fiona noticed that Brandon wasn't having much fun. He'd never been the most outgoing kid—he would spend entire days glued to computer games if Joanne let him—but Fiona sensed there was something more going on. When her dad and Katie decided to pay the penguins a second visit, Fiona stayed back with him, watching the belugas through the windows of the underground viewing area.

"Anything wrong, B?"

He was silent for a moment, then he asked, "How come you never come over anymore?"

Now it was Fiona's turn to go silent. "It's complicated," she finally replied.

"It's because you sexted, isn't it?" Fiona glanced at him. He was only eleven! What did he know about sexting? "Mom and Dad have been fighting about it," he said, without waiting for a reply. "Mom thinks you're a bad influence."

No surprise there. "What do you think?" she asked.

He hesitated before answering, then, blushing, he pulled something out of his jeans pocket. "I found this in Dad's car, under the seat."

Fiona stared in shock at her old cell phone, resting in the palm of his hand. She reminded herself to breathe.

"How long have you had this?" she asked, taking it from him.

"A few weeks." His face had gone tomato red.

"Did you look on it?" He nodded. "Did you find—?"

He nodded again, then blurted, "It was Tommy's idea to do it!"

"Do what?"

"Upload it. Onto Friendjam."

It took Fiona a moment to process what he was saying. *It was never Ryan!* she realized. *It was my own little brother!*

"Brandon," she said, too shocked to get mad, "you know how wrong it was to do that, right?"

From his tight expression, she couldn't tell if he was sorry or guilty or angry—or all three.

"Why did you take that picture?" he asked.

There were so many answers and half-answers to that question, Fiona opted for the simplest one.

"It was supposed to be private," she replied.

"Tommy says you're a whore."

The word had largely lost its sting over the past weeks, but coming from Brandon's mouth, it pierced her, right through the heart. Suddenly, she was burning with anger.

"Tommy is a little perv!" she told him. "Stop hanging out with him!"

"You can't tell me what to do!" he threw back.

"Brandon!"

"If you tell on me," he lashed out, "my mom's just going to blame you anyway!"

She watched him lope away with a surly stride, looking ridiculous in his child's body, acting like a teenager. But Fiona felt like crying, not laughing. She closed her hand over the cell phone, feeling it like fire in her palm.

WHEN FIONA GOT HOME later that afternoon, the first thing she did with her new smartphone was text Ryan to ask him to meet her at a neighborhood coffee place. She got there early to make sure she was waiting for him when he arrived. He looked nervous as he approached the table.

"Don't worry. I won't bite," she told him.

"I thought you weren't talking to me," he said as he sat down. "Is this some kind of ambush?"

"I owe you an apology," Fiona replied. "I know it wasn't you who posted that picture on Friendjam."

"That's what I've been trying to tell you."

"I know. I'm sorry. Turns out it was my little brother."

Ryan got a quizzical look. "That's...disturbing."

"Tell me about it."

Ryan sat back, relaxing in the chair. "It hasn't been easy for me, either, you know. You've got a lot of friends, and they all hate me."

"I figured you made a copy," Fiona offered lamely. "I thought you were getting back at me."

"I would never do that."

Looking at him now, open and uncomplicated, Fiona remembered why she'd once liked him.

"Here," she said, handing him her new smartphone. "Maybe this will make it up to you."

"Sweet phone," he said.

"Check out what's on it."

Before coming to meet Ryan, Fiona had set up a new Friendjam account. She posted that Ryan was not responsible for distributing the photo, that he was a good guy who had been unfairly accused. Then she asked people to repost the message, to make sure everybody saw it. While she was at it, she also asked that people do the decent thing and *stop* posting the boob shot. It was a start, at least.

Finished reading, Ryan glanced up at her. "Thanks," he said.

"You're welcome," she replied, holding out her hand for the phone. But Ryan wasn't ready to give it over. Fiona watched as he started playing with it. "Ryan, may I have my phone back, please?"

Instead of handing it back, he held it up and took her picture. He looked impressed as he examined the photo. "Awesome resolution."

"Ryan, give it."

"Cool! Look at this," he said, a curious smile spreading over his face as he passed the phone to her.

Fiona looked at the screen to see a photo of an Asian girl wearing a white smock and cap, a purple bruise around her left eye.

"I've heard of this," Ryan told her. "They test the phones in the factories in China, and sometimes they forget to wipe the memory."

"That's amazing," said Fiona, studying the picture of the factory girl. She was looking into the camera with a neutral expression—not smiling, not sad either. It was crazy, but there was something about her that seemed familiar.

"I wonder what happened to her eye," Ryan was saying.

Fiona wondered, too.

THAT NIGHT, in the privacy of her room, she took out her phone and looked at the factory worker's photo again. *A bruise...and a scar*, thought Fiona. *What have these girls been* *through?* She rolled off the bed and, sitting down at her laptop, clicked onto help_sylvie.com to find the picture of the African girl. The framing was identical in the two photos, head and shoulders, looking into the lens. *See me whole. See who I really am.* Two girls from two different continents, but the message was the same.

Fiona decided it was time to face up to something she'd been avoiding for months. She dug her old cell phone out from the bottom of her shoulder bag and found the charger in a drawer. In a moment, the phone was juiced enough that she could open the camera, and there it was—her very own famous photo. She forced herself to look at it—lips puckered, pajama top yanked up to reveal her breasts. She had a big drunken grin on her face, but her eyes weren't happy. Her eyes revealed something else. Fiona held the cell phone up between the picture of Sylvie on the laptop and the one of the factory girl on the smartphone. *See me whole*, said Fiona's eyes. *See who I really am.*

Make that three girls, she thought. *On three continents.*

LATE SUNDAY AFTERNOON, Fiona took the bus over to West Van and climbed the hill on foot to her father's house, her backpack slung over her shoulder. She wasn't sure if her dad's family would be home—but very sure that, if they were, Joanne would not be happy to see her. There were a few things that Fiona needed to set straight, though. She reached the house and rang the bell, waiting nervously on the doorstep. After a few moments, Brandon answered the door.

"Hi," said Fiona.

"Why are you here?" he asked suspiciously.

"Relax, B. I'm not going to rat on you. Although it's tempting."

He looked relieved. Fiona had given a lot of thought to whether or not she should tell her dad about Brandon's adventures on the Internet, and what he'd done. It wasn't about revenge—it was about how he was learning to treat and talk about girls. In the end, she'd decided that it was more important that he knew he could count on her to keep a secret.

"Sorry…for what I called you," he mumbled.

"Hmm," she replied. "We'll talk about what it means to call a girl that word another time. Say, when you start dating."

"I took that picture down, after Tommy posted it. But it was too late. It was already everywhere."

She nodded, not quite ready to forgive him, but acknowledging that he felt bad about what happened. "It took guts to come clean," she told him.

"Brandon? Who's at the door?" Joanne came into the hallway from the kitchen, and saw for herself. She forced a smile, of sorts. "Fiona! We didn't expect you tonight."

In her mind, Fiona shook her head. Who would have figured that her mom would wind up being so much cooler than Joanne?

"Is my dad here?" she asked. "I need to talk to him."

Joanne hesitated.

"We can talk outside, if it makes you feel safer," Fiona intoned with perfect sarcastic pitch, at which Joanne looked peeved.

"He's in the study," Brandon volunteered, and stood aside to let her come in.

Fiona's dad, at least, was happy to see her. He got up from where he was working at the computer and gave her a big hug.

"What a nice surprise! Everything okay?"

"Fine," she replied. "With me, at least."

"What do you mean?"

Fiona perched on the corner of his desk and took a stack of printed pages out of her backpack. Her dad eased back into his desk chair with a curious expression.

"Is that homework?"

"In a way. I've been doing some research on your company, Dad."

"For what? A school project?"

"Not exactly." She handed him an article she'd downloaded from the web. "Read this. It says that said as many as eight million people have died in the Democratic Republic of Congo, because of mining for conflict minerals."

He let out a groan. "Did your mother put you up to this?"

"Nope. *I* put me up to this. Did you know that the U.S. passed a law saying that American companies have to make sure the minerals they use to make cell phones and laptops are certified conflict-free?"

"Am I going to need a lawyer here?" he joked.

He was trying to make light, but Fiona was unrelenting.

"Is it true your company lobbied against the laws that tried to do the same thing here, Dad?"

He let out a sigh. "Where are you getting this stuff?" he asked.

"On the Internet."

"Right," he said, dismissively. "How many times have I told you, you can't trust what you read on the Internet?"

"So are you saying it isn't true, about your company?"

He scratched his forehead, avoiding her eyes.

"You're always on my case about taking responsibility, Dad."

"Look, when you grow up, you'll understand that things are a lot more complicated in the real world…"

"Let's talk about the real world," agreed Fiona. She took another sheet of paper from the pile of research. "This is Sylvie—you remember her," she said, holding up a copy of the famous photo, forcing her dad look at it. "She's my age, fifteen. Her father was killed because of coltan, and her village was burned to the ground. She was raped when she was ten years old by a soldier who also cut her face with a machete and gave her the scar. Coltan is one of the things your company mines, isn't it?" He flinched at this, but he didn't look away. "Her family's been living in a refugee camp ever since, and now if they don't get to come to Canada, they could all be murdered."

"Fiona, what do you expect me to do about it? It's just the way things work over there." The moment he spoke the words, he seemed to regret them. "I don't mean to sound callous," he said, "but we're just one company. We didn't kill this girl's father."

"Personal responsibility, Dad."

"Okay, let's talk personal responsibility. Are you saying you're willing to give up your new phone, your laptop—all of your electronics—in some useless gesture that isn't going to help anybody?"

"No. I'm saying the least you can do is try to get them out of that embassy, and into Canada."

A half-dozen different protests formed on his lips. He started to speak, sputtered, started again. Finally he gave up.

"Look, I know a guy pretty high up in the government," he told her. "Maybe I can talk him into intervening with immigration and speeding things up—but I'm not making any promises."

"Thank you," said Fiona, getting to her feet.

"Stay for dinner?"

Fiona thought about it for a moment. Was she really willing to put up with Joanne's glowering disapproval through an entire meal?

"Sure," she said at last.

She figured somebody had to stick around to watch out for Brandon and Katie. Somebody who *got* things.

AT THE END OF SEPTEMBER, the company at last released
Laiping's back pay. She wired it home, and her parents used
it to go to the hospital in Heyuan. When Laiping spoke to
her mother by phone after Baba's surgery, she was relieved
to hear that he was recovering well. But her mother complained that the cost of Baba's medicine would leave them
with barely enough yuan to buy food. Laiping promised she
would keep sending money from her paychecks, every two
weeks.

"You are a good daughter, Laiping," her mother
told her.

But Laiping didn't feel like a good daughter. She felt
angry and resentful. She remembered what Fen had said
about her mother—that she cared more about money
than she did about her. Laiping was beginning to feel that
way, too.

September was also the launch of the new product.
After that, work slowed down a little in the factory.
Laiping was switched back to her old job, soldering
capacitors to circuit boards, and usually got two days off
a week. But with Kai gone, and with her and Fen still not

speaking, Laiping was lonely. Min was her only friend, but when the trembling and weakness in her hands finally made it too painful for her to do her job polishing laptop cases, she applied to Human Resources to quit. She decided to return home to the village, where there was a boy who was interested in marrying her. Once she left, Laiping would have no one.

"You should quit, too," Min told her. "Find a better job, in a better factory."

But Min was still waiting to hear if permission to quit would be granted. If it didn't come through soon, she planned to give up the money she was owed and leave anyway. Laiping was tempted to do the same, but then she thought about who would pay for Baba's medicine, and realized she had no choice but to stay.

ONE EVENING when Laiping was coming down the wide staircase on her way out of the factory after her shift, she was surprised to see Fen waiting at the bottom. She looked older, smartly dressed in a slim skirt, a frilly blouse and heels, her hair pulled back neatly—there was nothing of the factory girl left. Laiping felt ordinary by comparison.

"Laiping!" she called to her. "Come here!"

Reluctantly, Laiping cut across the two streams of workers, one going up and the other coming down.

"What do you want?"

"There's something you need to see." She had a smartphone in her hand, the new product. "This email arrived in our office," she explained as she tapped an icon. "It was forwarded to me, because I understand English."

Laiping rolled her eyes, but Fen was too busy with the smartphone to see. She opened an email and showed it to Laiping, who was stunned to see herself on the screen. She was wearing the white smock of the testing line, and the bruise around her left eye was very noticeable—so the photo must have been taken about a month ago.

"Where did this come from?" asked Laiping, baffled.

"Some girl in Canada sent it. Look." Fen scrolled down the email to a second photo, of a *gweilo* girl with a broad face and curly brown hair, and some writing that Laiping supposed was English. "She found the photo of you on her new smartphone. She has a message for you. Here."

Fen handed Laiping a piece of paper, on which she had written a translation in Cantonese. Laiping read, "*Thank you for making my phone! I hope your eye is better. I am happy to know who you are. Love, Fiona.*"

"'I am happy to know who you are'?" Laiping said out loud, puzzled. "Are you sure that's what it says?"

"Yes, I'm sure!" replied Fen, defensively. "I looked it up." Then she said, shrugging, "Look at this—she sent another photo, too."

Fen scrolled down further on the screen. Laiping couldn't believe it—she was looking at the picture of the African girl with the scar, the photo that was on the prohibited website that Kai had shown her, all those weeks ago, when he told her that people in Europe and America cared about conditions in the factory. Laiping was wary— was Fen still spying for the company, trying to trap her into admitting she had looked at an illegal site? Would she be sent away, like Kai? But Fen prattled on, oblivious to the danger she was holding in her hand.

"This *gweilo* Fiona must have mental problems," she said. "Why would she send a picture of *that* girl?"

Laiping had no idea, except that obviously the *gweilo* girl thought there was a connection between them. She looked at Fen's translation again. *I hope your eye is better.* She found herself smiling. In a bizarre way, she realized, Kai had been right—somebody in another country *did* care about her.

"What does that girl with the scar have to do with you?" Fen pressed her. "Who is she?"

"Her name is Sylvie," Laiping told her. "She lives in Africa, where they get the tantalum powder that goes into the capacitors."

Fen looked impressed that Laiping would know this, and more than a little suspicious. "You better watch yourself," she said. "Some people already think you're a trouble-maker."

"Just like your father," Laiping replied, enjoying the furious look on Fen's face.

She walked out into the cool evening air and joined the mass of workers heading for the cafeteria, clutching the piece of paper on which Fen had written the translation. For the moment, at least, Laiping felt a little less alone.

FIONA AND HER MOTHER sat at either end of the living room sofa watching the nightly news on TV, feet up and meeting in the middle.

"It's about time!" remarked her mom, keeping up a running commentary on the night's lead story.

On the screen, Sylvie and her family could be seen coming through the arrival doors at Trudeau International Airport in Montreal. There was a zoo of cameras and reporters waiting for them. The two youngest kids had wide grins, and seemed to be enjoying the attention, but Sylvie had the dazed look of a deer caught in headlights, and her mother appeared tiny and terrified. There was another boy in the family, a teenager, who looked kind of hostile—until the young black doctor who'd been on the news for weeks fighting for the family to come to Canada greeted him with a hug. He got a big broad smile then, which made him look younger—and less scary.

Fiona's smartphone pinged. She picked it up from where it was lying beside her on the couch and checked to find a text from her dad.

"Happy now?" the text read.

"Very," she texted back, thumbs flying.

"Who's that?" her mom asked.

"Just Dad."

She took in Fiona's pleased look. Her eyes narrowed. "What's going on?"

"Nothing."

"Fiona?"

"He's just saying that he's glad Sylvie made it to Canada."

"Your father," she repeated, disbelieving. "Mister Mining. *He* said that."

"Jeez, Mom," Fiona replied. "People can change."

AFTERWORD

WHILE THE CHARACTERS in this novel are fictional, their experiences and circumstances reflect the lives of millions.

The death toll in the Democratic Republic of the Congo over the past two decades due to fighting over coltan and other conflict minerals was estimated at over five million in a report released by the International Rescue Committee in 2008. Many have characterized the mass killing as genocide. The systematic rape of women, children, and men has been used as a weapon of war in the ongoing fighting. The United Nations recently stated that one hospital alone in eastern Congo is treating three hundred rape survivors a month. Because of the cultural taboo against reporting sexual violence, authorities presume the actual number of rapes to be far higher.

So the violence goes on, affecting millions in the eastern DRC and causing thousands, like Sylvie and her family, to flee the country for refugee camps like Nyarugusu, where they struggle with family breakdown, poverty, and the effects of what can be seen as mass post-traumatic stress disorder. Without the rights of citizens, they live in limbo, facing uncertain futures. And girls like Sylvie are hardly safe in Nyarugusu, where between January and September of 2012, eighty-one rapes were reported—sixty-five of which involved girls under eighteen. One thirteen-year-old girl told the Women's Refugee Commission, "Even if they [the rapists] are reported, nothing is done to put them in jail. They still live among us. This happens often."

In China, statistics for 2012 indicate that in that year alone, 250 million migrant workers made the choice to leave rural villages in search of factory wages in cities like Shenzhen that specialize in high-tech manufacturing. Predominantly young and female, workers like Laiping set out with the dream of a better life, and in some ways they may achieve it—but it comes at the price of oppressive rules, illegally withheld wages, and punishing working conditions. Hundreds of workers have threatened to throw themselves off of dormitory roofs en masse in protest, and at least fourteen have committed suicide.

Workers like Laiping earn less in a month than North American workers do weekly, which is one of the reasons that factory jobs are disappearing in Canada and the United States—because labor costs are so much lower in places like China. While the factory I've created is fictional, its wages reflect those of higher-end factories operating in the Special Economic Zone of Shenzhen today. I have set the basic wage at 1800 yuan ($290 U.S.) per month, above the legal Shenzhen minimum wage of 1500 yuan ($240 U.S.) per month, which is the highest in China. In Shanghai it is the equivalent of $230 per month, and in Beijing $200.

Migrant workers become refugees of a sort, displaced from traditional family-based culture, and adrift in a make-shift society of isolation, anonymity, and endless striving that for most is ultimately fruitless. After a few years of being worn down by the assembly line, many return to their villages with little to show for the sacrifices they've made, while the disparity between the factory workers and China's burgeoning wealthy classes continues to grow.

In comparison with what happens to Sylvie and Laiping, the cyberbullying experienced by Fiona may seem a relatively minor trauma. But the death of even one young person driven to suicide by the vicious side of social media is too many, and there have been several. Fiona comes out all right. She's a strong girl with a positive self-image, supportive parents, and a core group of loyal friends. But not every young person possesses these buffers.

Am I advocating a boycott of the smartphones, tablets, and laptop computers whose manufacture causes exploitation in China, the Democratic Republic of the Congo, and other countries? Not for a minute. Like millions of people, in every nation on earth, I rely on these devices daily. What I *am* advocating, though, is that informed consumers be able to exercise their right to purchase ethical products that are exploitation-free.

Many groups and individuals are active internationally trying to instil ethical standards that will help the Sylvies and Laipings of the world lead safer and more secure lives. But the issues are incredibly complex. Even those tech companies that have made a commitment to work with their manufacturers to ensure that only conflict-free coltan is used in their products are thwarted by black markets and murky supply chains that make verification difficult. While Hervé Kayembe is an invented character, he and his soldiers are representative of multiple rogue militias that continue to attack villages in the eastern DRC over coltan, because they know they will find lucrative markets for it.

Factory wages and conditions in the Pearl Delta region of southern China have improved somewhat under pressure from certain American tech companies that take their business to manufacturers there; Foxconn, a major player, has promised to raise its basic wage from the current 2200 yuan ($350 U.S.) per month to 4400 yuan ($700 U.S.) per month. Yet many factories have instead relocated to more remote areas of China, where wages are reduced and sweatshops can more easily avoid international scrutiny.

So what can we as consumers do? We can ask our political leaders to enforce legislation requiring manufacturers to ensure that the coltan used in their products is conflict-free. Given that 70 percent of mining companies in the world are listed in Canada, Canadians can educate themselves about the practices of Canadian companies in the DRC, and around the world. Canada has recently joined other nations in introducing legislation that requires mining companies to disclose payments they make to foreign governments. It's a start toward exposing the kind of corruption that sees government-backed soldiers in places like the DRC attacking their own people.

And before making a decision about which brand of cell phone, laptop, or other tantalum capacitor–based product you or your parents plan to buy, do an Internet search to find out what that company's position is on the use of conflict minerals. If the company outsources manufacturing to factories in China and other countries, what standards does it hold them to? Some tech brands have a better record than others on the use of conflict-free raw materials and on trying to ensure decent conditions for workers. Ask the question, "Did anybody suffer during the making of this product?"

SUGGESTED READING AND WEBSITES

Factory Girls: From Village to City in a Changing China by Leslie T. Chang (New York: Spiegel & Grau/Random House, 2008).

The Bite of the Mango by Mariatu Kamara with Susan McClelland (Toronto: Annick Press, 2008).

Ethical Consumer: www.ethicalconsumer.org. This British site lists a wide range of products, including electronics, and provides background information on the companies that make them.

MiningWatch Canada: www.miningwatch.ca. As the name implies, this group monitors activities of Canadian mining companies in Canada and around the world.

Global Witness: www.globalwitness.org. This is an international group that for twenty years has campaigned against human rights abuses that are the result of natural resource–related conflict.

And, finally, there's an app for that. Buycott (www.buycott.com) allows consumers to use smartphones to scan bar codes on store shelves, and instantly provides details of the manufacturer's record on environmental abuse and human rights violations. The irony is not lost.

ABOUT THE AUTHOR

ELIZABETH STEWART's first young adult novel, *The Lynching of Louie Sam*, was based on the true story of a mob lynching of a Native American teen in 1884. It has received wide acclaim, including the 2013 Notable Books for a Global Society, the International Youth Library's White Ravens Collection 2013, the Skipping Stones Honor Award, the Geoffrey Bilson Award for Historical Fiction, and the John Spray Mystery Award.

During her lengthy career as a screenwriter, Stewart has received multiple awards for her television series scripts for young people, including *The Adventures of Shirley Holmes* and *Guinevere Jones*. She has also written movies for television, among them *Tagged: The Jonathan Wamback Story*, an examination of teen violence based on a true incident, and *Luna: Spirit of the Whale*, which chronicles the transformational effect a stray killer whale off the west coast of Canada has on a First Nations community. Both of these films were nominated for Geminis.

Stewart lives in Vancouver, British Columbia.